ROUND THE WORLD
IN EIGHTY DAYS

ROUND THE WORLD
IN EIGHTY DAYS

Jules Verne

TRANSLATED BY IRENE R. GIBBONS

Published by Priory Books, Bridlington.
A Peter Haddock Limited imprint.
© Blackie & Son Ltd.
Printed in Hungary

CONTENTS

In which Phileas Fogg and Passepartout accept each other as master and servant respectively

In 1872, No. 7 Savile Row, Burlington Gardens—the house where Sheridan died in 1816—was occupied by Phileas Fogg, Esq., one of the oddest and most conspicuous members of the Reform Club in London, although he appeared to make a point of never doing anything that could possibly attract attention.

Thus one of the greatest orators Britain has had the honour to possess was succeeded by that enigmatic personality Phileas Fogg. All that anyone knew about him was that he was a man of honour and one of the finest gentlemen in English high society.

He was said to resemble Byron—facially, that is, for no fault could be found with his feet. But this was a Byron complete with moustache and side-whiskers, an impassive Byron who could have lived for a thousand years without growing old.

Phileas Fogg was most certainly an Englishman, but perhaps not a Londoner. He had never been seen at the Exchange or at the Bank or in any of the counting-houses of the City. Nor had the docks of the Port of London ever accommodated a ship owned by Phileas Fogg. He did not appear on any committee. His name had never echoed through any of the Inns of Court—the Temple, Lincoln's Inn, Gray's Inn. He had never conducted a case at the Court of Chancery or the Queen's Bench or the Exchequer Court or in an ecclesiastical court. He was not a manufacturer or a businessman, a merchant or a farmer. He was not a member of the Royal Institution of Great Britain or the London Institute or the Workmen's Institute or the Russell Institute or the Western Literary Institute or the

Law Association or the Society of Arts, which is under the direct patronage of Her Gracious Majesty. In short, he did not belong to any of the countless societies that are to be found in the British capital and range from the Philharmonic Society to the Entomological Society, the latter having been established mainly for the purpose of destroying harmful insects.

Phileas Fogg was a member of the Reform Club, and that was all.

If anyone is surprised to find a gentleman as mysterious as Mr. Fogg among the members of that honourable society, I might tell him that Mr. Fogg was admitted on the recommendation of Baring Brothers, the bankers, with whom he had an account. As a result of this he enjoyed a certain standing and his cheques were regularly paid at sight from his current account which invariably showed a credit balance.

Was Phileas Fogg rich? Undoubtedly. But how he had made his fortune not even the best-informed people could say, and Mr. Fogg was the last man one would have turned to for information on the subject. He was not extravagant, but he was not mean either. Whenever help was required for some noble or useful or benevolent cause he would give it unostentatiously, and even anonymously.

No one could have been more uncommunicative than he was. He spoke as little as he possibly could and his silence made him seem all the more mysterious. Yet his life was an open book. He kept on doing the same things with mathematical uniformity, but people's imaginations could not accept this and they always searched for some ulterior motive.

Was he a travelled man? Probably he was. No one had a better knowledge of the map of the world than he had. No matter how remote a place was, he seemed to know all about it. Sometimes, with a few brief, well-chosen words, he would correct the various remarks made in the Club about travellers who were lost or missing; he would point out what had probably happened and his words often seemed to have been inspired by a kind of second sight, for events

would prove him right in the end. He was a man who must have travelled everywhere—in thought, at least.

But one thing was certain, and that was that Phileas Fogg had not left London for many years. Those who had the honour of knowing him rather better than the others could bear witness to that. No one could claim to have seen him anywhere except the Club—unless it was on the direct route he used every day to go there from his house. His only pastimes were reading the newspapers and playing whist. In that silent game, which was so much in keeping with his temperament, he often won, but his winnings never found their way into his own pocket. They represented, in fact, a considerable item in his charity budget. Mr. Fogg evidently played for the sake of playing and not in order to win. For him card-playing was a battle, a struggle against odds, but a struggle that involved no movement or shifting to another place or any fatigue, and that too was in keeping with his character.

As far as people knew, Phileas Fogg had neither wife nor children, and this can apply to the most honourable of men. And he had no relatives or friends, which is, of course, more unusual. Phileas Fogg lived alone in his house in Savile Row and no one ever entered it. There was never any mention of his household arrangements. One single man-servant was all he required. He had lunch and dinner at the Club with clockwork precision, always in the same room and at the same table. He did not entertain his fellow members or invite any outsider and at the stroke of midnight he went home merely to sleep. He never used the comfortable apartments which the Reform Club makes available to its members. Of the twenty-four hours, he spent ten at home, sleeping or attending to his toilet. Whenever he took a walk it was invariably across the marquetry floor of the entrance hall at a steady pace or in the circular gallery which was surmounted by a blue glass dome supported by twenty Ionic pillars fashioned in red porphyry. When he dined or had lunch, the tasty dishes for his table were supplied by the kitchens, the larder and the pantry of the Club and the fishmonger's and the dairy patronized by that establishment.

The servants of the Club, solemn black-coated figures wearing soft-soled shoes, served his meals from special china on excellent napery of Saxon linen. The Club glasses, of antiquated design, held his sherry or his port or his spiced claret. Finally, it was the Club ice—brought at great expense from the American lakes—that kept his drinks at the requisite degree of coldness.

If it is eccentric to live under conditions such as these, then one must admit that eccentricity is not a bad thing at all!

Without being luxurious, the house in Savile Row had the virtue of being extremely comfortable. Moreover, as the habits of its occupant were invariable, the service could be reduced to a minimum. But Phileas Fogg demanded an extraordinary degree of punctuality and regularity from his single servant. On that very day, 2nd October, Phileas Fogg had dismissed James Forster, whose crime had been that of bringing him his shaving water at 84° F, instead of 86°, and he was awaiting his successor who was to present himself between eleven o'clock and eleven-thirty.

Phileas Fogg was sitting squarely in his armchair with his feet together like a soldier on parade, his hands resting on his knees, his body erect and his head held high. He was watching the hand of the clock. It was a complicated time-piece that showed the hours, the minutes and the seconds, and also the day of the week, the day of the month and the year. As half past eleven was striking, Mr. Fogg would, as was his daily custom, leave the house and betake himself to the Reform Club.

At that moment there was a knock at the door of the small drawing-room in which Phileas Fogg was sitting.

James Forster, the servant who had been dismissed, came in.

'The new manservant is here,' he announced.

A fellow about thirty years of age stepped in and bowed.

'I understand you are French and your name is John,' said Phileas Fogg.

'Jean, if you please, sir,' replied the newcomer. 'Jean Passepartout. The nickname has stuck because I have a

12

natural aptitude for getting out of scrapes. I consider myself to be an honest fellow, sir, but, to be perfectly frank with you, I have followed several trades. I have been a strolling singer, a circus rider, a performer on the flying trapeze like Leotard and a tight-rope dancer like Blondin. Then I decided to make better use of my talents and so I became a teacher of gymnastics and, last of all, I was a sergeant in the fire brigade in Paris and I was at some remarkable fires. But I left France five years ago and I have been working as a valet in England because I wanted to have a taste of family life. Then I found myself without a position and I learned that Mr. Phileas Fogg was the most precise and the most sedentary man in the whole United Kingdom. And so I have come to see you because I want to lead a quiet life and forget my name of Passepartout and all that it implies . . .'

'Passepartout suits me,' the gentleman replied. 'You have been recommended to me and I have good testimonials concerning you. You know my terms of employment?'

'Yes, sir.'

'Good. What time would you say it was?'

'Eleven-twenty-two,' replied Passepartout, pulling a huge silver watch out of the depths of his waistcoat pocket.

'You are slow,' said Mr. Fogg.

'Excuse me, sir, but that is impossible.'

'You are four minutes slow. No matter. It is enough merely to note the difference. As from this moment, eleven-twenty-nine a.m. on Wednesday, 2nd October, 1872, you are in my employ.'

Having said this, Phileas Fogg rose, picked up his hat in his left hand, placed it on his head like an automaton and went off without another word.

Passepartout heard the outside door close once—it was his new master going out. Then he heard it a second time, which meant that his predecessor, James Forster, was departing.

And so Passepartout was left alone in the house in Savile Row.

In which Passepartout is convinced that he has found his ideal at last

'Upon my word,' Passepartout said to himself in slight bewilderment, 'I have seen some fellows every bit as alive as my new master at Madame Tussaud's!'

I should perhaps mention here that the 'fellows' at Madame Tussaud's are wax figures in London which attract a large number of visitors and really have everything except the power of speech.

During the few moments he had been with Phileas Fogg, Passepartout had made a rapid, but careful, examination of his future master. He was about forty with a handsome and distinguished appearance and a tall figure which was not marred by a slight tendency to stoutness. His hair and side-whiskers were fair and he had a smooth brow without any hint of wrinkles at the temples. His face was pale rather than ruddy and he had magnificent teeth. He seemed to possess to the highest degree what physiognomists call 'repose in action', a quality common to all those who go in more for work than for talking. He was calm and phlegmatic and his eyes were clear and unblinking. Indeed he was the perfect example of those imperturbable Englishmen one comes across fairly often in the United Kingdom, whose slightly academic bearing has been so wonderfully portrayed by the brush of Angelica Kauffman. Anyone who watched him carrying out the various actions of his daily life would get the impression that he was very well balanced in all his parts and accurately poised—indeed as perfect as a chronometer made by Leroy or Earnshaw. Phileas Fogg was accuracy personified. This could clearly be seen from the 'expression of his feet and hands', for in man, as well as in animals, the limbs can indicate the passions felt.

Phileas Fogg was one of those mathematically exact people who are never in a hurry and are always ready and so are economical in their footsteps and movements. He never took a stride more than he had to and he always went the shortest way. He never cast an unnecessary glance and would not allow himself to make any superfluous movement. No one had ever seen him upset or moved to emotion. He was the least hurried man in the world, but he always arrived on time. He lived alone and, as it were, outside the limits of all social relationships. He knew that in life one must allow for friction and, as friction has a retarding effect, he never let himself rub up against anyone.

As for Jean, with his nickname of Passepartout, he was a real Parisian and in the five years he had been working as a valet in London he had searched in vain for a master to whom he could become attached.

Passepartout was certainly not one of those impudent or unscrupulous valets depicted in French comedies. They are just impertinent rogues. They hold their shoulders high and their nose in the air and have a bold, hard look about them. Passepartout was a fine fellow with a likeable face and slightly protruding lips always ready to taste or to kiss, a gentle and obliging creature with one of those fine round heads one likes to see on the shoulders of a friend. He had blue eyes and a ruddy complexion, and his face was plump enough for him to be able to see his own cheek-bones. He was broad-chested and sturdily built, with powerful muscles. His herculean strength had been admirably developed by the training he had had in his younger days. His brown hair was rather unruly. It may be that the sculptors of antiquity knew of eighteen different ways of dressing Minerva's hair, but Passepartout knew of only one way of dressing his. Three flicks of the comb and that was all.

Would this fellow's natural exuberance be in keeping with Phileas Fogg's character? No one with the slightest claim to prudence would venture to say. Would Passepartout be the precise and meticulous servant that his master needed? One could only wait and see. After being

something of wanderer in his early years, he longed for a quiet life. He had heard praise of the methodical ways of the English and their proverbial *sang-froid* and so he had come to England to seek his fortune. But fate had not served him kindly up till then. He had not been able to take root anywhere. He had served in ten different houses. In each case his employers had been capricious or erratic, adventurers or wanderers. And that was not what Passepartout wanted. His last master, the young Lord Longsferry, a Member of Parliament, spent his nights in the shady oyster-rooms of the Haymarket and all too frequently had to be carried back to his lodgings by policemen. Passepartout wanted, above all, to be able to respect his master, so he ventured a few respectful comments which were ill received. So he left. Then he learned that Phileas Fogg, Esq., was looking for a servant. He gathered information about that gentleman. A person who led such an ordered life and never slept out or travelled or left home, even for a day, would be sure to suit him. So he applied and was taken on under the conditions described above.

After eleven-thirty had struck, Passepartout found himself alone in the house in Savile Row. He started on a tour of inspection at once. He went through the house from cellar to attic. He liked it. It was clean and tidy, austere and puritanical, and well-organized as far as the service was concerned. He thought it was like a beautiful snail shell, but a shell lighted and heated by gas. Carburetted hydrogen supplied all the lighting and heating requirements. On the second floor Passepartout had no trouble in finding the room intended for his use. He liked it. Electric bells and speaking tubes connected it with the rooms on the first floor and the mezzanine. On the mantelpiece was an electric clock to match the one in Phileas Fogg's bedroom. Both chronometers ticked out the seconds in unison.

'This suits me perfectly!' Passepartout said to himself.

In his room he also observed a notice fixed up above the clock. It was the daily programme of his duties. It gave all the details of his work from eight o'clock in the morning, the hour at which Phileas Fogg regularly got up, until half

past eleven, when he left the house and went to have lunch at the Reform Club—tea and toast at eight-twenty-three, shaving water at nine-thirty-seven, hair-dressing at nine-forty, etc. Then, from eleven-thirty in the morning until midnight, when that methodical gentleman went to bed, everything was noted and planned and organised. Passepartout studied the programme delightedly, impressing the various items on his mind.

As for Mr. Fogg's wardrobe, it was very well stocked and wonderfully organised. Each pair of trousers, each coat and waistcoat bore a number and that number was recorded in the register of incoming and outgoing garments, with an indication of the date on which, according to season, these items of apparel were to be worn in turn. The same rule applied to footwear.

In short, the house in Savile Row, which must have been a temple of disorder in the time of the illustrious, but dissipated Sheridan, was comfortably furnished in a manner befitting affluent circumstances. There was no library and no books. They would have been no use to Mr. Fogg. Two libraries were available to him at the Reform Club, one devoted to literature and the other to law and politics. In his bedroom he had a medium-sized safe which was fireproof and burglar-proof. There were no weapons in the house, no implement associated with hunting or war. Everything pointed to a peaceful way of life.

When he had examined the residence in detail, Passepartout rubbed his hands and his broad face beamed and he repeated in joyous tones:

'This suits me down to the ground! This is just what I want. We shall get on perfectly together, Mr. Fogg and I. He is a stay-at-home and so methodical. Just like a machine. And I have no objections at all to working for a machine!'

In which a conversation takes place that may cost Phileas Fogg dear

Phileas Fogg had left his house in Savile Row at eleven-thirty and, after putting his right foot five hundred and seventy-five times in front of his left foot, and his left foot five hundred and seventy-six times in front of his right foot, he reached the Reform Club, a huge building in Pall Mall that cost no less than £120,000 to build.

Phileas Fogg made his way at once to the dining-room. Its nine windows opened out on a beautiful garden where autumn had already turned the trees to gold. There he sat down at his usual table where a place had been laid ready for him. His lunch consisted of *hors-d'œuvre*, boiled fish seasoned with some first-class Reading Sauce, an underdone portion of roast beef garnished with mushrooms, a rhubarb and gooseberry tart and a piece of Cheddar cheese. The entire meal was washed down with a few cups of excellent tea, specially picked for the pantry of the Reform Club.

At twelve-forty-seven the gentleman rose and made his way towards the drawing-room, a luxuriously appointed room adorned with paintings in elaborate frames. There a servant handed him an uncut copy of *The Times* and Phileas Fogg carried out the laborious task of unfolding it with a sureness of touch that showed he was accustomed to the operation. He went on reading that newspaper until three-forty-five and then *The Standard*, which came next, kept him occupied till dinner-time. That meal was similar to lunch, except for the addition of Royal British Sauce.

At five-forty the gentleman reappeared in the large drawing-room and buried himself in the *Morning Chronicle*.

Half an hour later various members of the Reform Club entered and went up to the fireplace where a coal-fire was

burning. They were Phileas Fogg's usual partners at whist, and were, like him, inveterate players. There was the engineer Andrew Stuart, the bankers John Sullivan and Samuel Fallentin, the brewer Thomas Flanagan, and Gauthier Ralph, one of the directors of the Bank of England. They were all rich and highly respected men, even in this Club, which includes among its members the leading men of industry and finance.

'Tell me, Ralph,' Thomas Flanagan said. 'What has happened about the robbery?"

'Well,' replied Andrew Stuart, 'the Bank will just have to lose its money.'

'On the contrary,' said Gauthier Ralph, 'I hope we shall be able to lay our hands on the robber. Very clever police officers have been sent to America and over to the Continent to all the main ports of embarkation and disembarkation and the robber will find it difficult to elude them.'

'They have a description of the robber then, have they?' asked Andrew Stuart.

'The first point is that he is not a robber,' replied Gauthier Ralph in serious tones.

'What, not a robber—an individual who has taken fifty-five thousand pounds in banknotes?'

'No,' replied Gauthier Ralph.

'Is he a manufacturer then?' said John Sullivan.

'The *Morning Chronicle* states that he is a gentleman.'

The answer came from none other than Phileas Fogg, whose head had emerged just then from the sea of paper surrounding him. At the same time he nodded to his fellow-members and they returned his nod.

The exploit in question, which was being discussed with such interest by the various newspapers of the United Kingdom, had been carried out three days before, on 29th September. A bundle of banknotes, representing the enormous sum of fifty-five thousand pounds, had been removed from the counter of the head cashier of the Bank of England.

If anyone expressed astonishment at the ease with which the robbery had been carried out, the deputy governor,

Gauthier Ralph, would reply that at that very moment the cashier was busy entering the receipt of three shillings and sixpence and no one could be expected to keep an eye on everything at once.

But to make that whole incident more readily comprehensible I should perhaps mention here that that admirable institution, the Bank of England, lays great emphasis on the dignity of the public. There are no guards or old soldiers on duty and no metal gratings! The gold and silver and banknotes are freely exposed and are, so to speak, at the mercy of anyone who comes in. They could not cast any doubts upon the honesty of the public. A keen observer of British custom tells this story: in one of the rooms at the Bank where he happened to find himself one day, he wanted to have a closer look at a gold ingot weighing seven to eight pounds which was lying on the cashier's counter in full view of everyone. So he picked up the ingot and examined it, then he passed it to the man standing next to him and he in turn passed it to another and so the ingot went from hand to hand and finally reached the end of a dark corridor. And half an hour went by before it was put back in its place, without the cashier ever once raising his head.

But on 29th September things did not happen in quite that way. The bundle of banknotes did not return and when the magnificent clock over the payments department struck five o'clock, the hour when the offices closed, all the Bank of England could do was to enter the sum of fifty-five thousand pounds in the profits and losses account.

When it was properly established that a robbery had indeed taken place, some of the cleverest detectives were sent to the main ports, Liverpool, Glasgow, Le Havre, Suez, Brindisi, New York, etc., and, were promised, if successful, a bonus of two thousand pounds and five per cent of the sum recovered. While waiting for the results of the inquiry, which was opened at once, these inspectors had to scrutinize all travellers arriving or departing.

There was reason to suppose—and this was what the *Morning Chronicle* said—that the robber did not belong to

any of the gangs of thieves operating in England. On the day in question, 29th September, a well-dressed man with fine manners and an air of distinction had been observed walking to and fro in the payments department, where the robbery had taken place. As a result of the inquiry it had been possible to build up a fairly accurate description of that gentleman and that description was at once circulated to all the detectives in the United Kingdom and on the Continent. So some people—and Gauthier Ralph was one of them—believed there was good reason to expect that the robber would be caught.

As one can imagine, this was the main topic of conversation in London and all over England. People discussed it and debated excitedly whether the Metropolitan Police would be successful or not. So it is not at all surprising that the Members of the Reform Club should have been talking about it, especially as one of the deputy governors of the Bank was one of their number.

Gauthier Ralph had no doubts about the outcome of the investigations as he thought the bonus would greatly stimulate the zeal and intelligence of the detectives. But his friend Andrew Stuart was far from sharing his confidence. So the discussion went on after the gentlemen had sat down to play whist, Stuart facing Flanagan and Fallentin facing Phileas Fogg. The players did not speak during the game, but between the rubbers the conversation was resumed with fresh vigour.

'I maintain,' said Andrew Stuart, 'that the chances are loaded in the robber's favour. He certainly must be a clever man.'

'Come now!' replied Ralph. 'There is not a single country where he can take refuge.'

'Nonsense!'

'Where could he go?'

'I have no idea,' replied Andrew Stuart, 'but the earth is, after all, quite a large place.'

'It used to be . . . ' murmured Phileas Fogg. Then— 'Your cut, sir,' he added, holding out the cards to Thomas Flanagan.

The discussion was broken off during the rubber, but was soon revived by Andrew Stuart, who said:

'Used to be ? Do you mean to say that the earth has grown smaller ?'

'Certainly,' replied Gauthier Ralph. 'I share Fogg's view. The earth has grown smaller. Nowadays you can travel across it ten times as quickly as you could have done a hundred years ago. And, to go back to what we have been discussing, this will speed up the investigations being made.'

'And also make it easier for the robber to escape!'

'It is your turn to play, Stuart,' said Phileas Fogg.

But the disbelieving Stuart was not convinced and, when the game was over, he went on:

'You must admit, Ralph, that it is ludicrous to say that the earth has grown smaller. Just because you can go round the world in three months . . .'

'In eighty days only,' said Phileas Fogg.

'Quite true, gentlemen,' added John Sullivan. 'Eighty days now that the section of the Great Indian Peninsular Railway between Rothal and Allahabad has been opened. This is how the *Morning Chronicle* works it out:

London to Suez via the Mont Cenis and Brindisi, rail and steamer	7 days
Suez to Bombay, steamer	13 days
Bombay to Calcutta, rail	3 days
Calcutta to Hong Kong, steamer	13 days
Hong Kong to Yokohama, steamer	6 days
Yokohama to San Francisco, steamer	22 days
San Francisco to New York, rail	7 days
New York to London, steamer and rail	9 days
TOTAL:	80 days

'Yes, eighty days!' cried Andrew Stuart and, not watching what he was doing, he trumped a leading card. 'But that does not allow for bad weather, or contrary winds, or shipwrecks or derailments, and so on.'

'It allows for everything', replied Phileas Fogg, who went on playing. This time their conversation encroached upon the game.

'Even if the Hindus or the Red Indians take up the rails ?' cried Andrew Stuart. 'If they hold up the trains and loot the carriages and scalp the passengers ?'

'It allows for everything,' replied Phileas Fogg and, laying down his cards, he added, 'The two highest trumps.'

Andrew Stuart, whose turn it was to shuffle, picked up the cards, saying,

'You are right in theory, Fogg, but in practice . . .'

'In practice too, Stuart.'

'I would like to see you do it.'

'That is up to you. Let us go together!'

'God forbid!' cried Stuart. 'But I would certainly wager four thousand pounds that a journey undertaken under these conditions would be impossible.'

'Perfectly possible, I assure you,' replied Mr. Fogg.

'Well, do it then!'

'Go round the world in eighty days ?'

'Yes.'

'Very well then.'

'When ?'

'At once.'

'This is absolute madness!' cried Andrew Stuart, who was beginning to feel annoyed at his partner's insistence. 'Here, let us go on with the game!'

'Reshuffle the cards then,' replied Phileas Fogg, 'because it is a misdeal.'

Andrew Stuart picked up the cards again feverishly, then, all at once, he laid them on the table.

'Well, Fogg, I will,' he said. 'I will bet you four thousand pounds!'

'My dear Stuart,' said Fallentin, 'calm down! It is just a joke.'

'When I say I am going to bet,' replied Andrew Stuart, 'it is no joking matter.'

'I agree,' said Mr. Fogg. Then, turning to the others, he said:

'I have twenty thousand pounds deposited with Baring Brothers. I will gladly wager them . . . '

'Twenty thousand pounds!' exclaimed John Sullivan. 'Twenty thousand pounds which some unforseen delay may well snatch from your grasp!'

'Nothing is ever unforeseen,' Phileas Fogg replied simply.

'But, Fogg, that period of eighty days is just calculated as a minimum.'

'If it is put to good use, a minimum is all one requires.'

'But, if you are not going to exceed it, you will have to jump, quite literally, off the train and on to the steamer, and off the steamer on to the train!'

'That is just what I shall do.'

'You are joking!'

'A true Englishman never jokes about anything as serious as a bet,' replied Phileas Fogg. 'I am willing to bet twenty thousand pounds against anyone who cares to take me on that I shall go round the world in eighty days or less, that is to say, in nineteen hundred and twenty hours or one hundred and fifteen thousand two hundred minutes. Will you take the bet?'

'We will,' replied Stuart, Fallentin, Sullivan, Flanagan and Ralph after consulting together.

'Very well,' said Mr. Fogg. 'The train for Dover leaves at eight-forty-five. I intend to catch it.'

'Tonight!'

'Yes, tonight,' replied Phileas Fogg. 'So,' he added, consulting a pocket calendar, 'as today is Wednesday, 2nd October, I shall have to be back in London in this very drawing-room at the Reform Club on Saturday, 21st December, at eight-forty-five p.m. Failing that, the twenty thousand pounds in my account with Baring Brothers will belong to you *de facto* and *de jure*, gentlemen. Here is a cheque for that amount.'

A memorandum recording the bet was drawn up and signed on the spot by the six interested parties. Phileas Fogg was still as calm as ever. He had certainly not placed the bet merely for the sake of winning. He had staked only

24

these twenty thousand pounds—half of his fortune—because he foresaw that he might have to spend the other half on carrying out this difficult, if not impossible, scheme. As for his opponents, they seemed agitated, not because of the amount at stake, but because they had some misgivings about fighting him on those terms.

Seven o'clock was striking. The others gave Mr. Fogg the opportunity to stop playing so that he could make preparations for his departure.

'I am always ready,' was that impassive gentlemen's rejoinder and he proceeded to deal the cards.

'Diamonds are trumps,' he said. 'Your turn to play, Stuart.'

In which Phileas Fogg amazes his servant Passepartout

At seven-twenty-five, after winning twenty guineas or so at whist, Phileas Fogg bade his fellow-members farewell and left the Reform Club. At seven-fifty he opened the door of his house and went in.

Passepartout, who had studied his programme conscientiously, was rather surprised to see Mr. Fogg appear at that unaccustomed hour and thus show himself to be guilty of inaccuracy. According to the notice the occupant of No. 7 Savile Row ought not to have returned home till nearly midnight.

Phileas Fogg went up to his room first of all, then he called:

'Passepartout!'

Passepartout did not reply. The call could not be meant for him. It was not the right time.

'Passepartout!' repeated Mr. Fogg, without raising his voice at all.

Passepartout appeared.

'This is the second time I have called you,' said Mr. Fogg.

'But it is not midnight,' replied Passepartout with his watch in his hand.

'I know,' went on Phileas Fogg, 'and I do not blame you. We are leaving for Dover and Calais in ten minutes' time.'

The Frenchman's round face was distorted by a kind of grimace. It was obvious that he had not heard aright.

'Are you going away, sir?' he asked.

'Yes,' replied Phileas Fogg. 'We are going round the world.'

Passepartout, with his eyes gaping wide, his eyelids and eyebrows raised, his arms dangling and his whole body

sagging, presented all the symptoms of a state of amazement bordering on stupefaction.

'Round the world!' he muttered.

'In eighty days,' replied Mr. Fogg. 'So we have not a moment to lose.'

'But what about suitcases . . . ?' said Passepartout, his head swaying involuntarily from side to side.

'We shall not have any suitcases. Just a carpet-bag. And two flannel shirts and three pairs of stockings to go in it. The same for you. We shall buy things on the way. You will bring down my mackintosh and my travelling-rug. Wear a pair of strong shoes! In any case we shall be walking very little, if at all. Hurry now!'

Passepartout wanted to say something. But he could not. He left Mr. Fogg's room and went upstairs to his own, where he collapsed on to a chair, using a rather vulgar expression current in his native district:

'Well, here is a fine kettle of fish! And I wanted to have a quiet life . . . !'

He made his preparations for the journey mechanically. Round the world in eighty days! Was he dealing with a madman? No . . . was it a joke? They were going to Dover —all right! To Calais—all right! That would not worry him at all as he had not set foot on his native land for five years. Perhaps they would even go as far as Paris. My goodness, how delighted he would be to see the great capital again! But a gentleman who never took a step more than he had to would stop there . . . Yes, he definitely would, but it was none the less true that this gentleman who had been such a stay-at-home in the past was going away—he was setting out on a journey!

By eight o'clock Passepartout had packed the modest bag containing his own wardrobe and his master's. Then, still troubled in spirit, he left his room and, closing the door carefully behind him, he went to rejoin Mr. Fogg.

Mr. Fogg was ready. He was carrying under his arm Bradshaw's *Continental Railway Steam Transit and General Guide*, which was to supply him with all the information he needed for his journey. He took the carpet-bag from

Passepartout, opened it and slipped in a thick bundle of those beautiful banknotes that can be used in any country in the world.

'You have not forgot anything?' he asked.

'Nothing, sir.'

'What about my mackintosh and my travelling-rug?'

'Here they are.'

'Well, take this bag!'

And Mr. Fogg handed the bag over to Passepartout.

'Take care of it,' he added. 'There are twenty thousand pounds inside it.'

The bag nearly slipped from Passepartout's fingers, as if the twenty thousand pounds had been in gold and had weighed accordingly.

Then master and servant went downstairs and the outside door was locked behind them.

There was a cab-stand at the end of Savile Row and Phileas Fogg and his servant climbed into a cab which went off rapidly in the direction of Charing Cross Station, where one of the branch-lines of the South-Eastern Railway ends.

At eight-twenty the cab stopped outside the gate of the station. Passepartout jumped down. His master followed suit and paid the driver.

At that moment a poor beggar-woman holding a child by the hand came up to Mr. Fogg and asked him for money. She was walking barefoot in the mud and wore a battered hat from which dangled a pathetic feather and had a tattered shawl over her rags.

Mr. Fogg pulled out of his pocket the twenty guineas he had just won at whist and presented them to the beggar-woman.

'Here you are, my good woman!' he said. 'I am happy to have met you.'

Then he went on his way.

Passepartout felt his eyes grow moist. His master had started to win his affection.

Mr. Fogg and he went at once in the great hall of the station. There Phileas Fogg instructed Passepartout to buy two first-class tickets to Paris. Then, turning

round, he noticed his five acquaintances from the Reform Club.

'I am leaving, gentleman,' he said, 'and the various stamps put on the passport that I am carrying for the purpose will enable you to check my itinerary when I return.'

'Oh, that is unnecessary, Fogg,' Gauthier Ralph replied politely. 'We shall rely on your honour as a gentleman.'

'It is better to do it as I suggest,' said Mr. Fogg.

'You will not forget that you are to be back . . .' remarked Andrew Stuart.

'In eighty days,' replied Mr. Fogg, 'on Saturday, 21st December, 1872, at eight-forty-five p.m. Goodbye, gentlemen.'

At eight-forty Phileas Fogg and his servant took their seats in the same compartment. At eight-forty-five there was a resounding whistle-blast and the train started to move off.

It was a dark night and a fine drizzle was falling. Phileas Fogg, leaning back in his corner seat, did not speak. Passepartout, still stunned and bewildered, was automatically clutching to his bosom the bag containing the banknotes.

But the train had not passed Sydenham when Passepartout uttered a cry of real despair.

'What is wrong?' asked Mr. Fogg.

'The fact is . . . in my hurry . . . and all the upset . . . I forgot . . . "

'What?'

'I forgot to turn out the gaslight in my room!'

'Well, young man,' Mr. Fogg replied without emotion, 'it will just have to burn at your expense!'

*In which a new type of share appears on the London
Stock Exchange*

When he left London, Phileas Fogg had certainly no inkling
of the excitement that would be caused by his departure.
News of the bet spread first of all round the Reform Club
and created quite a stir among the members of that honourable society. Then the excitement passed from the Club to
the Press, by way of the reporters, and from the Press to
the public at large, in London and the whole of the United
Kingdom.

That business of 'going round the world' was commented
on and discussed and analysed with as much passion and
vehemence as if it had been a repetition of the affair of the
s.s. *Alabama*. Some sided with Phileas Fogg, and the
rest—who soon formed the great majority—were against
him. This journey round the world that had to be undertaken
in the bare minimum of time and with the means of transport available was not merely impossible—it was absolutely
mad, except on paper.

The Times, the *Standard*, the *Evening Star*, the *Morning
Chronicle* and twenty other newspapers with large circu-
lations were against Mr. Fogg. Only the *Daily Telegraph*
supported him up to a certain point. People called Phileas
Fogg a fool or a madman and his acquaintances at the
Reform Club were condemned for taking on a bet proposed
by someone who was not of sound mind.

Highly emotional, but logical, articles were published on
the subject. The British are well-known for the interest in
anything connected with geography. So there was not a
single reader in the land, irrespective of the class to which
he belonged, who did not read voraciously the columns
devoted to Phileas Fogg.

During the first few days some bold spirits—mainly women—were on his side, especially when the *Illustrated London News* published a portrait of him from the photograph he had deposited in the archives of the Reform Club. Certain gentlemen ventured to say: 'Well, well! Why not, after all? Stranger things have happened!' These were mainly people who read the *Daily Telegraph*. But one soon sensed that that paper was beginning to weaken in its allegiance too.

Indeed a long article appeared on 7th October in the *Journal of the Royal Geographical Society*. It discussed the question from all points of view and clearly demonstrated how mad the whole undertaking was. Everything was against the traveller—both man-made obstacles and natural obstacles. Before the plan could succeed there would have to be a miraculous degree of agreement between the hours of departure and arrival throughout—and this did not—indeed could not—exist. One could rely on trains arriving at a fixed time in Europe where the distances are relatively short, but they took three days to cross India and seven to cross the United States, so how could one rely on their always being on time? What about breakdowns and derailments and collisions? What about the rainy seasons and snowdrifts? Was not everything against Phileas Fogg? Was not one at the mercy of gales and fog on a ship in winter? Was it so unusual for even the fastest ships of the ocean lines to arrive two or three days late? And one single delay would be enough to break the chain of communication finally and irrevocably. If Phileas Fogg missed a sailing by only a few hours he would be forced to wait for the next steamer, and that would upset his journey completely.

That article caused a great stir. Nearly all the newspapers printed it and Phileas Fogg's stock dropped sharply.

During the first few days after his departure substantial sums of money had been staked on the outcome of his venture. In England the betting world is more intelligent and exalted than the gambling world. Betting is a part of the British temperament. So, not only did the various members of the Reform Club bet considerable sums for or

against Phileas Fogg—the general public entered into the spirit of things too. Phileas Fogg's name was entered on the lists as if he had been a race-horse. He became a Stock Exchange security which was at once quoted on the London market. 'Phileas Foggs' were on demand or on offer, outright or with an option, and huge deals were concluded. But five days after his departure, when the article in the *Journal of the Royal Geographical Society* had appeared, there was a glut of offers. The 'Phileas Foggs' went down. They were offered in bundles. They had been taken at five to one to begin with, then at ten, but soon they reached only twenty, fifty, one hundred!

Only one supporter remained loyal to him, and that was the old paralytic, Lord Albemarle. That worthy gentleman, who was confined to his chair, would have given his entire fortune to be able to go round the world, even if he took ten years to do it! He placed five thousand pounds on Phileas Fogg. And when people pointed out to him the folly, and also the pointlessness, of the whole project, he merely replied: 'If it can be done, an Englishman should be the first to do it.'

So that was how matters stood. Phileas Fogg's supporters were dwindling more and more. Everybody, and not without good reason, was turning against him. He was now only being backed at one hundred and fifty, or two hundred, to one. Then, seven days after his departure, a completely unexpected development made people stop backing him at all.

At 9 p.m. on the day in question the chief of the Metropolitan Police received a telegram worded as follows:

'Suez to London. *Rowan, Chief of Police, Central Office, Scotland Yard. Am shadowing Bank robber Phileas Fogg. Send warrant at once Bombay.*

Fix, Detective.'

That telegram had an immediate effect. The honourable gentleman vanished from the scene, making way for the Bank robber. His photograph, deposited at the Reform Club with those of all his fellow-members, was examined. It

　　　　　　　　　　(H880)

reproduced feature by feature the man whose description had been supplied by the inquiry. People recalled the mysterious life led by Phileas Fogg, his isolation from the world, his sudden departure. It seemed obvious that he was using the journey round the world as a pretext, basing it on a senseless wager. His sole object had been to throw the British police off the scent.

In which the detective Fix shows a very proper impatience

These are the circumstances under which the telegram concerning Mr. Phileas Fogg had been sent off.

On Wednesday, 9th October, the s.s. *Mongolia* of the Peninsular and Oriental Steam Navigation Company, an iron vessel of 2,800 tons and a nominal horse-power of 500, with a propeller and a spar-deck, was scheduled to arrive at Suez. The *Mongolia* made regular voyages from Brindisi to Bombay by way of the Suez Canal. She was one of the fastest ships of the Company and always exceeded her scheduled speeds, i.e., ten miles per hour between Brindisi and Suez, and nine and fifty-three hundredths between Suez and Bombay.

Whilst awaiting the arrival of the *Mongolia*, two men were walking about on the quayside among the crowds of natives and foreigners who have come flooding into that town, until recently little more than a village. The great scheme of M. de Lesseps will guarantee a great future for it.

One of these two men was the Consular agent of the United Kingdom in Suez. In spite of the unfavourable predictions of the British Government and the ominous forecast of the engineer Stephenson, he saw British ships passing through the Canal every day, thus reducing by half the old route from England to India by way of the Cape of Good Hope.

The other was a thin little man with quite an intelligent face. His nerves seemed to be on edge and he kept contracting his eyebrow muscles all the time. Very keen eyes glinted through long lashes, but he was able to extinguish the light in them at will. He was showing some signs of impatience and kept on walking to and fro, as if unable to stand still.

That man was called Fix and he was one of the British detectives who had been sent to the various ports of the world after the robbery at the Bank of England. Fix's task was to scrutinize all the travellers going on the Suez route and if any of them seemed suspicious he was to shadow that person until a warrant arrived for his arrest.

As it happened, Fix had received a description of the supposed Bank robber from the chief of the Metropolitan Police two days before. It was the description of that distinguished and well-dressed man who had been observed in the payments department of the Bank.

So the detective, obviously very much attracted by the substantial bonus promised in the event of an arrest, was waiting impatiently for the *Mongolia* to arrive.

'You say, sir,' he asked the Consul for the tenth time, 'that the ship cannot be long now?'

'No, Mr. Fix' replied the Consul. 'She was signalled yesterday off Port Said, and the hundred miles along the Canal are nothing to a ship as fast as she is. As I told you, the *Mongolia* has always won the £25 bonus awarded by the Government for every advance of twenty-four hours on the scheduled times.'

'Is the ship coming straight from Brindisi?' asked Fix.

'Yes, from Brindisi. She took on mail there for India. And she sailed at five o'clock on Saturday afternoon. So be patient. It will not be long now. But really I do not know how you will be able to recognize your man from the description you have, assuming that he is on board the *Mongolia* at all.'

'My good sir,' replied Fix, 'you do not *recognize* that sort of person. You sniff them out. You have to have a nose for it. It is like a special sense, with hearing and sight and smell all rolled into one. I have arrested more than one of these gentlemen in my time and, if my Bank robber is on board, he will not slip through my fingers, I can tell you.'

'I hope you are right, Mr. Fix. A large sum of money is involved.'

'A magnificent sum,' replied the detective enthusiastically. 'Fifty-five thousand pounds! We do not often have wind-

falls like that. Thieves are growing petty and niggardly. The old breed of thieves like Sheppard are dying out! They go and get themselves hanged nowadays just for a few shillings!'

'From all you say,' replied the Consul. 'I sincerely hope you will be successful. But I shall repeat what I said before. Under the circumstances I am afraid it is going to be difficult. Do you realize that, from the description you have received, the robber looks exactly like an honest man?'

'Sir,' replied the police inspector dogmatically, 'robbers who operate on a grand scale always do look like honest men. You see, men who look like rogues only have one course open to them. They must stay honest, otherwise they will be arrested. It is honest faces that have to be examined most carefully of all. It is a difficult task, I agree, and it is not an ordinary routine job—it is an art!'

You will see that Mr. Fix was not without a fair amount of *amour-propre*.

The quayside was growing gradually busier. Seamen of different nationalities, traders, brokers, street-porters and *fellahs* all came crowding on to it. The steamer was obviously due shortly.

It was quite a fine day, but the air was cold and the wind was blowing from the east. A few minarets stood out above the town under the pale rays of the sun. To the south a pier over a mile long extended like an arm into the Suez roadstead. Several fishing-boats and coastal vessels were tossing about on the Red Sea. Some of them had preserved in their own characteristic way the elegant lines of the galleys of olden times.

As he moved through the crowd, Fix scanned the passers-by with a rapid glance, a habit he owed to his profession.

It was then ten-thirty.

'Is the steamer never coming?' he cried when he heard the harbour clock striking.

'She cannot be far away,' replied the Consul.

'How long will she be staying at Suez?' asked Fix.

'Four hours. Just enough time to take on coal. It is thirteen hundred and ten miles from Suez to Aden, right

at the end of the Red Sea, so they have to take supplies of fuel on board.'

'And does the ship go straight to Bombay from Suez?' asked Fix.

'Yes, straight there, without breaking bulk.'

'Well,' said Fix, 'if the robber has taken this route and is on board this ship, he must be planning to land at Suez and reach the Dutch or French possessions in Asia by a different route. He must realize that he would not be safe in India, because it belongs to Britain.'

'Unless he is a very clever man,' replied the Consul. 'A British criminal is always better hidden in London, you know, than he would be abroad.'

With that remark, which gave Fix plenty of food for thought, the Consul went back to his office, which was situated not far away. The police inspector was left alone, in the grip of nervous impatience. He had a strange presentiment that the robber would indeed be on board the *Mongolia*. If the rogue had left England with the intention of making his way to the New World, the Indian route, which would not be so closely watched as the Atlantic route and would indeed be more difficult to watch, would no doubt have been the one preferred by him.

Fix did not have much time for thought. Shrill whistle-blasts announced the arrival of the steamer. The hordes of street porters and *fellahs* rushed towards the quay. All this commotion must have been a little worrying for the passengers and the safety of their limbs and clothing. About ten small boats moved away from the bank and went out to meet the *Mongolia*.

Soon they could see the gigantic hull of the *Mongolia* passing between the banks of the Canal. Eleven o'clock was striking as the steamer cast anchor in the roadstead, steam issuing noisily from the escape pipes.

There were a fair number of passengers on board. Some of them stayed on the spar-deck and gazed at the picturesque scene presented by the town. But the majority disembarked and boarded the little boats that had come alongside the *Mongolia*.

Fix made a careful study of all the passengers who stepped ashore.

Then one of them came up to him, after vigorously pushing away the *fellahs* who were pestering him with their offers of assistance, and asked him very politely if he could show him where the British Consulate was. And, as he did so, the passenger held out a passport which he no doubt wished to have stamped.

Fix instinctively took the passport and glanced briefly at it. But that was enough for him to read the description.

He almost gave a start. The page trembled in his hand. The description in the passport was identical to the one he had been given by the chief of the Metropolitan Police.

'This passport is not yours, is it?' he said to the passenger.

'No,' replied the latter, 'it is my master's passport.'

'And where is your master?'

'He stayed on board.'

'But,' the detective went on, 'he must go to the consulate in person to establish his identity.'

'What, is that necessary?'

'Absolutely essential.'

'And where is the Consulate?'

'There, on the corner of the square,' replied the inspector, pointing to a building less than a hundred yards away.

'Well then, I shall go and fetch my master, but he will not be at all pleased at this inconvenience.'

Thereupon the passenger bowed to Fix and returned to the steamer.

*Which illustrates once more how useless passports
are as far as the police are concerned*

The inspector went down on the quayside again and quickly
made his way to the Consul's office. He made an urgent
request to see that official and was at once ushered into his
presence.

'I have strong reason to believe, sir,' he said without
preamble, 'that our man has taken a passage on the
Mongolia.'

And Fix related what had passed between the servant
and himself regarding the passport.

'Well, Mr. Fix,' replied the Consul, 'I would not be at all
averse to seeing the rogue face to face. But perhaps he will
not appear at my office if he is the man you suppose him to
be. A thief does not like to leave any traces behind him and
the passport formality is no longer compulsory.'

'If he is a clever man,' replied the detective, 'as he must
be, he will come!'

'To have his passport stamped?'

'Yes. The only purpose served by passports is to inconvenience honest folk and help rogues to get away. I am
certain it will be in order, but I do hope you will not
stamp it . . .'

'And why not? If the passport is in order,' replied the
Consul, 'I have no right to refuse to stamp it.'

'But I must keep the man here till I have received a
warrant for his arrest from London.'

'Oh, as to that, Mr. Fix, that is your business. I cannot . . .'

The Consul did not finish his sentence. At that moment
there was a knock on the door and the office-boy ushered in
two strangers, one of whom was, as it turned out, the servant
who had spoken to the detective.

The master and servant had indeed come. The master handed over his passport and briefly asked the Consul to be good enough to put a stamp on it.

The latter took the passport and read it through carefully, while Fix watched the stranger from a corner of the office, or rather devoured him with his eyes.

When the Consul had finished reading it, he asked:

'Are you Mr. Phileas Fogg?'

'Yes, sir,' replied the gentleman.

'And that man is your servant?'

'Yes. He is a Frenchman called Passepartout.'

'You have come from London?'

'Yes.'

'And you are going . . . ?'

'To Bombay.'

'Very good, sir. You know that the stamp serves no purpose at all and we no longer require passports to be shown?'

'I do,' replied Phileas Fogg, 'but I want your stamp to prove that I have come through Suez.'

'Very good, sir.'

And the Consul signed and dated the passport and stamped it. Mr. Fogg paid the stamp dues and, bowing distantly, he went out, followed by his servant.

'Well?' asked the inspector.

'Well,' replied the Consul, 'he looks a perfectly honest man.'

'Possibly,' said Fix, 'but that is not the point. Do you not think that that phlegmatic gentleman is exactly like the robber whose description I have been given?'

'I agree, but all descriptions, you know . . . '

'I will get to the bottom of it,' replied Fix. 'The servant seems less of a closed book than his master. What is more, he is a Frenchman, so he will not be slow to speak. See you later, sir.'

So saying, the detective went out in search of Passepartout.

On leaving the Consulate, Mr. Fogg had made his way to the quay. There he gave some instructions to his servant.

Then he boarded a small boat and returned to the *Mongolia*, where he retired to his cabin. There he took out his notebook, which contained the following notes:

Left London, Wednesday, 2nd October, 8.45 p.m.
Arrived Paris, Thursday 3rd October, 7.20 a.m.
Left Paris, Thursday 8.40 a.m.
Arrived Turin via the Mont Cenis, Friday 4th October, 6.35 a.m.
Left Turin, Friday, 7.20 a.m.
Arrived Brindisi, Saturday 5th October, 4 p.m.
Sailed on *Mongolia*, Saturday, 5 p.m.
Arrived Suez, Wednesday 9th October, 11 a.m.
Total hours taken: 158½, i.e. 6½ days.

Mr. Fogg entered those dates in an itinerary arranged in columns and showing, from 2nd October to 21st December, the month, the day of the month, the day of the week and the schedules and actual times of arrival at each important point—Paris, Brindisi, Suez, Bombay, Calcutta, Singapore, Hong Kong, Yokohama, San Francisco, New York, Liverpool, London. This would enable him to calculate how much time he had gained or lost at each place on the way.

That methodical itinerary made allowance for everything and Mr. Fogg always knew if he was ahead of or behind schedule.

So on that day, Wednesday 9th October, he recorded his arrival at Suez. As it tallied with his scheduled time of arrival, it did not represent a gain or a loss.

Then he arranged for lunch to be served to him in his cabin. It never occurred to him to have a look at the town, as he belonged to that breed of Englishmen who view the countries they are crossing at secondhand, through their servants.

*In which Passepartout talks perhaps a little more
than he ought*

In a few moments Fix had caught up with Passepartout on
the quayside. The latter was strolling about and having a
look round, as, unlike his master, *he* felt under no obligation
to make a point of seeing nothing.

'Well, my friend,' said Fix, going up to him, 'has your
passport been stamped?'

'Oh, it is you sir,' replied the Frenchman. 'Thank you
very much. Everything is perfectly in order.'

'And you are having a look round, are you?'

'Yes, but we are going so fast that I feel as if the journey
is all a dream. And this is Suez?'

'Yes, this is Suez.'

'In Egypt?'

'Quite right—in Egypt.'

'In Africa?'

'Yes, in Africa.'

'In Africa!' repeated Passepartout. 'I cannot believe it.
Just imagine! I thought we would not be going beyond
Paris, and all I saw of that famous capital was the part
between the Gare du Nord and the Gare de Lyon through
the windows of a cab in lashing rain, between twenty
past seven and twenty to nine in the morning. I was sorry
about that. I would have loved to have seen the Père
Lachaise Cemetery and the circus on the Champs-Elysées
again!'

'You are in a great hurry then?' the police inspector
inquired.

'Not me—my master! And, by the way, I must go and
buy some socks and shirts. We set off without any cases,
just a carpet-bag.'

'I can take you to a bazaar where you will find all you need.'

'You really are too kind, sir,' replied Passepartout.

And so they set off together. Passepartout was still chattering on.

'I must be particularly careful,' he said, 'not to miss the boat.'

'You have ample time,' replied Fix. 'It is only twelve noon.'

Passepartout pulled out his large watch.

'Twelve noon?' he said. 'Nonsense! It is nine-fifty-two.'

'Your watch is slow,' replied Fix.

'My watch! A family heirloom that has been handed down from my great-grandfather! It does not go five minutes wrong in the whole year. It is an excellent time-keeper.'

'I see what it is,' replied Fix. 'You have kept to London time and it is about two hours behind Suez time. You should take care to set your watch to the meridian in every country.'

'What—touch my watch!' exclaimed Passepartout. 'Never!'

'Well, it will not agree with the sun.'

'Then it is just too bad for the sun. It is the sun that is wrong.'

And the worthy fellow replaced the watch in his waist-coat pocket with a flourish.

A few moments later Fix said:

'So you left London in a hurry, did you?'

'I should just think we did! Last Wednesday evening Mr. Fogg returned from his Club at eight o'clock, quite contrary to his usual practice, and three-quarters of an hour later we were off.'

'But where is your master going?'

'Straight on all the time. He is going round the world!'

'Round the world?' cried Fix.

'Yes, in eighty days. He says that it is for a bet, but, just between ourselves, I do not believe a word of it. There would be no sense in it. There is something else behind it.'

'Oh! This Mr. Fogg is an eccecntric, is he?'

'I think so.'

'He is rich then, is he?'

'Evidently. And he is carrying a tidy sum on him, in banknotes. And he does not stint himself on the way. Why, he has promised a fine bonus to the engineer of the *Mongolia* if we reach Bombay well ahead of schedule.'

'Have you known your master long?'

'Not me!' replied Passepartout. 'I entered his service on the very day of our departure.'

One can readily imagine the effect these replies had on the already over-active mind of the police inspector.

The hurried departure from London so soon after the robbery, the large sum of money taken away, this haste to reach distant lands, the pretext of an eccentric bet—all this could not but confirm Fix's suspicions. He let the Frenchman go on speaking and learned that that young fellow did not know his master at all, and that the latter lived a solitary life in London and was said to be rich although no-one knew the source of his wealth and he was a man of mystery, etc. But, at the same time, Fix could be certain that Phileas Fogg was not landing at Suez, but was really going on to Bombay.'

'Is Bombay a long way off?' asked Passepartout.

'Quite a long way,' replied the detective. 'You will have to spend another ten days or so at sea.'

'And where would you say Bombay is?'

'In India.'

'In Asia?'

'Of course.'

'Confound it! The fact is . . . there is something that is bothering me . . . it is the light!'

'What light?'

'My gaslight. I forgot to turn it out and it is burning at my expense. I have worked it out and it will cost me two shillings for every twenty-four hours, just sixpence more than I earn, and so, if the journey goes on much longer . . .'

Did Fix understand about the gas? Probably not. He was not listening. He was coming to a decision. The Frenchman

and he had reached the bazaar. Fix left his companion there to make his purchases with an injunction not to miss the boat and returned to the Consulate in all haste.

Now that Fix was convinced in his own mind he had reverted to his normal calm state.

'I have no doubt in my mind at all now,' he told the Consul. 'I have got my man. He is passing himself off as an eccentric who is trying to go round the world in eighty days.'

'In that case he is a cunning fellow,' replied the Consul. 'He means to return to London after he has thrown all the police forces of both continents off the scent.'

'We shall see about that,' said Fix.

'But might you not be mistaken?' the Consul asked once again.

'No, I am not.'

'Well then, why did the robber insist on having a passport stamp to prove that he had passed through Suez?'

'I have no idea,' replied the detective. 'But listen to this!'

And in a few words he outlined the main points of his conversation with Mr. Fogg's servant.

'All the evidence does indeed seem to be against the man,' said the Consul. 'What are you going to do?'

'I am going to send off a telegram to London urgently requesting a warrant to be sent to me in Bombay, and I shall sail on the *Mongolia* and follow the robber as far as India and there, on British soil, I shall go up to him politely with my warrant in my hand and place a hand on his shoulder.'

After making that cool statement the detective took his leave of the Consul and made his way to the telegraph office. From there he sent off his telegram to the chief of the Metropolitan Police.

A quarter of an hour later Fix, carrying light hand luggage and well supplied with money, went on board the *Mongolia* and soon the fast steamer was travelling full speed ahead over the waters of the Red Sea.

*In which the Red Sea and the Indian Ocean favour
the schemes of Phileas Fogg*

The distance between Suez and Aden is exactly thirteen hundred and ten miles and the sailing schedule of the Company allows its steamers one hundred and thirty-eight hours to cover it. The *Mongolia*, with her fires well stoked, was going so fast that she would arrive ahead of schedule.

Most of the passengers who had joined the ship at Brindisi were bound for India. Some were going to Bombay and the others to Calcutta, via Bombay, as, now that there was a railway line crossing the entire breadth of the Indian peninsula, it was no longer necessary to round the tip of Ceylon.

Among the passengers on the *Mongolia* there were several civil servants and officers of various ranks. Some belonged to the British Army, properly speaking, and the others commanded native Sepoys. All of them had high salaries although the Government had taken over the rights and duties of the old East India Company. Sub-lieutenants received £280, brigadiers £2,400 and generals £4,000. The pay of civil servants was even higher. Ordinary assistants, on the lowest rung of the ladder, received £480, judges £2,400, presiding judges £10,000, governors £12,000 and the Governor-General over £24,000.

So the passengers on the *Mongolia* lived well in that community of officials, with a sprinkling of young Englishmen with a fortune in their pockets who were going off to establish business houses a long way from home. The purser, the confidential agent of the Company and equal to the captain on board, arranged everything on a grand scale. At breakfast, and at the lunch at two o'clock, the tea at five-thirty and the dinner at eight the tables groaned

under dishes of fresh meat and *entremets* provided by the butcher's department and the pantries of the ship. There were a few lady passengers and they changed their dresses twice a day. There was music and even dancing, when the sea permitted it.

But the Red Sea is very unpredictable and often rough, like all long, narrow sea-ways. When the wind blew from the coast of Asia or the coast of Africa, the *Mongolia*, a long, sharp-built vessel with a propeller, was caught broadside on and rolled dreadfully. Then the ladies would disappear, the pianos fell silent and the singing and dancing would come to an end. But in spite of the squall and in spite of the swell, the steamer, carried forward by her powerful engine, sped on towards the Bab el Mandeb Straits.

What was Phileas Fogg doing all this time? One might imagine him to be in a perpetual state of worry and anxiety, concerned at the changes in the wind that would reduce the speed of the ship and at the wild, irregular motion of the swell that might damage the engine, and in fact all the possible mishaps that might force the *Mongolia* to put into the nearest port, so affecting the success of the journey.

Not at all! Or, at least, if the gentlemen did think of all these things that might happen he gave no sign of doing so. He was just as impassive as ever, the imperturbable member of the Reform Club who could not be caught off his guard by anything that happened. He seemed to be no more affected by it all than the ship's chronometers. He was rarely to be seen on deck. He had no desire to look at the Red Sea, so rich in memories, where the first scenes in the history of mankind were enacted. He made no attempt to identify the curious townships scattered along its shores, with their picturesque outlines carved upon the horizon. He never gave a thought to the perils of that gulf of Arabia, of which the historians of old, Strabo, Flavius Arrianus, Artemidorus and Edrisi always spoke in awestruck tones and over which the navigators of bygone days never ventured without first consecrating their voyage by means of sacrifices.

What was that eccentric gentleman doing while he was imprisoned on the *Mongolia*? First of all, he ate his four

meals every day. No rolling or pitching could upset that highly organised machine. And he also played whist.

Yes, he had come across players who were just as enthusiastic as himself. There was a tax collector going to his post in Goa, a minister of the church, the Reverend Decimus Smith, returning to Bombay, and a brigadier-general of the British Army who was rejoining his troops in Benares. These three passengers were just as passionately addicted to whist as Mr. Fogg and they played for hours on end in a silence as great as his own.

As for Passepartout, sea-sickness held no terrors for him. He occupied a cabin in the forepart of the ship and he too ate his meals conscientiously. To tell the truth, he no longer found the journey unpleasant. He made the best of it. He was well fed and had comfortable accommodation and he was seeing the world. And, what is more, he kept on telling himself that the fantastic adventure would come to an end in Bombay.

On the day after leaving Suez, 10th October, he was rather pleased to meet on deck the obliging man he had spoken to when he landed in Egypt.

'If I am not mistaken,' he said, going up to him with his nicest smile, 'you are the gentleman who was kind enough to act as my guide in Suez.'

'Quite right,' replied the detective. 'I remember you. You are the servant of that eccentric Englishman . . . '

'Quite so, sir.'

'My name is Fix.'

'Mr. Fix,' replied Passepartout, 'I am delighted to see you on board. Where are you going?'

'Why, to Bombay, like you.'

'That could not be better! Have you done this trip before?'

'Several times,' replied Fix. 'I am an agent of the Peninsular Company.'

'So you know India?'

'Oh, er . . . yes, I do,' replied Fix, not wanting to say too much.

'Is India a strange country?'

'Very strange. There are mosques and minarets, and temples and fakirs and pagodas, and there are tigers and snakes, not to mention dancing-girls. But I hope you will have time to see something of the country.'

'I hope so, Mr. Fix. You will realize that a man in his right mind cannot spend his life jumping from a ship into a train, and off a train on to a ship on the pretext that he is going round the world in eighty days. Oh no, all these antics will come to an end in Bombay. There is no doubt of that.'

'And is Mr. Fogg well?' asked Fix in his most natural tone of voice.

'Very well, Mr. Fix. And so am I. I am eating like an ogre who has been on a fast. It is the sea air.'

'I never see your master up on deck.'

'Never. He is not of an inquisitive turn of mind.'

'You know, Mr. Passepartout. This tour of the world in eighty days may well be a cover for some secret mission . . . a diplomatic mission perhaps.'

'Upon my word, Mr. Fix, I know nothing about it. And I really would not give so much as a half-crown to find out.'

From the time of that first meeting Passepartout and Fix often chatted together. The police inspector was anxious to strike up a friendship with Mr. Fogg's servant. It might turn out to be useful some day. So in the bar of the *Mongolia* he often treated him to glasses of whisky or pale ale, which the good fellow accepted without demur, and, not to be outdone, he took his turn of standing the drinks. He thought Fix was a very honest gentleman.

The ship was proceeding rapidly on her way. On the 13th they sighted Mocha within its girdle of ruined walls, above which rose green date-palms. Far away in the hills there were vast plantations of coffee-trees. Passepartout gazed at that famous city in delight. With its circular walls and the dismantled fort shaped like a handle it actually looked like an enormous coffee cup.

During the following night the *Mongolia* crossed the Bab el Mandeb Strait—its Arabic name means the 'Gateway of Mourning'—and on the next day, the 14th, she called at

Steamer Point, to the north-west of the Aden roadstead. There she was to take on fresh fuel.

This business of stoking the fires so far away from the centres of production is a serious and important matter. For the Peninsular Company alone it represents an annual expenditure of eight hundred thousand pounds. It has been necessary to establish depots at various points and in those far-off seas coal costs over £3 per ton.

The *Mongolia* still had sixteen hundred and fifty miles to go before reaching Bombay and she was to remain at Steamer Point for four hours to fill her bunkers.

But that delay could not have any adverse effect on Phileas Fogg's programme. It had been allowed for. Moreover, instead of arriving at Aden on the morning of 15th October, the *Mongolia* reached there on the evening of the 14th. This represented a gain of fifteen hours.

Mr. Fogg and his servant went ashore. The gentleman wanted to have his passport stamped. Fix followed him unobserved. When the formality of the passport had been attended to, Fogg returned to the ship in order to resume his interrupted game.

As for Passepartout, he went for a stroll, as was his habit. He wandered among the Somalis, the Banians, the Parsees, the Jews, the Arabs and the Europeans who make up Aden's population of twenty-five thousand. He marvelled at the fortifications which have made this town the Gibraltar of the Indian Ocean and the magnificent water tanks at which British engineers were still working two thousand years after the engineers of King Solomon.

'It is all very odd, very odd!' Passepartout said to himself as he returned to the ship. 'I can see that there is some point in travelling if one wants to see something new.'

At six o'clock in the evening the propeller blades of the *Mongolia* were flailing the waters of the Aden roadstead and soon she was speeding across the Indian Ocean. She was allowed one hundred and sixty-eight hours to make the crossing from Aden to Bombay. Conditions on the Indian Ocean were favourable. The wind was holding in the north-west and the sails came to the assistance of the steam.

The ship was now well-balanced and rolled less. The lady passengers reappeared on deck in fresh outfits. The singing and dancing began again.

So they had the best possible conditions for the voyage. Passepartout was delighted with the agreeable companion whom fate had sent his way in the person of Fix.

On Sunday, 20th October, towards noon, the coast of India was sighted. Two hours later the pilot climbed on board the *Mongolia*. On the horizon a background of hills was outlined harmoniously against the sky. Soon the lines of palm-trees, which are so abundant in the city, came clearly into view. The steamer entered the roadstead formed by the islands of Salsette, Colaba, Elephanta and Butcher's Island and at four-thirty she came alongside the quays of Bombay.

Phileas Fogg was at the time finishing the thirty-third rubber of the day and, thanks to a bold move, he and his partner had taken all thirteen tricks and so they ended that splendid crossing with a spectacular grand slam.

The *Mongolia* had reached Bombay on 20th October, although she had not been due there till the 22nd. So, since his departure from London, Phileas Fogg had gained two days and he recorded them methodically in his itinerary in the credit column.

*In which Passepartout is only too pleased to get
off with the loss of his shoes*

Everyone knows that India—that great inverted triangle
with its base in the north and its vertex in the south—
covers an area of fourteen hundred thousand square miles,
over which a population of one hundred and eighty million
inhabitants is unevenly distributed. The British Government exercises real control over a part of that immense
country. It maintains a Governor-General in Calcutta,
Governors in Madras, Bombay and Bengal, and a lieutenant-
Governor in Agra.

But British India, properly speaking, has an area of only
seven hundred thousand square miles and a population of
one hundred to one hundred and ten million inhabitants.
A considerable part of the country still does not come
under the authority of the Queen. In the domains of certain
rajahs in the interior, who are fierce and terrible men, the
independence of the Indians is still absolute.

From 1756—when the first British settlement was
established on the site now occupied by the city of Madras—
until the year when the great Sepoy insurrection broke out,
the celebrated East India Company was all-powerful. It
gradually annexed the different provinces, bought from the
rajahs in return for annual rents that were not paid in full, if
at all. It appointed its own Governor-General and all its
civil and military staff. But now it is no longer in existence
and the British possessions in India are held directly by the
Crown.

So the appearance and customs and ethnographic
divisions of the peninsula tend to change from day to day.
In former times one used to travel by all the old-fashioned
modes of transport—on foot, on horseback, in carts, hand-

chairs, palanquins or on men's backs or in a coach, etc. Now steamboats go along the Indus and the Ganges at great speed and a railway runs right across India, branching out as it goes along and bringing Bombay within three days' travelling time from Calcutta.

That railway does not go in a straight line across India. The distance is only one thousand to eleven hundred miles as the crow flies and trains driven at no more than average speed would not take three days to cross it. But the distance is increased by at least one-third as a result of the arc formed by the railway when it goes up to Allahabad in the north of the peninsula.

Here are, briefly, the main points along the route of the Great Indian Peninsular Railway. Leaving the island of Bombay, it crosses Salsette, jumps over to the mainland opposite Thana, crosses the range of the Western Ghats, runs north-eastwards as far as Burhanpur, proceeds through the virtually independent territory of Bundelkund, goes up to Allahabad, bends round to the east, reaches the Ganges at Benares, moves slightly away from it and, running down again to the south-east via Burdwan and the French town of Chandernagore, it reaches the end of the line in Calcutta.

The passengers from the *Mongolia* had landed at Bombay at four-thirty in the afternoon and the train for Calcutta was due to leave on the stroke of eight o'clock.

So Mr. Fogg said goodbye to his whist partners, left the steamer, gave his servant a note of several purchases to make with an injunction to be at the station by eight, and then made his way to the passport office at his steady pace, which was like the pendulum of an astronomical clock beating out the seconds.

He had no intention of viewing the wonders of Bombay, the municipal corporation building, the splendid library, the forts, the docks, the cotton-market, the bazaars, the mosques, the synagogues, the Armenian churches or the magnificent pagoda on Malabar Hill with its two polygon towers. He would not gaze in admiration at the masterpieces of Elephanta with its mysterious underground temples

53

lying hidden to the south-east of the roadstead, or the caves of Kanheri on the island of Salsette, which are remarkable relics of Buddhist architecture.

He would see nothing of all this. On leaving the passport office, Phileas Fogg walked calmly to the station and there had dinner. Amongst other dishes, the head waiter made a point of recommending an Indian rabbit stew which he praised highly.

Phileas Fogg agreed to have the stew and sampled it conscientiously. But, in spite of the highly spiced sauce, he found it absolutely horrible.

He rang for the head waiter.

'Is that rabbit?' he asked, looking him straight in the eye.

'Yes, my lord,' replied the rogue impudently, 'jungle rabbit.'

'And did the rabbit not mew when it was killed?'

'Mew? Oh, my lord! A rabbit! I swear to you . . .'

'Waiter,' Mr. Fogg replied coldly, 'do not swear and remember this! At one time cats were considered sacred animals in India—in the good old days.'

'Good for the cats, my lord?'

'And perhaps for travellers too!'

Having said that, Mr. Fogg went on dining calmly.

Fix the detective had landed from the *Mongolia* a few moments after Mr. Fogg and hurried to see the chief of police in Bombay. He established the fact that he was a detective and explained the mission with which he had been entrusted and his position with regard to the supposed robber. Had a warrant been received from London? No, nothing had been received. Indeed, as the warrant had left after Mr. Fogg, it could not possibly have arrived yet.

Fix was greatly put out. He wanted the chief of police to give him an order for the arrest of Mr. Fogg, but that he refused to do. It was a matter concerning the Metropolitan Police and only they could legally issue a warrant. Such rigid adherence to principle and strict observance of the law are part of the English way of life, which will admit of no arbitrary procedure where the liberty of the individual is involved.

Fix did not insist. He realised that he would have to resign himself to waiting for the warrant. But he determined not to lose sight of the enigmatic rogue during the whole time he remained in Bombay. He was certain that Phileas Fogg would stay on there, and, as we know, Passepartout had been convinced of that too. And so there would be time for the warrant to arrive.

But from the final orders given him by his master when he left the *Mongolia* Passepartout realized that the same thing would happen in Bombay as had happened in Suez and Paris. The journey would not end there; it would go on as far as Calcutta at least, perhaps even further. And he began to wonder if that bet of Mr. Fogg's was not a serious business after all and if fate would not drag him round the world in eighty days in spite of his desire for a quiet life.

After purchasing some shirts and socks, he went for a walk along the streets of Bombay. They were thronged with people. In the midst of Europeans of all nationalities he saw Persians with pointed headgear, Banians with round turbans, men of Sind with square caps, Armenians in long robes, Parsees with black mitres. A feast-day was in fact being celebrated by those very Parsees, or Guebers, direct descendants of the followers of Zarathustra, who are the most industrious, civilized, intelligent and austere of the Indians—a race to which the rich traders of Bombay belong. On that particular day they were holding a kind of religious carnival with processions and entertainments, including dancing-girls dressed in pink gauze brocaded with gold and silver who danced beautifully, and in a prefectly proper and decent manner, to the sound of viols and the beating of tom-toms.

Needless to say, Passepartout stopped to watch all these curious ceremonies and kept his eyes and ears wide open. In fact he looked for all the world like some country bumpkin who had come to town.

Unfortunately for himself and his master, whose whole project he was in danger of jeopardizing, his curiosity led him further than he ought to have gone.

After that glimpse of the Parsee carnival, Passepartout was making his way towards the station when he passed the wonderful pagoda on Malabar Hill and had the unfortunate idea of going inside.

He was unaware of two things. Firstly, that Christians are strictly forbidden to enter certain Hindu pagodas and, secondly, that even believers cannot go inside unless they leave their shoes at the door. I should mention here that it is a sound matter of policy on the part of the British Government to respect the religion of the country in every detail and ensure that others respect it too and anyone who violates this rule is severely punished.

Passepartout went in like an ordinary tourist, meaning no harm, and found himself surrounded by all the dazzle and show of Brahman ornamentation. Then suddenly he was flung down on the consecrated floor. Three priests with anger in their eyes rushed upon him, tore off his shoes and socks and began to beat him to the accompaniment of savage cries.

The Frenchman, who was strong and agile, sprang smartly to his feet. With a blow from his fist and a kick he brought down two of his opponents who were greatly handicapped by their long robes and, rushing out of the pagoda as fast as his legs would carry him, he soon outdistanced the third Hindu who had darted after him, rousing the crowd to action.

At five minutes to eight, just a few minutes before the train was due to leave, Passepartout reached the railway station barefoot and minus his hat. In the scuffle he had lost the parcel containing his purchases.

Fix was there on the platform. Following Mr. Fogg to the station, he realized that the rogue was about to leave Bombay. So he at once resolved to follow him to Calcutta, and further if necessary. Passepartout did not notice Fix, who was standing in the shadows, but Fix heard him give his master a brief account of his adventures.

'I hope this will not happen to you again,' Phileas Fogg replied simply, sitting down in one of the carriages.

The poor fellow, barefooted and embarrassed, followed his master without a word.

Fix was about to climb into a different carriage when a sudden thought stopped him and made him change his plans.

'No, I shall stay here,' he said to himself. 'A crime has been committed on Indian soil . . . I have got my man.'

And at that moment the engine gave a mighty whistle and the train disappeared into the night.

In which Phileas Fogg buys a mount at a fabulous price

The train had left on time. It was carrying a fair number of travellers, including some officers, civil servants and traders in opium and indigo whose business was taking them to the eastern part of the peninsula.

Passepartout was sitting in the same compartment as his master. A third traveller was occupying the opposite corner. It was the brigadier-general, Sir Francis Cromarty, one of Mr. Fogg's whist partners during the crossing from Suez to Bombay, who was rejoining his troops quartered at Benares.

Sir Francis Cromarty, a tall fair-haired man of about fifty who had distinguished himself greatly in the last revolt of the Sepoys, really deserved to be called a native of the country. He had lived in India from an early age and had only returned on a few occasions to the land of his birth. He was an educated man who would have been only too glad to give information about the customs, history and organisation of India if Phileas Fogg had been the kind of man to ask for it. But he asked no questions. He was not travelling—he was just going round the world. He was a heavy body describing an orbit round the earth in accordance with the laws of rational mechanics. At that moment he was going over again in his mind the hours he had spent since leaving London and he would have rubbed his hands if it had been in his nature to make an unnecessary movement of that kind.

Sir Francis Cromarty had not failed to realize that his travelling companion was an eccentric, although he had only had an opportunity to study him with his cards in his hand, between two rubbers. He therefore wondered, quite

justifiably, if a human heart did indeed beat behind that cold exterior, or if Phileas Fogg had a soul alive to the beauties of nature or to moral aspirations. He rather doubted this. Of all the eccentrics the brigadier-general had met, none could compare with this product of the exact sciences.

Phileas Fogg had made no secret of his plan of going round the world, or of the conditions under which he was doing it. But the brigadier-general merely saw in this wager an eccentric scheme that served no useful purpose and was devoid of the principle of *transire benefaciendo* that should guide the conduct of every reasonable man. Judging by the way in which that odd gentleman was going along, he would obviously do no good either to himself or to others.

One hour after leaving Bombay, the train, passing over the viaducts, had crossed the island of Salsette and was now running on the mainland. At the station of Kalyan it left on the right the branch that goes down to the south-east of India via Khandala and Poona and came to the station of Panwel. At that point it plunged into the complicated system of the Western Ghats, lines of mountains with trap and basalt at their base, the highest summits of which are densely wooded.

From time to time Sir Francis Cromarty and Phileas Fogg exchanged a few words and at that point on the journey the brigadier-general revived the conversation which was so often allowed to lapse, and said:

'A few years ago, Fogg, you would have had a delay here that would probably have upset your whole itinerary.'

'Why was that, Sir Francis ?'

'Because the railway stopped at the foot of the mountains and one had to cross them in a palanquin or on ponies as far as Khandala station, over on the opposite slope.'

'That delay would not have upset my programme in any way,' replied Mr. Fogg. 'I have made provision for certain obstacles occurring.'

'But, Fogg,' went on the brigadier-general, 'you nearly had a nasty business on your hands—I mean that little escapade of your servant.'

Passepartout, his feet wrapped in a travelling-rug, was sleeping soundly and had no idea that they were talking about him.

'The British Government is extremely severe, and rightly so, regarding that type of offence,' Sir Francis Cromarty went on. 'It is anxious, above all, that people should respect the religious customs of the Indians, and if your servant had been caught . . .'

'Well, if he had been caught, Sir Francis,' replied Mr. Fogg, 'he would have been tried and he would have served his sentence and returned quietly to Europe. I do not see how that business could have delayed his master.'

And, thereupon, the conversation was dropped once more. During the night the train crossed the Ghats and came to Nasik and on the next day, 21st October, it raced across the relatively flat area formed by the territory of Khandesh. The countryside was well cultivated and there was a sprinkling of townships over which the minarets of the pagodas rose in place of the characteristic church steeples of Europe. A large number of streams, most of them tributaries of the Godavari, watered that fertile country.

Passepartout had woken up and was looking out. He could not believe that he was crossing India in a train of the Great Peninsular Railway. It really seemed incredible to him. And yet it could not have been more real! The engine, driven by a British driver and fired with British coal, was sending out its smoke over the plantations of cotton and coffee, nutmeg, cloves and red peppers. The steam was twining round the clumps of palm-trees in the midst of which he could see picturesque bungalows, a few *viharas*, or derelict monasteries, and wonderful temples richly adorned with all the embellishments of Indian architecture. Then there were vast expanses of land stretching as far as the eye could see, jungles with snakes and tigers which were alarmed by the snorting of the train, and finally they came to forests through which the railway had been cut and there elephants watched with pensive gaze as the wild processions of wagons passed on its way.

In the course of the morning the travellers crossed that grim area beyond the station of Malegaon where blood had so often been shed by the followers of the goddess Kali. Not far away was Elura with its amazing pagodas and also the famous city of Aurangabad, the capital of the fierce ruler Aurangzeb, and now just the chief town of one of the detached provinces of the kingdom of the Nizam. It was over that region that Feringhea, leader of the Thugs and king of the Stranglers, held sway. These murderers had banded themselves together into a society who managed to elude capture and strangled victims of all ages in honour of the Goddess of Death, without ever shedding blood, and there was a time when one could not set foot anywhere in that area without coming across a dead body. The British Government has indeed been able to prevent these murders to a great extent, but the terrible society is still in existence and is still operating.

At twelve-thirty p.m. the train stopped at the station of Burhanpur and Passepartout was able to purchase for a fantastic sum a pair of Turkish slippers adorned with imitation pearls. He put them on with an air of vanity.

The travellers had a quick lunch and set out again for the station of Asirgarh. For a short time they went alongside the Tapti, a little river that later tumbles into the Gulf of Kambay near Surat.

It might be interesting to describe the thoughts that were passing through Passepartout's mind at the time. Till his arrival in Bombay he had believed, and had had every reason to believe, that the journey would end there. But now, as he was racing full steam ahead across India, he was aware of a change of heart. His old nature was returning with a rush. This was like the fanciful schemes of his youth. He was beginning to take his master's plans seriously and he was beginning to believe that the bet was real, and, as a result, he now believed in the journey round the world and the time-limit that must not be exceeded. He was anxious about possible delays or accidents that might occur on the way. He felt he was personally involved in the wager and shuddered to think how he might have prejudiced the whole

scheme the day before by loitering in Bombay. He was far less phlegmatic than Mr. Fogg and so he worried far more. He counted again and again the days that had passed and cursed the times when the train stopped and blamed it for being slow and he was secretly annoyed with Mr. Fogg for not promising the driver a bonus. He did not know that what could be done on a ship could not be done on the railway, where there has to be regulation speed.

Towards evening they plunged into the passes in the Satpura Mountains which separate the territory of Khandesh from Bundelkund.

On the next day, 22nd October, in answer to a question from Sir Francis Cromarty, Passepartout consulted his watch and said that it was three o'clock in the morning. That famous timepiece was still set according to the meridian of Greenwich which was about 77° to the west and the watch was in fact, four hours slow.

So Sir Francis corrected Passepartout and made the same comment as Fix had done. He tried to make him understand that he ought to adjust his watch to each new meridian and that, as he was going east all the time, i.e., to meet the sun, the days became four minutes shorter whenever they passed through a degree. It was no use. Whether the obstinate fellow really understood what the brigadier-general was saying or not, he refused to put his watch on and kept to London time as before. It was a harmless whim and could not hurt anybody.

At eight o'clock in the morning the train stopped fifteen miles outside Rothal in the middle of a vast clearning with some bungalows and workmen's huts standing round the edge of it. The uard gwent down the line of carriages and said:

'Will the passengers please get out here!'

Phileas Fogg looked at Sir Francis Cromarty who appeared to know nothing about this stop in the forest of tamarinds and date-palms.

Passepartout was no less surprised and rushed out on to the track. He returned almost at once, crying:

'There is no more railway, sir!'

'What do you mean?' asked Sir Francis Cromarty.

'The train is not going on!'

The brigadier-general climbed down from the carriage at once. Phileas Fogg followed him without hurrying. Both had a word with the guard.

'Where are we?' asked Sir Francis Cromarty.

'At the hamlet of Kholby,' replied the guard.

'Are we stopping here?'

'We have to. The railway has not been completed.'

'What! Not completed?'

'No! There is still a section about fifty miles long to be laid between here and Allahabad where the track continues.'

'But the papers announced the complete opening of the railway.'

'I cannot help that, sir. The papers were wrong.'

'And yet you issue tickets from Bombay to Calcutta!' went on Sir Francis Cromarty, who was beginning to feel annoyed.

'We do,' replied the guard, 'but the passengers know that they have to make their own way from Kholby to Allahabad.'

Sir Francis Cromarty was furious. Passepartout would gladly have knocked the guard down, although it was not his fault. He did not dare to look at his master.

'Sir Francis,' Mr. Fogg said simply, 'if you are agreeable, we shall try to find some way of reaching Allahabad.'

'Will this delay spoil your chances, Fogg?'

'No, Sir Francis, it has been allowed for.'

'What! You knew that the track . . .'

'Not at all! But I knew that some obstacle or other would crop up sooner or later. So nothing is spoiled. I have two days in hand and they can be sacrificed. There is a steamer sailing for Hong Kong from Calcutta at noon on the 25th. It is only the 22nd today, so we shall reach Calcutta on time.'

There was nothing to be said in face of this complete and utter assurance.

It was only too true that the finished track stopped at that point. Newspapers are like some watches. They have a curious habit of running on too fast and so they had announced the completion of line prematurely. Most of the

passengers know of this break in the track and, as soon as they had left the train, they commandeered all the vehicles that the village possessed—*palki-gharis* running on four wheels, carts pulled by zebu cattle, which are cattle with humps, travelling cars that looked like moving pagodas, palanquins, ponies, etc. So, after searching through the entire village, Mr. Fogg and Sir Francis Cromarty came back without finding anything.

'I shall walk,' said Phileas Fogg.

Passepartout, who had just rejoined his master, screwed up his face and looked down at his magnificent, but unpractical, slippers. Luckily he too had been exploring the various possibilities and, after a little hesitation, he said:

'Sir, I think I have found a means of transport.'

'And what might that be?'

'An elephant. It belongs to an Indian who lives a few yards away from here.'

'Let us go and see the elephant!' replied Mr. Fogg.

Five minutes later Phileas Fogg, Sir Francis Cromarty and Passepartout came to a hut beside an enclosure which was shut in by a high paling. In the hut there was an Indian and in the enclosure an elephant. In response to their request the Indian took Mr. Fogg and his two companions into the enclosure.

There they found themselves in the presence of a half-tamed animal which was being reared, not for use as a beast of burden, but as a fighting animal. And so he had begun to alter the naturally gentle disposition of the animal in order to bring it up gradually to that paroxysm of frenzy called *must* in Hindi, by feeding it for three months on sugar and butter. Such treatment may not seem very suitable for the purpose, but elephant-breeders find it is successful. Fortunately for Mr. Fogg, the elephant in question had only just been put on the diet and so *must* had not yet set in.

Kiouni—for that was the elephant's name—could, like all members of his species, keep on walking fast over a long period and, as no other conveyance was available, Phileas Fogg determined to use him.

But elephants are expensive in India, where they are growing scarce. Male elephants, which are the only ones suitable for circus work, are greatly in demand. These animals rarely have offspring in captivity and so they can only be obtained by hunting. As a result, they are very carefully looked after and when Mr. Fogg asked the Indian if he was willing to hire out the elephant the Indian refused point-blank.

Mr. Fogg insisted and offered the exorbitant price of ten pounds per hour. This was refused. Twenty pounds. That was refused too. Forty pounds ? No. Passepartout jumped at every rise in the bidding. But the Indian would not give way to temptation.

Yet it was a substantial sum. Assuming that the elephant would take fifteen hours to go to Allahabad, he would earn six hundred pounds for his owner.

Phileas Fogg, completely unruffled, then offered to buy the animal and first of all offered the Indian a thousand pounds.

The Indian refused to sell. Perhaps the rogue had sniffed out the opportunity of doing a fine deal.

Sir Francis Cromarty took Mr. Fogg aside and begged him to reflect a little before going any further. Phileas Fogg told his companion in reply that he was not in the habit of acting without due reflection and that, when all was said and done, a bet of twenty thousand pounds was at stake and he needed the elephant and he would have him, even if he had to pay twenty times his proper value.

Mr. Fogg went back to the Indian whose little eyes, alight with greed, showed that, as far as he was concerned, it was only a question of price. Phileas Fogg offered twelve hundred pounds, then fifteen hundred, then eighteen hundred, and finally two thousand pounds. Passepartout's normally ruddy face had turned pale with emotion.

At two thousand pounds the Indian gave way.

'By my slippers,' exclaimed Passepartout, 'he certainly puts a high price on elephant meat!'

The business having been concluded, all that remained was to find a guide. That was easier. A young Parsee with

an intelligent face offered his services. Mr. Fogg accepted and promised him generous remuneration, and that could not but double his intelligence.

The elephant was brought and fitted out without delay. The Parsee was quite familiar with the duties of a *mahout* or elephant driver. He covered the elephant's back with a kind of saddle-cloth and placed two rather uncomfortable panniers on either side of the animal.

Phileas Fogg paid the Indian in banknotes extracted from the famous bag. It really seemed as if they were being pulled out of Passepartout's guts. Then Mr. Fogg offered to convey Sir Francis Cromarty to the station of Allahabad. The brigadier-general accepted. One more passenger would not tire the huge animal.

Provisons were bought at Kholby. Sir Francis Cromarty sat down in one of the panniers and Phileas Fogg in the other. Passepartout then sat astride the saddle-cloth between his master and the brigadier-general. The Parsee perched himself on the elephant's neck and at nine o'clock the animal left the village and plunged into the dense forest of fan-palms.

In which Phileas Fogg and his companions venture through the forests of India and what befalls them there

To shorten the distance they had to cover, the guide left on his right the line followed by the track that was being laid. That line had to contend with the irregular pattern of the Vindhya Mountains and did not follow the shortest route, which it was in Phileas Fogg's interest to take. The Parsee, who was very familiar with the tracks and paths in the area, claimed that he could gain about twenty miles by cutting through the forest, and so they left the matter in his hands.

Phileas Fogg and Sir Francis Cromarty, plunged up to their necks in the paniers, were violently shaken by the elephant's rapid trot. The *mahout* was sending him along at a brisk pace. But they endured it with typically British phlegm. They talked little and indeed scarcely saw each other.

As for Passepartout, perched on the animal's back and directly exposed to every jolt and jerk, he took care not to hold his tongue between his teeth, on the advice of his master, as it would have been bitten right off. The good fellow was one moment flung on to the animal's neck, then back on to his rump the next, and went flying up and down like a clown on a springboard. But he laughed and joked in the midst of all these acrobatic antics and from time to time he took a lump of sugar out of his bag. The intelligent Kiouni would then take it in his trumpet without slackening his regular trot for a single instant.

After going on like this for two hours the guide stopped the animal and allowed him an hour's rest. Kiouni first quenched his thirst at a nearby pool and then started to devour branches of trees and bushes. Sir Francis Cromarty

did not complain about calling a halt. He felt worn out. But Mr. Fogg seemed as fresh as if he had just got out of bed.

'He must be made of iron!' said the brigadier-general with an admiring glance.

'Wrought iron,' remarked Passepartout, who was busy preparing a hasty lunch.

At noon the guide gave the signal for departure. The country soon assumed a very wild appearance. The great forests gave way to copses of tamarinds and dwarf palms, then came vast arid plains, bristling with meagre shrubs and with large blocks of syenite rock strewn about. All that area of upper Bundelkund, which is little visited by travellers, is inhabited by a fanatical people inured to the most terrible practices of the Hindu religion. The British have not been able to establish a regular system of control over this area which is ruled over by the rajahs tucked away in their inaccessible fastnesses in the Vindhya Mountains.

On several occasions they observed bands of wild-looking Indians who waved their arms about angrily when they saw the swift quadruped passing. The Parsee avoided them as best he could because he thought they were unpleasant characters to meet. They saw few animals during that day, just a few monkeys which scurried away with many contortions and grimaces to the great amusement of Passepartout.

But one problem was worrying Passepartout in the midst of many others. What would Mr. Fogg do with the elephant when he reached the station of Allahabad ? Would he take the elephant with him ? Impossible! The cost of transport added to the price he had paid for him would make the animal a tremendous liability. Would he sell him ? Would he give him back his liberty ? That fine beast deserved to be treated with consideration. If Mr. Fogg happened to present the elephant to him, Passepartout, it would be a great embarrassment. He worried about this all the time.

At eight o'clock in the evening the main range of the Vindhya Mountains had been crossed and the travellers

halted at the foot of the northern slope where they sought shelter in a ruined bungalow.

They had covered about twenty-five miles during that day and they had as much to do again before they reached Allahabad station.

It was a cold night. Inside the bungalow the Parsee lit a fire of dry branches and the warmth from it was most welcome. Their supper consisted of the provisions bought at Kholby. The travellers felt they were worn out and aching all over as they ate their meal. There were a few broken phrases of conversation and then loud snores. The guide watched beside Kiouni who fell asleep on his feet, leaning against the trunk of a large tree.

That night was not marked by any untoward incident. The silence was sometimes broken by the growling of cheetahs and panthers, mingling with the shrill chattering laughter of monkeys. But the carnivores did no more than call out and made no attempt to attack the occupants of the bungalow. Sir Francis Cromarty was sleeping heavily like a soldier weary after a hard day. Passepartout was sleeping restlessly and began to toss about in his dreams as he had done on the day before. As for Mr. Fogg, he rested as peacefully as if he had been in his quiet house in Savile Row.

At six o'clock in the morning they set out again. The guide hoped to reach the station of Allahabad that very evening. In that way Mr. Fogg would lose only part of the forty-eight hours he had saved since the start of his journey.

They went down the final slopes of the Vindhya Mountains. Kiouni had resumed his rapid pace. Towards noon the guide by-passed the village of Kalinjar, situated on the Ken, one of the minor tributaries of the Ganges. He always avoided inhabited places and felt safer in those empty stretches of country that mark the first depressions of the basin of the mighty river. The station of Allahabad was less than twelve miles to the north-east. They halted under a clump of banana-trees, the fruits of which are as wholesome as bread and 'as succulent as cream', as travellers say, and were much appreciated on this occasion.

At two o'clock the guide entered a dense forest which they had to go through for several miles. He preferred to travel in the shelter of the trees. In any case they had had no unpleasant encounters so far and there was every likelihood that the journey would end uneventfully when the elephant showed some signs of uneasiness and suddenly stopped.

It was then four o'clock.

'What is wrong?' asked Sir Francis Cromarty, raising his head over the side of his pannier.

'I do not know, sir,' replied the Parsee, listening to a confused murmur that could be heard passing along under the thick branches.

A few moments later the murmur became clearer. It was like a concert going on a long way off, with human voices and brass instruments.

Passepartout was all eyes and ears. Mr. Fogg waited patiently without saying a word.

The Parsee jumped down, tied the elephant to a tree and plunged into the densest part of the undergrowth. A few minutes later he returned and said:

'A Brahman procession is coming this way. We must avoid being seen, if at all possible.'

The guide untied the elephant and led him into a thicket and advised the travellers not to step down on to the ground. Then he held himself in readiness to mount the animal quickly if it became necessary to flee. But he thought the band of worshippers would pass by without seeing him, as he was completely hidden by the thick foliage.

The discordant noise of voices and instruments came nearer. Monotonous chanting mingled with the sound of drums and cymbals. Soon the head of the procession appeared under the trees some fifty feet away from the hiding-place of Mr. Fogg and his companions. They could easily see through the branches the odd collection of people taking part in the religious ceremony.

The first to pass were priests wearing mitres on their heads and clad in long gaudy robes. They were surrounded by men, women and children who were singing a kind of

dirge, interrupted at regular intervals by the beating of
tom-toms and the clash of cymbals. Behind them, on a
vehicle with wide wheels, the spokes and rims of which
were decorated with a pattern of inter-twined snakes,
appeared a hideous statue drawn by two pairs of richly
caparisoned zebu cattle. The statue had four arms and its
body was coloured dark red. The eyes were wild, the hair
was tangled and its tongue was hanging out, and the lips
were stained with henna and betel. Round its neck was
wound a necklace of skulls and round its waist was a girdle
of severed hands. It was standing on a prostrate giant
without a head.

Sir Francis Cromarty recognized the statue.

'It is the goddess Kali,' he whispered, 'the goddess of
love and death.'

'Of death maybe—but love, never!' said Passepartout.
'Ugly old hag!'

The Parsee signed to him to be quiet.

Round the statue a group of old fakirs were jumping
about and contorting themselves violently. They were
smeared with bands of ochre and were covered with
cross-shaped incisions from which the blood came oozing
drop by drop. These stupid fanatics still throw themselves
under the wheels of the car of Juggernaut during important
Indian ceremonies.

Behind them came a few Brahmans in all the splendour of
their oriental costumes, dragging along a woman who was
hardly able to stand up.

The woman was young and fair-skinned like a European.
Her head, neck, shoulders, ears, arms, hands and toes were
all heavily laden with jewels, necklaces, bracelets, rings and
ear-rings. A gold tunic, covered with light muslin, displayed the contours of her figure.

Behind that young woman, and providing a violent visual
contrast, were guards with unsheathed sabres stuck in their
belts and long damascened pistols. They were carrying a
palanquin on which lay a dead man.

He was an old man dressed in the rich apparel of a rajah
and wearing, as he had done during his lifetime, a turban

71

embroidered with pearls, a robe woven from silk and gold thread, a belt of diamond-studded cashmere and the magnificent weapons of an Indian prince.

Musicians and a rear-guard of fanatics, whose cries sometimes drowned the deafening clamour of the instruments, marked the end of the procession.

Sir Francis Cromarty viewed all that pomp with an oddly sad air and, turning to the guide, he said:

'It is a suttee!'

The Parsee nodded and laid a finger on his lips. The long procession moved slowly along under the trees and soon the last of it disappeared into the depths of the forest.

Little by little the chanting died away in the distance. There were still a few far-off cries and then after all the tumult came profound silence.

Phileas Fogg had heard the word uttered by Sir Francis Cromarty and, as soon as the procession had disappeared, he asked:

'What is a suttee?'

'A suttee, Fogg,' replied the brigadier-general, 'is a human sacrifice, a voluntary sacrifice. The woman you have just seen will be burned early tomorrow morning.'

'Oh, the scoundrels!' exclaimed Passepartout, who could not suppress a cry of indignation.

'And what about the dead man?' asked Mr. Fogg.

'It is the body of the prince, her husband,' replied the guide, 'an independent rajah of Bundelkund.'

'What!' said Phileas Fogg, his voice not betraying the least trace of emotion. 'Do these barbarous customs still go on in India without the British being able to stamp them out?'

'In the greater part of India,' replied Sir Francis Cromarty, 'these sacrifices are no longer carried out, but we have no influence over certain savage areas, least of all here in Bundelkund. Murders and looting take place all the time on the whole of this northern side of the Vindhya Mountains.'

'That poor woman!' murmured Passepartout. 'Burnt alive!'

'Yes,' the brigadier-general went on, 'burnt alive, and, if she were not, you cannot imagine what a pathetic condition

she would be reduced to by her relatives. Her hair would be shaved off and she would be kept barely alive on a few handfuls of rice. She would be an outcast, an unclean creature, and she would die in some corner like a mangy dog. So it is the prospect of such a terrible life that often leads these unfortunate women to undergo torture, rather than any feelings of love or religious fanaticism. But sometimes the sacrifice is really voluntary and can only be prevented by vigorous action on the part of the Government. A few years ago, for example, I was living in Bombay and a young widow came to the Governor and asked permission to be burned with the body of her husband. As you can well imagine, the Governor refused. So the widow left town and took refuge with an independent rajah and there she was able to perform her sacrifice.'

As the brigadier-general was telling his story, the guide was shaking his head and when he had finished speaking he said:

'The sacrifice that is going to take place at dawn tomorrow is not voluntary.'

'How do you know?'

'Everybody in Bundelkund knows the story,' replied the guide.

'But the unfortunate woman did not seem to be resisting,' remarked Sir Francis Cromarty.

'That was because they had doped her with the smoke of hemp and opium.'

'But where are they taking her?'

'To the pagoda of Pillaji, two miles from here. She will spend the night there until it is time for her to be sacrificed.'

'And when will that be?'

'At first light tomorrow.'

After that reply the guide brought the elephant out of the dense thicket and hoisted himself on to the animal's neck. But just as he was going to urge him on with a special whistle Mr. Fogg stopped him and said to Sir Francis Cromarty:

'How about rescuing that woman?'

'Rescuing her, Fogg!' exclaimed the brigadier-general.

'I still have twelve hours in hand. They can be used for that purpose.'

'Good gracious! You are a brave man!' said Sir Francis Cromarty.

'Sometimes,' replied Phileas Fogg simply. 'When I have time to be.'

*In which Passepartout proves once again that
fortune favours the brave*

The plan was a bold one and bristling with difficulties
and was perhaps impracticable. Mr. Fogg was going to
risk his life, or at the very least his liberty and consequently
the success of his plans, but he did not hesitate. And
he found, moreover, a resolute ally in Sir Francis
Cromarty.

Passepartout was prepared too. They could count on him.
He found his master's idea inspiring, and sensed that there
was a heart and soul behind that frigid exterior. He was
beginning to grow fond of Phileas Fogg.

There remained the guide. What side would he take?
Would he not be inclined to favour the Indians? If he
would not help them, they would at least have to assure
themselves of his neutrality.

Sir Francis Cromarty put the question to him openly.

'Sir,' replied the guide, 'I am a Parsee and that woman is a
Parsee too. You can rely on me.'

'Good,' said Mr. Fogg.

'But I must point out,' the Parsee went on, 'that we are
not only risking our lives. We shall suffer terrible torture if
we are caught. So consider it well.'

'I have,' replied Mr. Fogg, 'and I think we should wait
till it is dark before taking any action.'

'I think so, too,' replied the guide.

The Indian then gave a few details about the victim. She
was an Indian woman famed for her beauty—a Parsee, the
daughter of a rich merchant in Bombay. There she had had
a completely English upbringing and from her manners and
her education one would have thought she was a European.
Her name was Aouda.

She was an orphan and had been married against her wishes to the old rajah of Bundelkund. Three months later she was a widow. Knowing the fate that awaited her, she escaped, but was recaptured at once, and the relatives of the rajah, in whose interest it was that she should die, had doomed her to that torture from which it seemed that there was no escape.

That story could not but strengthen the generous determination of Mr. Fogg and his companions. It was decided that the guide should take the elephant to the pagoda of Pillaji and go as close to it as possible.

Half an hour later they halted in a clump of trees about five hundred feet away from the pagoda. They could not see it, but the yells of the fanatics were clearly audible.

They then discussed ways and means of getting to the victim. The guide knew the pagoda of Pillaji where the young woman was imprisoned. Could they go in through one of the doors when all the assembled throng had sunk into a drunken sleep or would they have to make a hole in one of the walls ? That could not be decided until they were actually on the spot and the time had come for action. But the kidnapping would certainly have to be carried out that very night—not when dawn came and the victim was being led to her place of torture. At that stage no human intervention could possibly save her.

Mr. Fogg and his companions waited for darkness to fall. As soon as the shadows deepened, around six o'clock in the evening, they decided to carry out a reconnaissance round the pagoda. The last cries of the fakirs were dying away. In accordance with their custom, the Indians would now be in a heavy drunken stupor brought on by *bhang*—liquid opium mixed with an infusion of hemp—and it might be possible to slip through their ranks and so reach the temple.

The Parsee, guiding Mr. Fogg, Sir Francis Cromarty and Passepartout, moved forward noiselessly through the forest. After creeping along for ten minutes under the branches they reached the bank of a small river and there they saw, in the light of iron torches with resin burning at their tips, a pile of wood. It was the funeral pyre, built of

precious sandalwood and already impregnated with perfumed oil. On the top of it lay the embalmed body of the rajah who was to be burned at the same time as his widow. A hundred feet or so away from the funeral pyre stood the pagoda, the minarets of which could be seen rising through the treetops in the gloom.

'Come with me!' said the guide in a low voice.

And, redoubling his precautions, he slipped silently through the tall grass, followed by his companions.

The silence was now broken only by the murmur of the wind in the branches.

Presently the guide stopped at the end of a clearing. It was lit by a few resin torches. The ground was strewn with sleeping figures, weighed down by drunken stupor. It looked like a battlefield covered with dead bodies. There were men, women and children all jumbled together. A few of them were still making gurgling noises.

In the background the indistinct outline of the temple of Pillaji rose up among the trees. But, to the great disappointment of the guide, the rajah's guards were posted at the doors in the light of smoking torches or were patrolling with drawn swords. One could well imagine that the priests would be on guard inside too.

The Parsee did not advance any further. He had realized that it would be impossible to force an entry into the temple, so he led his companions back.

Phileas Fogg and Sir Francis Cromarty were aware, like him, that nothing could be attempted from that quarter.

They stopped and talked together in whispers.

'Let us wait!' said the brigadier-general. 'It is only eight o'clock and these guards may grow drowsy later on.'

'That is possible,' replied the Parsee.

So Phileas Fogg and his companions lay down at the foot of a tree and waited.

The time seemed to drag. The guide sometimes left them and went to the edge of the forest to have a look. The rajah's guards were still keeping watch by the light of the torches and a faint glimmer was filtering through the windows of the pagoda.

They went on waiting till midnight, but the situation remained unchanged. Watch was still being kept outside. It was clear that they could not rely on the guards growing drowsy. They had probably not been allowed to become intoxicated with *bhang*. So they would have to adopt a different course of action and get in through an opening in the walls of the pagoda. They still had to find out if the priests were watching over their victim as carefully as the soldiers at the door.

After some final discussion the guide said he was ready to go. Mr. Fogg, Sir Francis and Passepartout followed him. He made a fairly wide detour so that they would arrive at the sanctuary end of the temple.

About half-past twelve they reached the foot of the walls without meeting a soul. No watch had been set on that side, but there were no doors or windows there at all.

It was a dark night. The moon, then in its last quarter, had hardly risen above the horizon, which was piled high with clouds. The height of the trees added still further to the gloom.

But it was not enough to have reached the foot of the walls. They still had to make a breach in them. For that operation Phileas Fogg and his companions had nothing but their pocket-knives. Fortunately the walls of the temple were constructed from a mixture of bricks and wood that would not be difficult to pierce. Once the first brick was removed, the others would come out easily.

They set to work, making as little noise as possible. The Parsee on one side and Passepartout on the other worked hard to loosen the bricks, in order to make an opening two feet wide.

The work was progressing well when a cry was heard from inside the temple and answering cries came almost at once from outside.

Passepartout and the guide broke off what they were doing. Had they been discovered? Had the alarm been given? Prudence bade them withdraw. And they did so, along with Phileas Fogg and Sir Francis Cromarty. They huddled down once more under cover of the trees to wait

until the alarm, if such it was, had passed and held themselves in readiness to resume their task.

But, by a stroke of ill-fortune, guards appeared outside the sanctuary of the pagoda and took up their positions in such a way that it was impossible to go near.

It would be hard to describe the disappointment those four men felt at being halted in their work. Now that they could no longer reach the victim, how would they rescue her? Sir Francis Cromarty was fuming with frustration and Passepartout was beside himself. In fact the guide found it difficult to restrain him. But the impassive Mr. Fogg waited there without showing his feelings.

'Have we no option but to leave?' asked the brigadier-general in a low voice.

'That is all we can do,' replied the guide.

'Wait!' said Mr. Fogg. 'It will be all right if I reach Allahabad before twelve noon.'

'But what can you hope to do? asked Sir Francis. 'Daylight will be breaking in a few hours from now and . . .'

'The opportunity that is eluding us now may present itself at the last moment.'

The brigadier-general would have liked to have been able to read what was in Phileas Fogg's eyes at that moment.

On what was that imperturbable Englishman pinning his hopes? Did he mean to rush up to the young woman at the moment she was being delivered up to her torment and wrest her openly from her executioners?

That would be madness, and was the man as mad as that? However, Sir Francis Cromarty agreed to wait for that terrible scene to take place. The guide did not let his companions stay in the place where they had taken refuge. He took them back to the front of the clearing. There, in the shelter of a clump of trees, they could observe the sleeping groups.

But Passepartout, perched in the branches of a tree, was working out an idea. It had flashed across his mind and then sank deep into his brain.

To begin with he had said: 'What madness!' But now he kept repeating to himself: 'Why not, after all? There is

just a chance and perhaps it is the only one we shall get, and with all the people in that doped state . . .'

At all events Passepartout did not change his mind and soon slithered down like a snake on to the lowest branches, the ends of which bent down to the ground.

The hours passed and soon a few faint glimmers announced that daylight was approaching. But it was still very dark.

The moment had come. The slumbering throng rose as if from the dead. The groups came to life again. There was a beating of tom-toms and the chanting and shouting started up once more. The hour had come for the unfortunate woman to die.

The doors of the pagoda opened. A brighter light shone out from inside. Mr. Fogg and Sir Francis Cromarty could see the victim with the light glinting upon her. Two priests were dragging her outside. It even seemed as if she was trying to shake off the numbness and stupor by some instinct of self-preservation and was making an effort to escape from her executioners. Sir Francis Cromarty's heart was pounding and he seized Phileas Fogg by the hand. In that hand was an open knife.

The crowd fell back. The young woman was once more in the state of torpor produced by the fumes of hemp. She passed through the ranks of the fakirs to the accompaniment of their fanatical cries.

Phileas Fogg and his companions, mingling with the tail-end of the crowd, followed her.

Two minutes later they reached the bank of the river and stopped less than fifty feet away from the funeral pyre on which lay the body of the rajah. In the semi-darkness they could see that the victim was lying absolutely still by the side of her husband's body.

Then a torch was set to the pyre and the wood, impregnated with oil, began to flare up at once.

It was then that Sir Francis and the guide had to hold Phileas Fogg back. In a moment of mad generosity he was preparing to rush towards the funeral pyre . . .

Phileas Fogg pushed them aside. But then the scene

changed suddenly. There was a cry of terror. The whole crowd threw itself to the ground in fear.

The old rajah was not dead after all. They saw him rise all at once like a ghost and pick the young woman up in his arms and climb down from the funeral pyre amid the swirling smoke which gave him the appearance of a spectre.

The fakirs and the guards and the priests, all seized with terror, lay face downwards on the ground, not daring to raise their eyes and witness the miracle.

The unconscious woman was carried forward in strong arms as if she weighed nothing at all. Mr. Fogg and Sir Francis Cromarty were still standing. The Parsee had bowed his head and Passepartout was no doubt just as amazed as the rest of them . . .

The figure that had risen from the dead came close to the spot where Mr. Fogg and Sir Francis were standing and said abruptly:

'Let us be off!'

It was Passepartout himself who had made his way to the funeral pyre through the dense smoke. It was Passepartout who had taken advantage of the semi-darkness to rescue the young woman from the jaws of death. It was Passepartout who had played his part boldly and had succeeded in passing through the frightened crowd.

A moment later all four disappeared into the wood and the elephant carried them off at a rapid trot. But a great shouting and uproar arose and a bullet pierced Phileas Fogg's hat, so the ruse had been discovered.

The body of the old rajah could now be seen on the flaming pyre. The priests had recovered from their fright and realized that their victim had been kidnapped.

They rushed into the forest at once, followed by the guards. Shots were fired, but the kidnappers were moving fast and in a few moments were out of range of the bullets and arrows.

In which Phileas Fogg goes down the whole of the lovely valley of the Ganges without giving it a glance

The bold kidnapping venture had succeeded. An hour later Passepartout was still laughing at his achievement. Sir Francis Cromarty shook the intrepid fellow by the hand. His master said: 'Well done!'—which was high praise coming from his lips. And Passepartout said that all the credit was due to his master. All he had done was to have an amusing idea and he laughed to think that, for a few moments, he Passepartout, the one-time gymnast and ex-sergeant of the fire brigade, had played the part of an old embalmed rajah, the late husband of a charming wife!

As for the young Indian woman, she was unaware of what had happened. Wrapped up in the travelling rugs, she was resting in one of the panniers.

Under the capable guidance of the Parsee, the elephant was running swiftly through the forest, which was still in darkness. One hour after leaving the pagoda of Pillaji he was rushing across a vast plain. At seven o'clock they called a halt. The young woman was still in a state of utter prostration. The guide made her drink a few sips of water and brandy, but the stupefying effect of the drugs did not wear off for some time.

Sir Francis Cromarty, who knew about the intoxicating effect of inhaling hemp vapours, was not at all worried on her account.

The brigadier-general was not concerned about the young woman's recovery, but he was uneasy about the future. He told Phileas Fogg that if Aouda remained in India she would inevitably fall into the hands of her executioners again. Those fanatics were to be found throughout the

peninsula and they would be sure to recapture their victim in spite of the British police—in Madras or Bombay or Calcutta. And, to support this, Sir Francis quoted a similar incident that had occurred recently. In his opinion the young woman would not really be safe until she had left India.

Phileas Fogg said he would bear that in mind and would take the necessary steps.

Around ten o'clock the guide announced that they were reaching Allahabad station. There the railway track started again. The trains covered the distance between Allahabad and Calcutta in less than a day and a night.

Phileas Fogg would therefore reach there in time to board the steamer which would be sailing at noon on the following day, 25th October, for Hong Kong.

The young woman was deposited in a room at the station. Passepartout was instructed to go and buy various articles of apparel for her—a dress, a shawl, furs, etc., in fact, whatever he could find. And for this his master allowed him an unlimited supply of cash.

Passepartout set out at once and roamed through the streets of the town. Allahabad, the City of God, is one of the most venerated places in India because it is built at the confluence of two sacred rivers, the Ganges and the Jumna, which attract pilgrims from all parts of the peninsula. According to the legends of Ramayana the Ganges has its source in Heaven and is brought down to earth by Brahma.

As he made his purchases, Passepartout took a quick look at the town, formerly guarded by a magnificent fort, turned into a state prison. There is no more trade or industry in this town, which was once such a centre for both. Passepartout looked in vain for a draper's shop, as if he had been in Regent Street within a stone's throw of Farmer & Co., and only managed to find the item he was looking for at the shop of a secondhand dealer, a fussy old Jew. He got a dress in a plaid material, a large cloak and a magnificent sealskin pelisse for which he paid £75 without demur. Then he returned in triumph to the station.

Aouda was beginning to regain consciousness. The drugs administered to her by the priests of Pillaji were losing their effect little by little and her beautiful eyes had regained their soft Indian loveliness.

The poet king Yusuf Adil, extolling the charms of the queen of Ahmednagar, wrote: 'Her gleaming tresses, divided symmetrically into two parts, frame the harmonious contours of her delicate white cheeks, all shining and fresh. Her ebony eyebrows have the shape and power of the bow of Kama, the god of love, and under her long silky lashes, in the dark pupils of her large and limpid eyes the purest reflections of the light of Heaven are mirrored as in the sacred Himalayan lakes. Her teeth, fine and even and white, gleam between her smiling lips like the drops of dew in the half-closed bosom of a pomegranate blossom. Her tiny ears, symmetrically curved, her rosy hands, her small feet, arched and tender as lotus buds, are resplendent with the loveliest pearls of Ceylon and the fairest diamonds of Golconda. Her slender and supple waist, just large enough for a hand to encircle, sets off the elegant curve of her rounded hips and the richness of her bosom where blossoming youth displays her most perfect treasures, and under the silken folds of her tunic it would seem that she had been modelled in pure silver by the divine hand of Viswakarma, the architect of the gods.'

Discarding all that poetic verbiage, it is enough to say that Aouda, the widow of the rajah of Bundelkund, was a charming woman in the true European sense of the word. She spoke very pure English and the guide had not exaggerated in any way when he said that the young Parsee woman had been transformed by her upbringing.

But the train was about to leave the station of Allahabad. The Parsee was waiting. Mr. Fogg paid him his wage at the agreed rate, without a farthing over. Passepartout was a little surprised. He knew how greatly his master was indebted to the guide's devotion. The Parsee had indeed risked his life voluntarily in the affair at Pillaji and if the Indians found this out later on it would be difficult for him to escape their vengeance.

There remained too the question of Kiouni. What would he do with an elephant for which he had paid such a high price?

But Phileas Fogg had already made up his mind on the subject.

'Parsee', he said to the guide, 'you have served me well and devotedly. I have paid you for your services, but not for your devotion. Would you like to have this elephant? He is yours.'

The guide's eyes shone.

'Your honour is giving me a fortune!' he exclaimed.

'Take him, guide,' replied Mr. Fogg, 'and I shall still be in your debt.'

'Bravo!' cried Passepartout. 'Take him, my friend! Kiouni is a fine brave beast.'

And, going to the elephant, he gave him a few lumps of sugar, saying: 'Here you are, Kiouni—here, boy!'

The elephant gave a few grunts of satisfaction. Then, taking hold of Passepartout by the waist and twining his trunk round him, he lifted him up as high as his head. Passepartout was not at all frightened and patted the animal, which then set him gently down on the ground again. And Passepartout returned Kiouni's 'trunk-shake' with a vigorous handshake.

A few moments later Phileas Fogg, Sir Francis Cromarty and Passepartout were ensconced in a comfortable carriage, with Aouda occupying the best seat, and were rushing full steam ahead towards Benares.

That town was eighty miles at most from Allahabad and the distance was covered in two hours.

During that part of the journey the young woman regained consciousness completely. The drowsy vapours of *bhang* melted away. How astonished she was to find herself in a railway compartment and wearing European clothes in the company of complete strangers! To begin with, her companions lavished attention upon her and tried to revive her with a few drops of spirits. Then the brigadier-general told her what had happened. He stressed the devotion of Phileas Fogg who had unhesitatingly risked his

life to save her and the dramatic ending of the adventure, which was due to the bold imagination of Passepartout.

Mr. Fogg let him go on without saying a word. Passepartout, who was covered with confusion, kept on repeating that 'it was nothing at all'.

Aouda thanked her rescuers effusively, with tears more than by words. Her lovely eyes conveyed her gratitude better than her lips could ever have done. Then she remembered the scenes of the suttee and, as her gaze fell once more on Indian soil where so many perils still awaited her, she gave a shudder of terror.

Phileas Fogg realized what was passing through Aouda's mind and, to set it at rest, he offered —in a very detached tone, let it be said—to take her to Hong Kong where she could stay until the whole affair had died down.

Aouda accepted the offer gratefully. A relative of hers happened to live in Hong Kong, a Parsee like herself and one of the leading merchants of the town, which is completely British although it lies off the coast of China.

At twelve-thirty the train stopped at Benares station. According to Brahman legend this town occupies the site of the ancient Kasi, which was at one time suspended in space between the zenith and the nadir, like the tomb of Mahomet. But, during the more realistic age of Victoria, Benares, which orientalists call the Athens of India, was reposing prosaically on the earth and Passepartout had a momentary glimpse of its brick houses and wattle huts, which gave it an appearance of utter desolation without any local colour.

It was there that Sir Francis Cromarty's journey came to an end. The troops he was rejoining were encamped a few miles to the north of the town. So the brigadier-general said goodbye to Phileas Fogg. He wished him every success and hoped that the remainder of his journey would be less unusual and more profitable than the preceding stage. Mr. Fogg gave his companion's fingers a slight squeeze. Aouda's leave-taking was more affectionate. She would never forget what she owed to Sir Francis Cromarty. As for Passepartout, the brigadier-general honoured him with a hearty handshake. Touched by this, he said he would

gladly be of service to him wherever and whenever the occasion arose. Then they parted.

From Benares onwards the railway followed the valley of the Ganges to some extent. The weather was fairly clear and through the carriage windows they could see the varied scenery of Behar, green mountains, fields of barley, maize and wheat, pools and streams peopled with greenish alligators, well-kept villages, and forests that were still green. A few elephants and zebu cattle with huge humps were washing in the waters of the sacred river and, in spite of the lateness of the season and the cold temperature, groups of Indians of both sexes were piously carrying out their holy ablutions. They are fierce enemies of Buddhism and are fervent disciples of the Brahman religion, which is represented by three persons: Vishnu the sun god, Shiva, who is the divine personification of natural forces, and Brahma the supreme master of priests and lawgivers. But what must Brahma, Shiva and Vishnu think of this anglicized India, where steamboats come snorting along to trouble the sacred waters of the Ganges and scare away the gulls flying over its surface and the tortoises swarming on its banks, and the believers lying by the water's edge!

The scenery went flashing past, its details often hidden by a cloud of white steam. The travellers obtained hardly a glimpse of the fort of Chanar twenty miles to the south-east of Benares, the ancient fortress of the rajahs of Behar, Ghazipur with its important rose-water factories, the tomb of Lord Cornwallis which rises on the left bank of the Ganges, the fortified town of Buxar, Patna, the great industrial and trading town and site of the main opium market in India, Monghyr, a town which is more than just European and is as English as Manchester or Birmingham, famous for its iron-foundries and its factories for making edge tools and side-arms, where the tall chimneys befoul Brahma's Heaven with their black smoke—a real slap in the face for the land of dreams!

The night came and, amid the roaring and howls of tigers and bears and wolves fleeing before the engine, the train sped on its way and soon nothing could be seen of the

wonders of Bengal, not a glimpse of Colgong or the ruins of Gaur, or Murshidabad, which was once a capital city, or Burdwan, or Hooghly, or Chandernagore, that French dot on the map of India, where Passepartout would have been proud to see the flag of his native land fluttering.

Finally, at seven o'clock in the morning, they reached Calcutta. The steamer bound for Hong Kong was not due to weigh anchor till noon. So Phileas Fogg had five hours to spare.

According to his itinerary, that gentleman should have reached the capital of India on 25th October, twenty-three days after leaving London, and he actually did arrive on the appointed day. He was neither ahead of nor behind the scheduled time. Unfortunately the two days he had gained between London and Bombay had been lost—we know how—as he was crossing the Indian peninsula. But one would assume that Phileas Fogg would have no regrets about that!

*In which the bag of banknotes loses another few
thousand pounds*

The train had stopped in the station. Passepartout stepped
down from the carriage first, followed by Mr. Fogg who
helped the young woman down on to the platform. Phileas
Fogg intended to go straight to the Hong Kong steamer and
instal Aouda comfortably on board. He did not want to
leave her as long as she was in a country that was so dangerous for her.

Just as he was about to leave the station a policeman came up to him and said: 'Are you Mr. Phileas Fogg?'

'Yes, I am.'

'And is that man your servant?' added the policeman,
indicating Passepartout.

'Yes.'

'Please follow me.'

Mr. Fogg gave no sign of surprise. The policeman was a
representative of the law and, for all Englishmen, the law
is sacred. Passepartout, being a Frenchman, wanted to
argue, but the policeman touched him with his stick and
Phileas Fogg signed to him to obey.

'May this young lady accompany us?' asked Mr. Fogg.

'Yes, she may,' replied the policeman.

The policeman led the way to a *palki-ghari*, a kind of
carriage with four wheels and four seats, drawn by a pair of
horses. They set off. No one spoke during the ride, which
lasted about twenty minutes.

First the carriage went through the native quarter with its
narrow streets lined with hovels, swarming with a dirty and
ragged cosmopolitan population. Then it passed through
the European town, gay with brick houses and shaded by
coconut palms. It was bristling with flagstaffs. In spite of

the early hour elegant horsemen and fine carriages were going about.

The *palki-ghari* stopped in front of a plain-looking building that did not have the appearance of a private house. The policeman asked his prisoners—for that was what they were—to descend from the carriage and he led them into a room with barred windows and said to them:

'You will appear before Judge Obadiah at eight-thirty.'

Then he withdrew and closed the door.

'We are prisoners!' cried Passepartout, dropping on to a chair.

Aouda turned at once to Mr. Fogg and, trying in vain to disguise her emotion, she said: 'You must abandon me, sir! You are being prosecuted because of me. It is because you rescued me.'

Phileas Fogg merely replied that that was not possible. Prosecuted because of the suttee? Quite out of the question! How could the plaintiffs dare to come forward? No, it was all a mistake. Mr. Fogg added that in any case he would not dream of abandoning the young woman. He would take her to Hong Kong.

'But the boat sails at noon!' remarked Passepartout.

'We shall be on board by noon,' was all the gentleman said.

He stated this so categorically that Passepartout could not help saying to himself: 'Of course! It is an absolute certainty. We will be on board by twelve noon!' But he did not feel at all reassured.

At half past eight the door opened. The policeman reappeared and conducted the prisoners into the adjoining hall. It was a courtroom and there were a fair number of people there already, Europeans and natives.

Mr. Fogg, Aouda and Passepartout sat down on a bench facing the seats set aside for the magistrate and the clerk of the court.

The magistrate, Judge Obadiah, entered almost immediately, followed by the clerk of the court. He was a fat man as round as a ball. He unhooked a wig which had been hanging on a nail and put it on quickly.

'Call the first case,' he said.

But then he lifted his hand to his head and said: 'Why! This is not my wig!'

'Indeed it is not, Mr. Obadiah, it is mine,' replied the clerk.

'My dear Mr. Oysterpuff, how can you expect a judge to pass judgement properly if he is wearing a clerk's wig!'

The wigs were exchanged. During these preliminaries Passepartout was seething with impatience, as the hand of the large courtroom clock seemed to be marching at a frightful speed across the dial.

'The first case,' repeated Judge Obadiah.

'Phileas Fogg?' said the clerk, Oysterpuff.

'Here,' replied Mr. Fogg.

'Passepartout?'

'Present,' replied Passepartout.

'Good,' said Judge Obadiah. 'Prisoners of the court, the police have been watching all trains from Bombay for you.'

'But what are we accused of?' cried Passepartout impatiently.

'You will find out,' replied the judge.

'Sir,' said Mr. Fogg, 'I am a British subject and I have a right . . .'

'Have you been treated without proper consideration?' asked Mr. Obadiah.

'Not at all!'

'Very well then! Bring in the plaintiffs!'

At that order from the judge a door opened and three Hindu priests were shown in by a court officer.

'It *was* that, after all!' murmured Passepartout. 'These are the rogues who wanted to burn our young lady alive.'

The priests stood before the judge and the clerk read out a charge of sacrilege made out against Phileas Fogg, Esq., and his servant, who was accused of having violated a place hallowed by the Brahman religion.

'Have you heard the charge?' the judge asked Phileas Fogg.

'Yes, sir,' replied Mr. Fogg, consulting his watch, 'and I plead guilty.'

'Oh! So you plead guilty?'

'I plead guilty and I am waiting for these three priests to confess in turn what they planned to do at the pagoda of Pillaji.'

The priests looked at one another. It seemed as if they did not understand what the defendant was saying.

'Yes indeed!' cried Passepartout impetuously. 'At that pagoda of Pillaji where they were going to burn their victim alive!'

Fresh bewilderment on the faces of the priests and profound amazement on the part of Judge Obadiah.

'What victim?' he demanded. 'Burn whom? In the middle of Bombay?'

'Bombay?' cried Passepartout.

'Of course. We are not speaking about the pagoda of Pillaji, but the pagoda on Malabar Hill, Bombay.'

'And as circumstantial evidence here are the shoes of the profaner,' added the clerk, placing a pair of shoes on his desk.

'My shoes!' cried Passepartout who, in his amazement, had been unable to hold back that involuntary exclamation.

One can imagine the mental turmoil of master and servant. They had forgotten that incident at the pagoda in Bombay—and yet it was the very incident that had led to their appearance before the magistrate in Calcutta.

Fix the detective had realized how that unfortunate business could be turned to good account. Delaying his departure by twelve hours, he had advised the priests of Malabar Hill what to do. He had promised them substantial damages, knowing full well that the British Government was very severe in the handling of that type of crime. Then he had sent them out after the profaner on the next train. But, because of the time taken to rescue the young widow, Fix and the Hindus had reached Calcutta before Phileas Fogg and his servant, whom the magistrates were instructed by telegram to arrest as they got off the train. One can imagine Fix's disappointment when he learned that Phileas Fogg had not arrived in the Indian capital. He was forced to the conclusion that the robber had stopped at one

of the stations on the Peninsular Railway and had taken refuge in the northern provinces. For twenty-four hours Fix had watched for him at the station, a prey to mortal anxiety. How delighted he was, therefore, when he saw him step down from the train that morning, accompanied, it is true, by a young lady whose presence he could not account for. He at once sent a policeman after him and that is how Mr. Fogg, Passepartout and the widow of the rajah of Bundelkund came to be led before Judge Obadiah.

And if Passepartout had been less taken up with his own affairs he would have noticed the detective following the debate in a corner of the courtroom with lively interest, for the warrant he needed in Suez and Bombay still had not reached him in Calcutta.

However, Judge Obadiah had taken note of Passepartout's involuntary confession. He would have given all he possessed to have been able to take back these ill-considered words.

'Have the facts of the case been admitted?' asked the judge.

'They have,' replied Mr. Fogg calmly.

'Whereas English law,' resumed the judge, 'sets out to protect with equal strictness all the religions of the populations of India and the charge has been admitted by Mr. Passepartout, who is accused of having defiled with sacrilegious feet on 20th October the paved floor of the pagoda on Malabar Hill, Bombay, the said Passepartout is sentenced to two weeks' imprisonment and a fine of three hundred pounds.'

'Three hundred pounds?' cried Passepartout who had really only noticed the fine.

'Silence!' barked the court officer.

'And,' added Judge Obadiah, 'whereas it has not been proved that there was no connivance between the servant and his master, and the latter should in any case be held responsible for the speech and actions of a servant in his employ, the said Phileas Fogg is hereby detained and sentenced to one week's imprisonment and a fine of one hundred and fifty pounds. Call the next case!'

Fix, sitting there in his corner, was absolutely overjoyed. Phileas Fogg was being detained for a week in Calcutta and this would allow more than enough time for the warrant to reach him.

Passepartout was absolutely dumbfounded. That sentence spelt ruin for his master. A bet of twenty thousand pounds had been lost and all because he had idled about and gone into that accursed pagoda!

Phileas Fogg, who was in perfect control of himself, just as if the sentence did not concern him at all, did not even frown. But, as the clerk was calling the next case, he rose and said:

'I wish to offer bail.'

'You have a right to do so,' replied the judge.

Fix felt a cold shiver go down his back, but his confidence was restored when he heard the judge say that, 'whereas Phileas Fogg and his servant were strangers' he would fix the bail for each of them at the enormous figure of one thousand pounds.

It would cost Mr. Fogg two thousand pounds if he did not serve his sentence.

'I will pay it,' said the gentleman.

And from the bag that Passepartout was carrying he drew out a bundle of banknotes which he deposited on the clerk's desk.

'That sum will be restored to you when you leave prison,' said the judge. 'In the meantime you are released on bail.'

'Come!' said Phileas Fogg to his servant.

'But they might at least give me back my shoes!' cried Passepartout furiously.

His shoes were duly returned to him.

'What expensive shoes they are!' he muttered. 'They have cost over a thousand pounds each. And they actually pinch my feet.'

The pathetic figure of Passepartout walked out behind Mr. Fogg who had offered his arm to the young woman. Fix still hoped that the robber would not be willing to forfeit the sum of two thousand pounds and would duly serve his term of imprisonment. So he followed on the trail of Fogg.

Mr. Fogg took a cab, and Aouda, Passepartout and he climbed in at once. Fix ran behind the carriage which soon stopped on one of the quays.

Half a mile away in the roadstead the *Rangoon* lay at anchor, her Blue Peter flying from the top of the mast. Eleven o'clock was striking. Mr. Fogg had one hour still to go. Fix saw him get down from the carriage and climb into a boat with Aouda and his servant. The detective stamped his foot.

'The scoundrel!' he cried. 'He is going away! Two thousand pounds thrown away! He is as extravagant as only a thief can be! Oh, but I will trail him to the end of the world if need be, although, the way he is going on, all the proceeds of the robbery will soon be used up.'

The inspector had good reason to think along these lines. Since leaving London, Phileas Fogg had scattered over five thousand pounds along the way, in travelling expenses and bonuses, payment for the elephant and money for bail and fines, so the percentage of the sum recovered that would be allotted to the detective was declining steadily.

*In which Fix does not seem as if he knows what he
is speaking about at all*

The *Rangoon*, one of the steamers used by the Peninsular
& Oriental Steam Navigation Company in the seas off
China and Japan, was an iron vessel with a propeller and a
gross tonnage of seventeen hundred and seventy tons and
a nominal horsepower of four hundred. She equalled the
Mongolia in speed, but not in comfort. So Aouda was not as
well accommodated as Phileas Fogg would have wished.
But it was only a crossing of three thousand five hundred
miles, lasting eleven to twelve days, and the young woman
did not prove to be a difficult passenger.

During the first few days of the trip Aouda was able to
get to know Phileas Fogg better. She always showed how
deeply grateful she was to him. The phlegmatic gentleman
would listen quite impassively to what she had to say,
without betraying the slightest trace of emotion by any
gesture or tone of his voice. He took pains to see that the
young woman had everything she needed. He came regularly
at certain times of day, if not to chat, at least to listen to her.
He carried out all the duties that courtesy demanded, but
with as much grace and spontaneity as an automaton whose
movements had been co-ordinated for that purpose.
Aouda did not know what to think, but Passepartout
explained to her a little about his master's eccentric
personality. He told her about the bet that was taking the
gentleman round the world. Aouda smiled. But, when all
was said and done, she owed him her life and her rescuer
did not lose anything by being viewed through the rosy
haze of her gratitude.

Aouda confirmed the Indian guide's account of her
moving story. She belonged to a race occupying the leading

place among the native population. Several Parsee merchants had made large fortunes in India in the cotton trade.

One of them, Sir James Jejeebhoy, had been knighted by the British Government and Aouda was a relative of that rich man, who lived in Bombay. It was in fact a cousin of Sir James, the Honourable Jejeeh, to whom she was going in Hong Kong. Would she be able to take refuge with him? She could not say definitely. But Mr. Fogg said that she had no cause for worry. Everything would work itself out 'mathematically.' That was his slogan.

Did the young woman understand that horrible adverb? We do not know. But her large eyes gazed at Mr. Fogg—those large eyes 'limpid as the sacred Himalayan lakes'! But the unapproachable Fogg, as reserved as ever, did not seem to be the type of man to fling himself into those waters.

The first part of the crossing on the *Rangoon* passed off under excellent conditions. The weather was moderate. All that part of the immense bay, which the sailors call 'the Bengal fathoms', was favourable and the ship made good progress. The *Rangoon* soon sighted Great Andaman, the main island of the group, whose picturesque mountain called the Saddle Peak, two thousand four hundred feet high, is a landmark to sailors from a long way off.

They sailed quite close to the shore. The savage Papuans on the island did not put in an appearance. They are on the bottom rung of the human ladder and people at one time wrongly thought they were cannibals.

The scenery of those islands was superb. Immense forests of fan-palms, areca, bamboo, nutmeg and teak trees and gigantic mimosas and tree-like ferns covered the land in the foreground, and away at the back one could see the majestic outline of the mountains. On the coast there were thousands of those valuable sea-swallows whose edible nests are considered a choice delicacy in the Celestial Empire. But the varied spectacle of the Andaman group soon passed and the *Rangoon* sailed on quickly towards the Strait of Malacca, which gives access to the China seas.

And Inspector Fix, unfortunate enough to find himself involved in a voyage of circumnavigation—what was he

4   (H 880)

doing during the crossing? In Calcutta he had instructed that the warrant, if it did arrive in the end, should be sent on to him in Hong Kong and then he had managed to go on board the *Rangoon* without being seen by Passepartout. He hoped to be able to conceal his presence until the steamer reached port. It would be difficult to explain why he was on board without arousing the suspicions of Passepartout, who must imagine him to be in Bombay. But the logic of circumstances led to his renewing his friendship with that worthy fellow. How did that come about? You will soon see.

All the hopes and desires of the police inspector were now centred on one single spot in the world, Hong Kong. The steamer would stop at Singapore for too short a time for him to take any action there. So it was in Hong Kong that the robber would be arrested—or would slip from his grasp for ever.

Hong Kong was, of course, a British territory, but the last one they would come to on the journey. Beyond it Mr. Fogg could find a virtually safe refuge in China, Japan or America. If Fix did in the end receive the warrant that was obviously following him round in Hong Kong, he would arrest Fogg and hand him over to the local police. There would be no difficulty about that. But after Hong Kong an ordinary warrant would not be enough. He would need an extradition order. This would lead to delays and obstacles of every kind, which the rogue would be sure to take advantage of, and so he would escape altogether. If the deed could not be done in Hong Kong it would be very difficult, if not impossible, to attempt it again with any prospect of success.

'So,' Fix repeated to himself during those long hours he spent in his cabin, 'either the warrant will be in Hong Kong and I shall arrest my man, or it will not be there and I shall have to delay his departure at all costs! I failed in Bombay and I failed again in Calcutta! If the scheme misfires in Hong Kong my reputation will be ruined. I must succeed, whatever the cost! But how can I delay the departure of that accursed Fogg, if that proves to be necessary?'

In the last resort Fix had made up his mind to confess everything to Passepartout and let him know the kind of master he was serving. He was certainly not an accomplice. After such a revelation Passepartout would undoubtedly be afraid of becoming involved and would side with him, Fix. But this was a risky solution and could only be used if there was no alternative. One word from Passepartout to his master would be enough to upset matters once and for all.

The inspector of police was in an extremely worrying position, but the presence of Aouda on board the *Rangoon* and in the company of Phileas Fogg opened up new prospects of success.

Who was she? What combination of circumstances had made her Fogg's travelling companion? The meeting had obviously taken place between Bombay and Calcutta. But where about in the peninsula? Had fate thrown Phileas Fogg and the young woman together? Or had the journey across India been undertaken by that gentleman for the express purpose of meeting that charming person? For she certainly was charming! Fix had noticed this in the courtroom in Calcutta.

One can imagine how the problem intrigued him. He wondered if it might not be a criminal case of kidnapping. Yes, that must be it! The idea began to take root in Fix's brain and he realised how well it could be turned to account. Whether the young woman was married or not, she had been kidnapped and things could be made so hot for the kidnapper in Hong Kong that he would not be able to get away, no matter how much money he offered.

But he ought not to wait for the *Rangoon* to reach Hong Kong. That fellow Fogg had a detestable habit of jumping from one boat to another and he might be a long way off before the matter could be broached.

The important thing to do was therefore to notify the British authorities and warn them of the arrival of the *Rangoon* before the passengers landed. Nothing could, in fact, be simpler as the steamer was calling at Singapore and Singapore is linked with the Chinese coast by telegraph.

However, before acting Fix wanted to be on surer ground, so he resolved to question Passepartout. He knew that it was not very difficult to make the fellow talk and so he decided to abandon the incognito he had maintained until then. He had no time to lose. It was 31st October and the *Rangoon* was due at Singapore the very next day.

So Fix emerged from his cabin and went up on deck with the intention of making the first move and going up to Passepartout with signs of extreme surprise. Passepartout was strolling about in the forepart of the ship when the inspector rushed up to him, crying:

'Fancy meeting you on the *Rangoon*!'

'Mr Fix, are you here too?' replied Passepartout, absolutely amazed to recognize his shipboard acquaintance from the *Mongolia*. 'What! I thought I left you behind in Bombay and yet here you are on the way to Hong Kong! Are you going round the world too?'

'No, no,' replied Fix, 'I expect to be staying on in Hong Kong—for a few days at least.'

'Oh!' said Passepartout, who seemed surprised for a moment. 'But why have I not seen you since we left Calcutta?'

'Dear me, I was indisposed—a touch of sea-sickness . . . I was lying down in my cabin . . . The Bay of Bengal does not suit me as well as the Indian Ocean. And how is your master, Mr. Phileas Fogg?'

'He is in perfect health and keeping up with his itinerary. Not a day late! Oh, but Mr. Fix, you will not know this, but we have a young lady with us.'

'A young lady?' replied the detective, looking as if he did not understand.

But Passepartout soon told him her story. He told him about the incident at the pagoda in Bombay, the purchase of the elephant for two thousand pounds, the affair of the suttee, the abduction of Aouda, the sentences passed at the court in Calcutta, their release on bail. Fix, already familiar with the final part of the story, gave the impression that he knew nothing at all about it and Passepartout was delighted to recount his adventures to such a good listener.

'But,' asked Fix, 'does your master intend to take the young woman to Europe?'

'Oh no, Mr. Fix! We are merely going to hand her over to one of her relatives, a rich Hong Kong merchant.'

'There is nothing I can do about that,' the detective said to himself, concealing his disappointment. 'A glass of gin, Mr. Passepartout?'

'I would love one, Mr. Fix. The least we can do is to drink to our meeting here on the *Rangoon*.'

The various things that happen during the voyage from Singapore to Hong Kong

From that day onwards Passepartout and the detective met frequently, but the latter was very reserved towards his companion and did not try to make him talk. Once or twice he caught a glimpse of Mr. Fogg who was happy to remain in the large saloon of the *Rangoon*, keeping Aouda company or playing whist, as was his wont.

As for Passepartout, he was beginning to wonder very seriously about the strange stroke of fate that had caused Fix to cross his master's path once more. It was more than a little surprising. The very kind and obliging gentleman he had met first of all at Suez and who had then sailed on the *Mongolia* and landed in Bombay, where he said he would be staying, had turned up on the *Rangoon* on the way to Hong Kong. He was, in short, following Mr. Fogg's itinerary stage by stage. It was certainly worth thinking about. At the very least it was a curious coincidence. What was Fix up to ? Passepartout was ready to bet his fine Turkish slippers, which he had carefully preserved, that Fix would leave Hong Kong at the same time as they did, probably on the same steamer.

Passepartout could have pondered over all this for a hundred years without ever guessing what the detective's mission was. He would never have imagined that Phileas Fogg was being shadowed like a thief round the earth. But, as it is part of human nature to try and find an explanation for everything, Passepartout, in a sudden flash of inspiration, found a reason for the permanent presence of Fix and it really was a very plausible one. Fix could be none other than an agent sent out after Mr. Fogg by his fellow-members at the Reform Club to make sure that the

journey round the world was being carried out properly, in accordance with the agreed itinerary.

'It is perfectly obvious!' the good fellow said to himself more than once, very proud of his perspicacity. 'He is a spy sent out by these gentlemen to follow us. And that is not a very fair thing to do. Mr. Fogg is such an upright, honourable man. Arrange to have him spied on—the very idea! Oh, you gentlemen of the Reform Club, you will have to pay sweetly for this!'

Passepartout, delighted with his discovery, decided, however, not to say anything to his master, as he feared the latter would feel hurt, and rightly so, at this mistrust on the part of his adversaries. But he promised himself that he would play a joke on Fix, using veiled allusions and not committing himself.

On the afternoon of Wednesday, 30th October, the *Rangoon* entered the Strait of Malacca which separates the peninsula bearing that name from Sumatra. Picturesque rugged islets hid the large island from view.

At four o'clock on the following morning the *Rangoon* put into Singapore half a day ahead of schedule in order to replenish her stocks of coal.

Phileas Fogg noted that half-day in the 'gains' column and went ashore on this occasion, as Aouda had expressed a desire to drive about for a few hours.

Fix, in whose eyes every action of Mr. Fogg's seemed open to suspicion, followed him without being seen. Passepartout, who laughed quietly to himself when he saw Fix's manoeuvre, went shopping as usual.

The island of Singapore is neither large nor imposing in appearance. It has no mountains, which means that it has no contours. But it is charming nevertheless. It is like a park divided up by beautiful roads. A fine carriage drawn by those elegant horses that have been imported from Australia, conveyed Aouda and Phileas Fogg through the clumps of palm-trees with brilliant foliage, and clove-trees, the actual cloves being formed by the buds of the half-open flowers. There were pepper-plants in place of the thorny hedPes that are so characteristic of the European country-

side. Sago-trees and large ferns with magnificent branches lent variety to the appearance of that tropical region. Nutmeg-trees with shiny leaves saturated the air with their all-pervading perfume. There were nimble troupes of grimacing monkeys in the woods and perhaps there were tigers in the jungle. People may be surprised to learn that these terrible carnivores have not all been destroyed on this relatively small island, but the reason is that they swim across the strait from Malacca.

After roaming through the countryside for two hours, Aouda and her companion—who looked about a little without really seeing anything—returned to the town, a huge conglomeration of heavy squat houses, surrounded by charming gardens where mangosteens and pineapples and all the finest fruits in the world can be grown.

At ten o'clock they returned to the steamer, having been followed without their knowledge by the inspector who must have had the expense of hiring a carriage too.

Passepartout was waiting for them on the deck of the *Rangoon*. He had bought a few dozen mangosteens, which are as big as a medium-sized apple, dark brown outside and bright red inside. As the white pulp melts in the mouth true gourmets obtain a sense of enjoyment unequalled by any other food. Passepartout was only too delighted to offer them to Aouda who thanked him most gracefully.

At eleven o'clock the *Rangoon* had taken on a full load of coal and let go her mooring-ropes. And a few hours later the passengers lost sight of those high mountains of Malacca and the forests in which the finest tigers in the world roam.

It is about thirteen hundred miles from Singapore to the island of Hong Kong, a small British territory quite separate from the Chinese mainland. Phileas Fogg was interested in covering that distance in six days at most so that he could sail from Hong Kong on the boat due to leave for Yokohama on 6th November.

The *Rangoon* was heavily laden. Many passengers had come on board in Singapore—Indians, Ceylonese, Chinese, Malays and Portuguese, most of whom were in second-class accommodation.

The weather, which had been quite fine until then, changed with the last quarter of the moon. There were rough seas. It sometimes blew a moderate gale, from the south-east quarter fortunately, and that helped the steamer on her way. When practicable, the captain hoisted the sails. The *Rangoon*, rigged as a brig, often used her two topsails and her foresail and she moved along faster, thanks to the twofold action of steam and wind. And so they skirted the coasts of Annam and Cochin-China on a choppy and sometimes very tiring sea.

But it was the steamer, and not the sea, that the passengers, most of whom were sick, ought to have blamed for all they had to undergo.

The ships of the Peninsular Company which sail the China seas have a serious structural defect. The ratio of their draught when laden to their depth has been miscalculated and, as a result, they offer poor resistance to the sea. Their water-tight volume is inadequate, so they become waterlogged. If they ship only a few seas, that is sufficient to alter their trim. These ships are thus greatly inferior to those used by the French lines, for example, the *Impératrice* and the *Cambodge*, as regards their mode of construction, if not as far as the engine and steam equipment are concerned. According to the calculations of the engineers, the latter can ship a weight of water equivalent to their own weight before they will sink, whereas the boats of the Peninsular Company, the *Golconda*, the *Korea* and the *Rangoon*, could not ship even a sixth of their weight without going to the bottom.

So, when the weather was bad, they had to take great precautions. It was sometimes necessary to lay-to under half-steam. The loss of time did not appear to affect Phileas Hogg in any way, but it irritated Passepartout very much. At such times he would blame the captain and the engineer and the Company and consign to the Devil all who had anything to do with the transportation of travellers. The thought of the gaslight still burning at his expense in the house in Savile Row no doubt added greatly to the impatience he felt.

'You are in a great hurry to reach Hong Kong, are you not?' the detective asked him one day.

'Yes, in a great hurry!' replied Passepartout.

'Do you think Mr. Fogg is in a hurry to catch the steamer for Yokohama?'

'Yes, in a frightful hurry.'

'So you believe in this odd journey round the world?'

'Absolutely. Do you, Mr. Fix?'

'Me? No, I do not believe in it at all.'

'Oh, very funny indeed!' replied Passepartout with a wink.

Those words set the detective thinking. They worried him, he did not know why. Had the Frenchman guessed who he was? He did not quite know what to think. But how had Passepartout been able to recognize that he was a detective? It was a secret known only to himself. And yet, when he spoke to him like that, there was certainly something behind it.

The good fellow went even further on another day. He could not help it. He just could not hold his tongue. 'Tell me, Mr. Fix,' he said to his companion in a mischievous tone, 'are we going to be unfortunate enough to leave you behind when we reach Hong Kong?'

'Well,' replied Fix in some embarrassment, 'I do not know. Perhaps . . .'

'Oh!' said Passepartout. 'I should be delighted to have you with us. An agent of the Peninsular Company surely could not stop on the way. You were only going as far as Bombay, but now you will soon be arriving in China. America is not far away you know, and it is just a step from America to Europe!'

Fix looked closely at his friend and saw he was wearing his nicest smile. He decided to laugh with him. Passepartout was in very good form and asked him if he 'earned a lot of money in his line of business'.

'Yes and no,' replied Fix, without turning a hair. 'Sometimes business is good and sometimes it is bad. But you will realize that I am not travelling at my own expense.'

106

'Oh no, I am sure you are not!' cried Passepartout, laughing more than ever.

After that conversation Fix returned to his cabin and began to think. He had obviously been found out. In some way or other the Frenchman had discovered that he was a detective. But had he warned his master? What part was he playing in all this? Was he an accomplice or not? Had they got wind of the whole affair? That would spoil everything. The detective spent a few trying hours. There were moments when he believed that all was lost and there were others when he felt that Fogg might be unaware of the situation. In the end he did not know what course to take.

Then he grew calm again and resolved to be perfectly frank with Passepartout. If he were not in a position to arrest Fogg in Hong Kong and if Fogg were preparing to leave British soil once and for all, he, Fix, would tell Passepartout the whole story. The servant was either the accomplice of his master—in which case the latter would know everything and the affair would be ruined once and for all—or the servant had had no part in the robbery and it would thus be in his interest to abandon the robber.

Such were the respective positions of the two men and far above them soared the supremely indifferent Phileas Fogg. He was following his orbit round the world in a perfectly rational manner, without troubling about the asteroids that were gravitating round him.

And yet, close beside him, there was, as an astronomer might have said, a disturbing body which ought to have upset that gentleman's heart to some extent. But it had not! The charm of Aouda had no effect, much to the surprise of Passepartout, and the disturbances, if they existed at all, would have been more difficult to calculate than those of Uranus which led to the discovery of Neptune.

Yes, it was a daily source of wonder to Passepartout, who saw such deep gratitude towards his master shining in the young woman's eyes. Phileas Fogg definitely had no heart, beyond what was needed for deeds of heroism; as for love— oh no! And he showed no sign of worrying about the outcome of the journey, whereas Passepartout was living in a

state of constant apprehension. One day Passepartout was leaning on the engine-room superstructure. He was watching the mighty machine which sometimes ran away, when there was a violent pitching movement, with the propeller racing round out of the water. The steam would then escape from the valves and that roused the good fellow to anger.

'The valves are not charged enough!' he exclaimed. 'We are not moving. That is just like the British! Now, if it was an American ship, we would blow up maybe, but we would certainly go faster!'

In which Phileas Fogg, Passepartout and Fix each goes about his own business

During the final days of the crossing the weather was fairly bad. The wind became very strong. It remained fixed in the north-west quarter and interfered with the progress of the steamer. The *Rangoon*, which was not a stable vessel, was leaking considerably and the passengers grew heartily sick of the everlasting long waves whipped up by the wind.

During the 3rd and 4th November there was something of a storm. The sea was lashed by a squall, and the *Rangoon* had to lie to for half a day and keep going with only ten turns of the propeller so that she could lean with the waves. All the sails had been taken in and, even so, there was too much rigging whistling in the stormy gusts.

As one can imagine, the speed of the steamer was considerably reduced. and it was estimated that they would reach Hong Kong twenty hours behind the scheduled time, and even later if the storm did not cease.

Phileas Fogg watched the spectacle of the angry sea, which seemed to be fighting him personally, with his usual impassivity. His brow did not cloud for a single moment and yet a delay of twenty hours might throw his whole journey out of joint and cause him to miss the steamer for Yokohama. But he seemed to be devoid of nerves and felt no resentment or annoyance. It really did seem as if the storm formed part of his programme and had been allowed for. Aouda spoke to him about that stroke of bad luck, but she found him just as calm as he had been in the past.

Fix did not look at things in the same light at all. Quite the reverse! He was delighted with the storm. And his satisfaction would have known no bounds if the *Rangoon* had been obliged to run before the storm. All these delays

suited him. They would compel Mr. Fogg to stay on in Hong Kong for a few days. The heavens, with their squalls and gusts, were playing into his hands. He did indeed feel a little sick, but what did that matter! His feelings of nausea were unimportant and when his body writhed under the onslaught of sea-sickness his heart was dancing with delight.

As for Passepartout, one can well imagine his ill-concealed anger during that time of trial. Everything had gone so well until then. Land and water seemed to be devoted to his master. Steamers and railways obeyed him. Wind and steam joined forces to assist him in his journey. Had the hour of adversity struck for him at last? Passepartout had lost his *joie de vivre*. It was as if the twenty thousand pounds wagered had to come out of his own pocket. The storm exasperated him and the fierce squall enraged him. He would have liked to have given that disobedient sea a good thrashing. Poor fellow! Fix carefully concealed from him the personal satisfaction he felt and he was wise to do so, for, if Passepartout had had any suspicion of Fix's secret joy, Fix would have been in for a nasty time.

Throughout the squall Passepartout stayed on the deck of the *Rangoon*. He could not have stayed below. He climbed up the masts to the amazement of the crew and helped them to carry out their various duties with the agility of a monkey. He questioned the captain and the officers and the sailors a hundred times and they could not help laughing when they saw he was so put out. Passepartout wanted to know exactly how long the storm would last. He was told to consult the barometer, but it could not make up its mind to go up. Passepartout shook the barometer, but the shaking and the insults he heaped on the harmless instrument were all to no avail.

Finally the storm died down. The state of the sea changed during 4th November. The wind jumped two quarters and became favourable, because now it was blowing from the south.

Passepartout calmed down with the weather. The topsails and the lower sails could be hoisted and the *Rangoon* went on her way once more at a spanking pace.

But they could not make up all the time lost. They just had to resign themselves to that fact. Land was not sighted till five o'clock in the morning of the 6th. According to Phileas Fogg's itinerary, the steamer should have arrived on the 5th. But they would not be reaching port till the 6th. They were twenty-four hours late and would inevitably miss the sailing to Yokohama.

At six o'clock the pilot came aboard the *Rangoon* and took his place on the bridge in order to steer the ship through the channels and into the port of Hong Kong. Passepartout was dying to question the man and ask him if the steamer for Yokohama had left Hong Kong, but he did not dare to and preferred to hold on to a small remnant of hope until the last moment. He had confided his worries to Fix and that cunning fox had tried to comfort him by saying that Mr. Fogg would simply have to take the next steamer. That put Passepartout into a blind fury.

Passepartout did not venture to question the pilot, but Mr. Fogg, after consulting his Bradshaw, asked that worthy in his calm unruffled way if he knew when a boat would be leaving Hong Kong for Yokohama.

'Tomorrow on the morning tide,' replied the pilot.

'Oh!' said Mr. Fogg, not showing any surprise.

Passepartout felt like hugging the pilot and Fix would have liked to wring his neck.

'What is the steamer's name?' asked Mr. Fogg.

'The *Carnatic*,' replied the pilot.

'Was she not due to sail yesterday?'

'Yes, sir, but she had to have one of her boilers repaired and the sailing has been put off until tomorrow.'

'Thank you,' replied Mr. Fogg and walked down into the saloon of the *Rangoon* with his usual measured gait.

As for Passepartout, he seized the pilot's hand and shook it vigorously, saying: 'You are a fine man, pilot!'

The pilot probably never found out why his replies had inspired that friendly outburst. A whistle was blown and he went up on the bridge again and steered the steamer through the flotilla of junks, native *tankas* and fishing-boats

and ships of all kinds that were cluttering the narrow entrance to Hong Kong harbour.

At one o'clock the *Rangoon* was alongside the quay and the passengers went ashore.

On this occasion fate had played strangely into Phileas Fogg's hands, one must admit. If the *Carnatic* had not needed to have her boilers repaired, she would have sailed on 5th November and the travellers bound for Japan would have had to wait for the next ship to depart. Mr. Fogg was twenty-four hours behind schedule, it was true, but that delay would not have unfortunate repercussions on the rest of the journey.

The steamer crossing the Pacific from Yokohama to San Francisco connected with the steamer from Hong Kong and could not sail until the latter arrived. There would clearly be a delay of twenty-four hours in Yokohama, but during the twenty-two days they would need to sail across the Pacific it would be easy to make up the time lost. So Phileas Fogg was within twenty-four hours of fulfilling his programme thirty-five days after leaving London.

As the *Carnatic* was not due to sail till five o'clock on the following morning, Mr. Fogg had sixteen hours ahead of him in which to attend to his business, that is, the business concerning Aouda. When they landed he offered his arm to the young woman and conducted her to a palanquin. He asked the bearers to show him a hotel and they suggested the Club Hotel. So the palanquin set off, followed by Passepartout, and twenty minutes later they reached their destination.

An apartment was reserved for the young woman and Phileas Fogg made sure that she would not go short of anything. Then he told Aouda that he was going off at once in search of the relative to whom he was going to entrust her. At the same time he instructed Passepartout to stay at the hotel till he returned so that the young woman would not be left alone.

The gentleman asked to be taken to the Exchange. There they would be certain to know a man like Mr. Jejeeh, who was one of the richest merchants in the city.

The broker to whom Mr. Fogg addressed his query did indeed know the Parsee trader. But he had not been living there for two years. Having made his fortune, he had taken up his abode in Europe—in Holland, it was thought, because of the many contacts he had established in that country during his business life.

Phileas Fogg returned to the Club Hotel. He at once asked to see Aouda and, without preamble, told her that Mr. Jejeeh was no longer resident in Hong Kong and was probably living in Holland.

Aouda made no answer to begin with. She passed her hand over her brow and remained deep in thought for a few moments. Then she said softly: 'What am I to do, Mr. Fogg?'

'That is very simple,' replied the gentleman. 'Come back to Europe.'

'But I cannot take advantage . . .'

'You are not doing that and your presence is not upsetting my programme in the slightest.'

'Passepartout?'

'Yes, sir,' replied Passepartout.

'Go to the *Carnatic* and reserve three cabins.'

Passepartout was delighted that they were going to be continuing their journey in the young woman's company, as she had treated him so kindly, and he set out from the Club Hotel at once.

*In which Passepartout takes too lively an interest
in his master and what happens then*

Hong Kong is just a small island which became a British
possession as a result of the Treaty of Nanking which
followed the war of 1842. In a few years the British, with
their colonising genius, had established an important city
there and had created the port of Victoria. The island is
situated in the estuary of the Canton River and only sixty
miles separate it from the Portuguese city of Macao, built on
the other side. Hong Kong vanquished Macao in the
commercial struggle and now most of the Chinese traffic
goes through the British city. Docks, hospitals, wharves,
warehouses, a Gothic cathedral, a Government House and
Macadamised roads are to be found there—in fact, it would
all make one think that one of the commercial towns in Kent
or Surrey had moved round the globe and come to rest of
the coast of China, almost at the other side of the world.

With his hands in his pockets, Passepartout made his way
towards the port of Victoria and looked at the palanquins
and the chairs with sails still in favour of the Celestial
Empire, and the crowds of Chinese, Japanese and Europeans thronging the streets. Except for a few things, he felt,
as he walked along, that he might have been in Bombay,
Calcutta or Singapore. There is, in fact, a whole string of
British towns scattered round the world.

Passepartout reached the port of Victoria. There, at the
mouth of the Canton River, he saw a swarm of ships of all
nationalities—British, French, American, Dutch—war-
ships and merchant vessels, Japanese and Chinese boats
junks, sampans, *tankas* and even flower-boats, which were
like flower-beds floating on the water. As he walked along,
Passepartout saw a fair number of natives, all very elderly,

dressed in yellow. He went into a Chinese barber's for a shave in Chinese style and learned from the local Figaro, who spoke fairly good English, that these old men were all eighty years of age at least, and that at that age they had the privilege of wearing yellow, the Imperial colour. Passepartout thought that was very odd, without quite knowing why.

When he had had his shave he went to the landing stage of the *Carnatic* and there he observed Fix walking up and down. This did not surprise him at all. But there were signs of keen disappointment on the inspector's face.

'Good!' said Passepartout to himself. 'Things are going badly for the gentlemen of the Reform Club.'

And he went up to Fix with a gay smile, not taking any notice of the vexed expression on the other's face.

The detective had good reason to curse at the devilish luck that had been dogging his footsteps. The warrant had not come! It was obvious that it was following him up and could not reach him there unless he stayed in the city for a few days. As Hong Kong was the last British territory on the way, Mr. Fogg would escape him once and for all if he did not manage to detain him there.

'Well, Mr. Fix, have you made up your mind to come with us to America?' asked Passepartout.

'Yes,' replied Fix from between clenched teeth.

'Well, well!' exclaimed Passepartout with a loud guffaw. 'I knew for a fact that you could not leave us. Come and book your cabin! Come on now!'

And the two men went into the shipping office and reserved cabins for four people. But the clerk pointed out that, as the repairs on the *Carnatic* had been completed, the steamer would sail that very evening at eight o'clock, not the next morning, as had been announced.

'Grand!' replied Passepartout. 'That will suit my master. I must go and tell him.'

At that moment Fix came to a momentous decision. He resolved to tell Passepartout everything. It was perhaps the only way of keeping Phileas Fogg in Hong Kong for a few days.

As they left the office, Fix invited his companion to have a drink in a tavern. Passepartout had time for this. So he accepted Fix's invitation.

There was a tavern right on the quayside. It had an inviting appearance and so they both went in. They found themselves in a huge, well-decorated room with a camp bed strewn with cushions at one end. A number of men were sleeping on it.

About thirty customers were sitting in the large room at little tables of plaited cane. Some were drinking pints of English beer, ale or porter, others had jugs of spirits, gin or brandy. And the majority were also smoking long pipes of red clay, filled with small balls of opium mixed with attar of roses. From time to time some smoker would slide limply under the table and the waiters would pick him up by his head and feet and carry him to the camp bed where they would set him down alongside another sleeper. About twenty intoxicated men were stretched out side by side in the final stages of stupor.

Fix and Passepartout realized that they had entered a smoking-house frequented by those miserable and besotted and emaciated idiots to whom commercially minded Britain sells £10,400,000 worth of that dreadful drug opium every year. These are sad millions levied on one of the deadliest vices of human nature.

The Chinese Government has tried in vain to check this abuse by means of severe laws, but all to no avail. From the rich class, to whom the use of opium was formally reserved to begin with, the custom has descended to the lower orders and the ravages of the drug can no longer be arrested. Opium is smoked everywhere and all the time in the Middle Empire. Men and women become addicted to this deplorable craze and, once they have grown used to inhaling it, they cannot do without it, for if they stopped they would experience horrible contractions of the stomach. A heavy smoker can smoke as many as eight pipes per day, but he dies in five years.

Well, it was one of these smoking-houses, of which there are so many, even in Hong Kong, that Fix and Passepartout

had entered with the intention of having a drink. Passepartout had no money, but he gladly accepted the hospitality of his companion, which he could return at some other time and place,

They ordered two bottles of port, which the Frenchman did full justice to, and Fix, who was more reserved by nature, watched his companion very carefully indeed. They chatted about a variety of things and, above all, about what an excellent idea it was for Fix to book a passage on the *Carnatic*. And, speaking of the steamer, whose sailing time had been brought forward by a few hours, Passepartout rose to his feet, now that the bottles had been drained dry, as he wanted to go and tell his master.

Fix stopped him. 'Just a minute,' he said.

'What is it, Mr. Fix?'

'I have some serious matters to discuss with you.'

'Serious matters?' cried Passepartout, draining a few drops of wine remaining at the bottom of his glass. 'We shall speak about them tomorrow. I have no time today.'

'Stay a minute!' replied Fix, 'They concern your master.'

When he heard that, Passepartout looked closely at the other man. He thought there was an odd expression on Fix's face. Then he sat down again.

'What is it that you have to tell me?' he asked.

Fix rested his hand on his companion's arm and, lowering his voice, he asked:

'You have guessed who I am?'

'Of course I have,' said Passepartout with a smile.

'Well, I am going to tell you the whole story . . . '

'Now that I know everything, my friend! That is not much good! But, tell me just the same! But, before you start, just let me tell you that those gentlemen have put themselves about needlessly.'

'Needlessly?' said Fix. 'It is all very well for you to talk! It is clear to be seen that you do not know the sum involved.'

'Of course I know it,' replied Passepartout. 'It is twenty thousand pounds.'

'Fifty-five thousand!' said Fix, grasping the Frenchman's hand.

'What!' cried Passepartout. 'Mr. Fogg dared to . . . ! Fifty-five thousand pounds . . . ! Well, that is all the more reason why I should not lose a moment,' he added, rising to his feet once again.

'Fifty-five thousand pounds!' repeated Fix, ordering a flask of brandy and making Passepartout sit down again. 'And if I succeed, I shall gain a bonus of two thousand pounds. You can have five hundred on condition that you help me.'

'Help you?' cried Passepartout, wide-eyed.

'Yes, help me to keep Mr. Fogg in Hong Kong for a few days.'

'What!' said Passepartout. 'What are you saying? Do you mean to say that, not content with having my master followed and casting doubts on his integrity, those gentlemen want to place obstacles in his path? I am ashamed of them!'

'Now then, what do you mean by that? asked Fix.

'I mean that it shows a complete lack of finer feelings. It is just like robbing Mr. Fogg and taking the money out of his pocket!'

'Oh, but that is what we mean to do!'

'But it is all a plot,' cried Passepartout, who was getting worked up under the influence of the brandy that Fix was pouring out for him. 'Just a plot! And they are supposed to be gentlemen! Colleagues of his!'

Fix began not to follow.

'Colleagues!' cried Passepartout. 'Members of the Reform Club! I would have you know, Mr. Fix, that my master is an honest man and when he makes a bet he means to win it honourably.'

'But who do you think I am?' asked Fix, staring at Passepartout.

'Why, an agent sent out by the members of the Reform Club to check up on my master's itinerary. It is perfectly humiliating! I guessed what you were up to, but I took good care not to say anything to Mr. Fogg.'

'He knows nothing about it?' Fix asked anxiously.

'Nothing,' replied Passepartout, emptying his glass once more.

The police inspector passed a hand over his brow. He hesitated before speaking again. What was he to do? Passepartout's error seemed to be a genuine one, but it made his plan more difficult. It was obvious that the fellow was speaking in perfectly good faith and was not an accomplice of his master, which Fix might have feared to be the case.

'Well,' he said to himself 'as he is not his accomplice, he will help me.'

The detective had made up his mind a second time. Moreover, he could not wait any longer. At all costs he had to arrest Mr. Fogg in Hong Kong.

'Listen to me,' said Fix curtly, 'and listen carefully! I am not what you think—I am not an agent sent out by the members of the Reform Club . . .'

'Hmm!' said Passepartout, looking at him with a mocking expression.

'I am a police inspector, sent out by the Metropolitan Police . . .'

'You . . . an inspector of police!'

'Yes, and I can prove it,' Fix went on. 'Here are my credentials.'

And the detective took out of his wallet and showed to his companion a document signed by the chief of the Metropolitan Police. Passepartout looked at Fix in bewilderment, unable to utter a single word.

'Mr. Fogg's bet,' went on Fix, 'is just a pretext which has taken you in, you and his fellow-members at the Reform Club. You see he was anxious to have you as his unwitting accomplice.'

'But why?' cried Passepartout.

'I will tell you. On 29th September last, fifty-five thousand pounds were stolen from the Bank of England by an individual whose description was noted. Here is the description and it tallies feature by feature with that of Mr. Fogg.'

'Nonsense!' cried Passepartout, bringing his sturdy fist down on the table. 'My master is the most honest man in the world!'

'What do you know about it?' replied Fix. 'You do not even know him! You entered his service on the day he left and he went off in a hurry on an absurd pretext without luggage and carrying a large sum in banknotes. And you dare to maintain that he is an honest man!'

'Yes! Yes!' repeated the poor fellow mechanically.

'Do you want to be arrested as his accomplice then?'

Passepartout was holding his head in his hands. He was not like the same person. He did not dare to look at the police inspector. Phileas Fogg a robber—Fogg, the rescuer of Aouda—Fogg who was so brave and generous? And yet there was so much circumstantial evidence against him. Passepartout tried to thrust these suspicions aside, as they insinuated themselves into his mind. He did not want to believe in his master's guilt.

'Well, what do you want of me?' he asked the detective, controlling himself by a supreme effort.

'I will tell you.' replied Fix. 'I have shadowed Mr. Fogg as far as this place, but I have not yet received the warrant for his arrest which I have requested from London. So you must help me to keep him in Hong Kong . . .'

'Me! Keep him . . .'

'And I will give you a share of the bonus of two thousand pounds promised by the Bank of England.'

'Never!' replied Passepartout, who made as if to get up and fell back. He felt that his mental and physical faculties were departing from him simultaneously.

'Mr. Fix,' he said falteringly, 'even if all you have told me is true . . . if my master is the robber you are looking for . . . which I deny . . . I have been . . . I am in his service . . . I have found him a good and generous master . . . me betray him? Never, not for all the gold in the world . . . I come from a place where people don't do that sort of thing!'

'You refuse?'

'Yes, I refuse.'

'Let us pretend I said nothing,' replied Fix. 'And let us have a drink!'

'Yes, let us have a drink!'

Passepartout was aware that he was becoming more and more intoxicated. Fix, realizing that it was necessary at all costs to separate him from his master, meant to finish the job properly. On the table were a few pipes filled with opium. Fix slipped one into Passepartout's hand and he took it and raised it to his lips and lit it, took a few puffs and fell back, his head heavy with the effect of the narcotic.

'Ah,' said Fix, seeing that Passepartout was unconscious, 'Mr. Fogg will not be warned in time of the sailing of the *Carnatic* and, even if he does leave, it will at least be without this accursed Frenchman!'

Then he paid the bill and went out.

In which Fix has direct dealings with Phileas Fogg

During that scene which would perhaps have serious repercussions on his future Mr. Fog g was walking through the streets of the British city with Aouda. Since Aouda had accepted his offer to take her to Europe he had had to think of all the items that would be necessary for such a long journey. An Englishman like himself could go round the world with nothing more than a carpet-bag, but a woman could not undertake a journey like that without luggage. So it was essential to buy clothes and other items needed for the journey. Mr. Fogg carried out that task with the calm imperturbability characteristic of him and to all the excuses or objections made by the young widow, who was overcome with all his kindness, he would reply invariably:

'It is in the interests of my journey. It is all part of the programme.'

Having made their purchases, Mr. Fogg and the young woman returned to the hotel and sat down to a sumptuous dinner. Then Aouda, feeling a little tired, went up to her room, after shaking her imperturbable rescuer by the hand in true English style.

During the whole of that evening the gentleman engrossed himself in *The Times* and the *Illustrated London News*.

If he had been the kind of man to be surprised at anything, it would have been at the non-appearance of his servant at bedtime. But, knowing that the steamer was not due to leave Hong Kong for Yokohama till the following morning, he did not worry. The next day Passepartout did not come when Mr. Fogg rang.

What the gentleman thought when he learned that his servant had not returned to the hotel nobody can say. Mr.

Fogg merely picked up his bag, sent a message to Aouda and ordered a palanquin.

It was then eight o'clock. High water, which was to enable the *Carnatic* to pass through the channels, was advertised for nine-thirty.

When the palanquin arrived at the hotel door, Mr. Fogg and Aouda climbed into that comfortable conveyance and their luggage followed on a barrow.

Half an hour later the travellers climbed out on the landing stage and there Mr. Fogg learned that the *Carnatic* had sailed the day before.

Mr. Fogg, who had been counting on finding both steamer and servant there, was obliged to make do without either. But there was no hint of disappointment on his face and, when Aouda looked at him in concern, all he said was:

'It is just an incident, madam—nothing more.'

At that moment someone who had been watching him closely came up to him. It was Inspector Fix. He bowed and said to him:

'Were you not, sir, a fellow-passenger of mine on the *Rangoon* which docked here yesterday?'

'Yes, sir,' replied Mr. Fogg distantly, 'but I do not have the honour . . . ?'

'Excuse me, but I thought I would find your servant here.'

'Do you know where he is?' the young woman asked anxiously.

'What!' replied Fix with feigned surprise. 'Is he not with you?'

'No,' replied Aouda. 'He has not put in an appearance since yesterday. Do you think he has gone on board the *Carnatic* without us?'

'Without you, madam . . . ?' replied the detective. 'But, pardon my question, did you intend to sail on that ship?'

'Yes, sir.'

'That was my intention too, madam, and you find me a very disappointed man. Repairs on the *Carnatic* were completed early and she left Hong Kong twelve hours ahead of time without notifying anyone, and now we shall

have to wait a week for the next sailing.' As he said, 'a week' Fix felt his heart leap with joy. A whole week! Fogg kept in Hong Kong for a week! That would leave time for the warrant to come. At long last, fate was on the side of the representative of the law.

So one can judge what a devastating blow it was for him when Phileas Fogg said in his calm voice: 'But there are surely other ships besides the *Carnatic* in the port of Hong Kong.'

And Mr. Fogg, offering his arm to Aouda, made his way towards the docks in the search of a ship about to sail.

Fix followed him in bewilderment. It was as if there was a wire attaching him to that man.

But fate really did seem to have forsaken the man she had served so well until then. For three hours Phileas Fogg went round the harbour area in all directions, determined, if necessary, to charter a vessel to take him to Yokohama. But he only saw ships loading or unloading and they would not be sailing yet. Fix began to feel hopeful again.

But Mr. Fogg was not put out and was going to continue his search, even if it took him as far as Macao, when a seaman came up to him in the outer harbour area.

'Is your honour looking for a boat?' the seaman said, raising his cap.

'Have you a boat ready to leave?' asked Mr. Fogg.

'Yes, your honour, a pilot-boat, No. 43, the best of the flotilla.'

'Does she go fast?'

'She can do between eight and nine miles or thereabouts. Do you want to see her?'

'Yes.'

'Your honour will be pleased with her. Are you going on a sailing trip?'

'No, a voyage.'

'A voyage?'

'Would you be willing to take me to Yokohama?'

At those words the seaman just stood there with his arms dangling limply by his sides and his eyes starting out of his head.

'Your honour is joking,' he said.

'No! I have missed the *Carnatic* and I have to be in Yokohama on the fourteenth at the latest to take the steamer to San·Francisco.'

'I am sorry,' replied the pilot, 'but that is quite out of the question.'

'I am offering you a hundred pounds per day and a bonus of two hundred pounds if I arrive on time.'

'Are you in earnest?' asked the pilot.

'Very much so,' replied Mr. Fogg.

The pilot went away to one side. He was looking at the sea and was obviously torn between the desire to earn that enormous sum and the fear of venturing so far. Fix was in mortal torment. In the meantime Mr. Fogg had turned round to Aouda.

'You will not be afraid, madam?' he asked.

'Not with you, Mr. Fogg,' replied the young woman.

The pilot came up to the gentleman again. He was turning his cap round and round in his hands.

'Well, pilot?' said Mr. Fogg.

'Well, your honour,' replied the pilot, 'I cannot risk my men or myself or your life on such a long crossing on a boat of barely twenty tons at this time of year. And we would not arrive in time. It is sixteen hundred and fifty miles from Hong Kong to Yokohama.'

'Just sixteen hundred,' said Mr. Fogg.

'It comes to the same thing.'

Fix drew a deep breath.

'But,' added the pilot, 'there might perhaps be another way of doing it.'

Fix held his breath.

'How?' asked Phileas Fogg.

'By going to Nagasaki, which is on the southern tip of Japan and is eleven hundred miles away, or just, to Shanghai, which is eight hundred miles from Hong Kong. For that last trip we would be keeping close to the Chinese coast and that would be a great advantage, all the more so if you bear in mind that the currents would carry the boat to the north.'

'Pilot,' replied Mr. Fogg, 'it is at Yokohama that I have to take the American mail-ship, and not at Shanghai or Nagasaki.'

'Why not?' replied the pilot. 'The San Francisco steamer does not sail originally from Yokohama. She calls at Yokohama and Nagasaki, but her port of departure is Shanghai.'

'Are you certain of that?'

'Quite certain.'

'And when does the steamer leave Shanghai?'

'At seven o'clock in the evening of the eleventh. So we have four days ahead of us. Four days, that is, ninety-six hours, and at an average of eight miles per hour, all being well, and if the wind holds in the south-east and the sea is calm, we can cover these eight hundred miles between here and Shanghai.'

'When could you leave?'

'In an hour. That would leave just enough time to buy in provisions and set sail.'

'Very well. Are you the owner of the boat?'

'Yes, I am. John Bunsby, owner of the *Tankadere*.'

'Do you want something on account?'

'If your honour does not mind.'

'Here are two hundred pounds. And sir,' added Phileas Fogg, turning to Fix, 'if you would care to avail yourself . . .'

'Sir,' replied Fix resolutely, 'I was just about to ask you that very favour.'

'Good. We shall be on board in half an hour.'

'But what about poor Passepartout?' said Aouda, who was extremely worried about his disappearance.

'I shall do everything I can for him,' replied Phileas Fogg.

And as Fix, in a feverish state of anger and nerves, was making his way to the pilot-boat, the others went to the police offices in Hong Kong. There Phileas Fogg gave a description of Passepartout and left sufficient money to take him back to Europe. He did the same at the French Consulate and, after calling at the hotel, the travellers returned by palanquin to the outer harbour.

Three o'clock was striking. Pilot-boat No. 43, with her crew and provisions on board, was ready to sail.

The *Tankadere* was a charming little schooner of twenty tons, very narrow in the bows and very long along the water line and with an easy sweep. She was like a racing yacht. Her shining brass, her galvanized ironwork and her deck, which was as white as ivory, all showed that her owner, John Bunsby, knew how to keep her in good order. Her two masts slanted slightly sternwards. She carried a spanker, a foresail, a lateen sail, jibs, topsails and could rig a cross-jack if the wind was behind her. She would certainly move fast and had indeed won several prizes in competitions between pilot-boats.

The crew of the *Tankadere* consisted of the owner, John Bunsby, and four men. They belonged to that breed of seamen who venture out in all weathers in search of ships and know these seas very well indeed. John Bunsby, a man of about forty-five, sturdy and deeply tanned, had a keen eye and a strong face and was level-headed and good at his job. He would have inspired confidence in even the most timid of souls.

Phileas Fogg and Aouda went on board. Fix was there already. They went down the after companion-way into a square room, the walls of which were hollowed out to form berths above a circular divan. In the middle was a table lit by a swinging lamp. It was small, but clean.

'I am sorry I cannot offer you anything better,' said Mr. Fogg to Fix, who bowed without replying.

The police inspector felt rather humiliated at having to take advantage of Mr. Fogg's kindness in that way.

'He is certainly a very courteous rogue,' he thought, 'but he is a rogue all the same.'

At three-ten the sails were hoisted. The British flag was fluttering from the schooner's gaff. The passengers were sitting on deck. Mr. Fogg and Aouda cast a final glance at the quay to see if Passepartout would appear.

Fix had some feelings of apprehension because fate might have brought the unfortunate fellow whom he had treated so shabbily to that very spot and then there would have been unpleasant explanations, from which the detective would not have come out well at all. But there was no sign

of the Frenchman. No doubt he was still under the dulling influence of the narcotic.

Finally, John Bunsby reached the open sea, and with the wind filling her spanker and her foresail and her jibs, the *Tankadere* went dancing over the waves.

In which the owner of the Tankadere *is in great danger of losing his bonus of two hundred pounds*

That voyage of eight hundred miles on a twenty-ton craft was an adventurous undertaking, especially at that time of year. The China seas are usually rough and are exposed to terrible winds, especially during the equinoctial gales, and it was still only early November.

It would clearly have been to the advantage of the pilot to have taken his passengers as far as Yokohama, as he was being paid by the day. But it would have been unwise to have attempted such a crossing under these conditions. It was indeed daring, if not foolhardy, to go up as far as Shanghai. But John Bunsby had confidence in his *Tankadere,* which rose on the waves like a seagull, and perhaps he was right.

During the final hours of that day the *Tankadere* sailed through the uncertain channels of Hong Kong and, wherever the wind was coming from, she behaved splendidly.

'I need not remind you, pilot,' said Phileas Fogg when the schooner reached the open sea, 'to go as quickly as you can.'

'You can rely on me, your honour,' replied John Bunsby. 'We are carrying all the canvas that the wind will let us. Our topsails would add nothing. They would just overburden the craft and reduce her speed.'

'This is your trade, and not mine, and I am relying on you.'

Phileas Fogg, with his body erect and his legs apart, was standing looking at the swell with the balance of a practised seaman and no sign of any unsteadiness. The young woman, who was sitting aft, was moved by the sight of the ocean, darkening in the shades of twilight, on which she had

ventured in that frail craft. Above her head the white sails were spread and seemed to be carrying her off through space like great wings. The schooner, lifted by the wind, seemed to be flying through the air.

Night came. The moon was entering its first quarter and its feeble light would soon be blotted out by the mists on the horizon. Clouds were scudding along from the east and were already covering part of the sky.

The pilot had put his lights in position—an essential precaution to take in these busy seas so near to the land. Collisions were not a rare occurrence and, at the speed she was going, the schooner would have been shattered by the slightest impact.

Fix was musing in the forepart of the vessel. He held himself aloof, knowing that Fogg was taciturn by nature. Also, he found it repugnant to speak to a man from whom he was accepting favours under such circumstances. He was thinking of the future too. He was sure that Mr. Fogg would not stop in Yokohama, but would take the steamer to San Francisco at once and so reach America which was vast enough to ensure his safety and freedom. Phileas Fogg's plan seemed as clear as daylight.

Instead of sailing from England to the United States, like any ordinary rogue, Fogg had done a grand tour and had traversed three-quarters of the globe, so that he could reach the American continent in greater safety. There he would quietly work his way through the fifty-five thousand pounds from the Bank, having thrown the police completely off the scent. But once on American soil, what would Fix do? Would he abandon his man? No, certainly not! He would not move a step away from him until he had obtained an extradition order. There lay his duty and he would perform it to the end. But there was one happy feature in the whole business—Passepartout was no longer at his master's side. Especially after the confidential information Fix had imparted to him, it was important that master and servant should not meet again.

Phileas Fogg too was thinking about his servant who had disappeared under such odd circumstances. It seemed quite

possible that there had been a misunderstanding and the poor fellow had boarded the *Carnatic* at the last moment. That was Aouda's opinion too. She missed the honest servant to whom she owed so much. But they might meet him again in Yokohama and it would be easy to find out if he had gone there on the *Carnatic*.

Around ten o'clock the breeze began to freshen. It might have been wise to take in a reef, but, after carefully observing the sky, the pilot left the sails set. The *Tankadere* was carrying her sails admirably, as she had a deep draught, and they were all ready to haul down the sails quickly in the event of a squall.

At midnight Phileas Fogg and Aouda went down into the cabin. Fix was already there and had lain down in one of the berths. As for the pilot and his men, they spent the whole night on deck.

At sunrise on the next day, 8th November, the schooner covered over a hundred miles. The log was often heaved and it showed that the average speed was between eight and nine miles. The *Tankadere* had a free wind reaching her sails, which were all drawing, and so she was able to run along at her maximum speed. If the wind held like that, she would win through.

During the whole of that day the *Tankadere* did not move far from the coast and the currents were favourable. It was, at most, five miles away on her port beam and the irregular outline of the coast could sometimes be seen through clear patches. As the wind was blowing off the land, the sea was not rough. This was fortunate as vessels of low tonnage suffer, above all, from the swell, which cuts down their speed and 'kills' them, as a French seaman would say.

Around noon the breeze slackened a little and shifted to the south-east. The pilot had the topsails set, but they had to be taken in after two hours, as the wind was freshening once more.

Mr. Fogg and the young woman were fortunately not susceptible to sea-sickness and they ate with gusto the preserved food and biscuits supplied. Fix was invited to share their meals and he was obliged to accept, knowing

full well that it is just as necessary to ballast stomachs as ships, but it vexed him! To travel at the expense of this man and feed on his provisions was rather dishonest, he thought. He ate—very little, it is true—but he did eat nevertheless.

However, when the meal was over, he thought he ought to take Mr. Fogg aside and he said to him:

'Sir . . .'

That 'sir' burned his lips and he had to restrain himself from seizing the 'gentleman' in question by the throat.

'It was very obliging of you to offer me a passage on board your ship. But, although my resources do not permit me to do things on such a grand scale, I mean to pay my share . . .'

'Do not let us speak of that, sir,' replied Mr. Fogg.

'But I insist . . .'

'No, sir,' repeated Mr. Fogg in a tone indicating that the matter was closed. 'It all comes under general expenses.'

Fix gave in, but he felt as if he were choking, and went to lie down in the forepart of the schooner. During the rest of that day he did not say another word.

They were moving fast. John Bunsby had high hopes. On several occasions he told Mr. Fogg that they would reach Shanghai in time. Mr. Fogg merely replied that he was relying on that. And the whole crew of the little schooner were putting their hearts into it. The bonus was an incentive to these good people. So every sheet was conscientiously hauled taut. Every sail was vigorously hoisted home. The man at the wheel could not be accused of letting the vessel yaw. They could not have manoeuvred more strictly if they had been taking part in a Royal Yacht Club regatta.

In the evening the pilot ascertained from the log that they had travelled two hundred and twenty miles from Hong Kong, and Phileas Fogg could expect to reach Yokohama without having to record any delays in his itinerary. So the first serious mishap he had had since leaving London would probably have no adverse effect.

In the small hours of the morning the *Tankadere* sailed

into the Fo-Kien Channel, which separated the large island of Formosa from the Chinese coast, and she crossed the Tropic of Cancer. The sea was very rough in that channel and full of eddies formed by the counter-currents. The schooner was labouring along. The choppy seas were impeding her course and it became very difficult to stand upright on deck.

With daybreak the wind freshened further. The sky looked as if there was going to be a whole gale. And the barometer indicated that there was shortly going to be an atmospheric change. The needle was moving in an irregular manner and the mercury was fluctuating. They could also see the sea rising towards the south-east in long swells, which was a sign of storm. On the day before, the sun had set in a red haze amid phosphorescent scintillations on the sea.

The pilot studied that ominous sky for a long time and muttered unintelligible things between his teeth. Then, finding himself beside his passenger, he said to him in a whisper:

'Can I be honest with your honour?'

'You can,' replied Phileas Fogg.

'Well, we are going to have a full gale.'

'Will it be coming from the north or the south?' was all that Mr. Fogg asked.

'From the south. I will tell you straight. There is a typhoon on the way.'

'Very well then, we are having a typhoon and it will come from the south,' replied Mr. Fogg. 'It will push us in the right direction.'

'If you take it like that,' replied the pilot, 'I have nothing more to say.'

John Bunsby's forebodings had been right. In an earlier part of the year the typhoon would have passed like a 'luminous cascade of electric flames', as a celebrated meteorologist once put it, but during the winter equinox it might be violent.

The pilot took the necessary precautions in advance. He ordered all the sails to be taken in and the yards to be

lowered on to the deck. The top masts were struck. The boom was brought in. The hatch-covers were battened down securely. From that moment onwards not a drop of water could enter the hull of the vessel. One single triangular sail, a storm-jib made of strong canvas, was hoisted as a lateen sail to keep the schooner travelling with the wind astern. And they waited.

John Bunsby had requested his passengers to go down into the cabin. But that confined space, which was almost without air and was subjected to the jolting motion of the swell, was not a pleasant place to be imprisoned in. Neither Mr. Fogg nor Aouda, nor Fix himself, would agree to leave the deck.

Around eight o'clock the squall of wind and rain was upon them. With its one small piece of canvas hoisted the *Tankadere* was lifted like a feather in the wind. One cannot give an exact idea of its speed when it is blowing a gale, but if one compared its speed to four times that of a railway engine driven at full speed it would be an understatement.

Throughout that day the craft sped on towards the north, carried onward by the monstrous waves and fortunately maintaining a speed equal to theirs. A score of times she was nearly pooped by one of those mountains of water towering up astern, but an adroit movement of the wheel on the part of the pilot warded off disaster. The passengers were sometimes covered with spray, but they accepted this philosophically. Fix was no doubt fuming, but the intrepid Aouda, her eyes fixed on her companion, whose composure she could not but admire, showed herself worthy of him and braved the storm at his side. As for Phileas Fogg, it seemed as if the typhoon too had been included in his programme.

Till then the *Tankadere* had always been travelling north, but, towards evening, as they had feared, the wind shifted three quarters and was now blowing from the north-west. The schooner was then broadside on to the waves and she was being dreadfully jarred. The sea beat on her with a violence calculated to alarm anyone who did not know how strongly all the different parts of a boat are secured together.

With the coming on of night the storm grew more severe. When he saw the darkness descending and the storm growing in intensity, John Bunsby felt very anxious. He wondered if it would not be time to put into harbour and he consulted his crew.

When he had consulted his men, John Bunsby went up to Mr. Fogg and said:

'I think, your honour, we would do well to make for one of the ports on the coast.'

'I think so too,' replied Phileas Fogg.

'Oh!' said the pilot. 'But which one?'

'I only know of one,' Mr. Fogg replied calmly.

'Which one?'

'Shanghai.'

For a few moments the pilot seemed unable to understand his reply and the obstinacy and determination it revealed. Then he shouted: 'All right then! Your honour is right! On to Shanghai!'

And they kept the *Tankadere* going steadily northwards.

It was a really terrible night. It was a miracle that the little schooner did not capsize. Twice she was swamped and everything would have been swept off her if it had not been lashed on. Aouda was feeling worn out. but she uttered no word of complaint. More than once Mr. Fogg had to rush up to her to protect her from the fury of the waves.

Day dawned once more. The storm was still blowing with unabated fury. But the wind was now in the south-east. This was a change for the better and the *Tankadere* was now advancing once more over that turbulent sea, and the waves crashed into other waves whipped up by the change in wind direction. So there was a clash of counter-swells that would have crushed a craft less sturdily built than the *Tankadere*.

From time to time they could see the coast through the tatters of mist, but there was not a single ship in sight. The *Tankadere* must have been the only one to weather the storm out at sea.

At noon there were some signs of calmer weather and, as the sun sank on the horizon, they became more definite.

The storm had been of short duration because of its very violence. The passengers, absolutely worn out, were able to eat a little and have some rest.

The night was relatively calm. The pilot ordered the sails to be double-reefed again. The speed of the craft was considerable. At daybreak on the following morning, the 11th, John Bunsby examined the coast-line and was able to state that they were less than a hundred miles from Shanghai.

A hundred miles and they had only this one day to do it in! Mr. Fogg would have to arrive at Shanghai that very evening if he did not want to miss the steamer for Yokohama. If it had not been for that storm, in the course of which he lost several hours, he would have been barely thirty miles away from that port.

The breeze was slackening appreciably, but fortunately the sea was falling with it. The schooner now had all her sails unfurled. The topsails, staysails and the middle jib were all drawing and the sea was foaming under the stem.

At noon the *Tankadere* was no more than forty-five miles from Shanghai. She had six hours left to reach port before the steamer sailed for Yokohama.

There was keen anxiety on board. They wanted to reach it at all costs. All of them—except, no doubt, Phileas Fogg—felt their hearts pounding with impatience. The little schooner would have to maintain an average speed of nine miles per hour and the wind was still slackening. It was an irregular breeze, with capricious gusts coming from the coast. They passed and the sea became smooth as soon as they had gone by.

But the craft was so light and her high sails, which were of fine canvas, gathered these random breezes so well that, with the help of the current, John Bunsby calculated that they were only ten miles from the Shanghai River at six o'clock. The city itself is situated at least twelve miles above the estuary.

At seven o'clock they were still three miles from Shanghai. A formidable oath escaped from the pilot's lips. It seemed that the two hundred pounds bonus was going to elude him.

He looked at Mr. Fogg but Mr. Fogg seemed quite composed—and yet his entire fortune was at stake at that very moment . . .

Just then a long slender shape topped with a plume of smoke appeared on the water. It was the American steamer leaving at the appointed time.

'Damnation!' cried John Bunsby, flinging back the wheel in despair.

'How about signals?' was all that Phileas Fogg said.

A small bronze cannon jutted out from the bows of the *Tankadere*. It was used for signalling in misty weather. The cannon was loaded right to the muzzle, but, just as the pilot was about to apply a lighted coal to the touch-hole, Mr. Fogg said:

'Bring the flag down to half-mast!'

The flag was duly brought down to half-mast. It was a distress signal and it was to be hoped that the American steamer would notice it and would change course and come to their help.

'Fire!' said Mr. Fogg.

And the little bronze cannon boomed out.

In which Passepartout sees clearly that even in the Antipodes it is wise to have some money in one's pocket

After leaving Hong Kong at six-thirty p.m. on 7th November the *Carnatic* sailed full steam ahead in the direction of Japan. She was carrying a full complement of cargo and passengers. Two cabins aft were unoccupied. They were the ones that had been reserved for Mr. Phileas Fogg.

The next morning the men in the forepart of the ship were surprised to see a passenger with dazed eyes and a staggering gait and dishevelled hair emerge from the second-class hatchway, totter along the deck and then sit down.

That passenger was none other than Passepartout. This is what had happened. A few moments after Fix left the smoking-house, two waiters lifted Passepartout, who was sound asleep, and laid him on the bed placed there for the smokers. But three hours later Passepartout, pursued even in the midst of his nightmares by one single thought, woke up and began to struggle against the stupefying effect of the narcotic. The idea of his unfulfilled duty shook him out of his torpor. He left the bed and stumbled his way along, leaning against the walls. He would fall and then get up again, but still he seemed to be urged on by an irresistible instinct. And so he emerged from the smoking-house, calling out as if in a dream:

'The *Carnatic*! The *Carnatic*!'

The ship was there with steam up, ready to sail. Passepartout only had a few steps to go. He dashed on to the landing-stage, crossed the gangway and fell unconscious in the bows, just as the *Carnatic* was casting off. A few of the sailors, who were accustomed to scenes of that kind,

carried the poor fellow down to a second-class cabin and Passepartout did not wake up till the next morning, one hundred and fifty miles away from China.

That is how Passepartout came to be on the deck of the *Carnatic* that morning, breathing in great mouthfuls of fresh sea air. The pure air was clearing his head. He began to collect his thoughts and found this a laborious task. But, in the end, he managed to recall the scenes of the day before, Fix's confidences and the smoking-house, etc. . . .

'I must have been dreadfully intoxicated,' he said to himself. 'What is Mr. Fogg going to say? But the main thing is that I did not miss the boat.' Then, thinking of Fix, he said to himself: 'I hope we have got rid of him and that he has not dared to follow us on board the *Carnatic* after the suggestions he made to me. A police inspector, a detective close on my master's heels and accusing him of that robbery at the Bank of England! What utter nonsense! Mr. Fogg is no more a thief than I am a murderer!'

Should Passepartout tell his master the whole story? Ought he to inform him of the part played by Fix in the affair? Would it not be better to wait till he reached London before he told him that a detective from the Metropolitan Police had followed him round the world? Then they could have a good laugh about it together. Yes, that was the thing to do. It was, at all events, something for him to think about. The first thing he had to do was to go and find Mr. Fogg and ask him to accept his excuses for his unpardonable conduct.

So Passepartout rose to his feet. There was a swell and the ship was rolling badly. The good fellow, his legs still feeling weak, made his way as best he could to the stern of the ship.

On deck he saw no-one bearing any resemblance to his master or Aouda.

'Not to worry,' he said. 'Mrs. Aouda will still be in bed and Mr. Fogg will have found someone to play whist with and, as usual, he will . . . '

And Passepartout went below to the saloon. Mr. Fogg was not there. There was only one thing Passepartout could do

and that was to ask the purser which cabin was Mr. Fogg's. But the purser told him that he did not know any passenger of that name.

'Excuse me,' said Passepartout, insisting, 'but he is a tall gentleman who is very quiet and reserved and he has a young lady with him . . .'

'We have no young ladies on board,' replied the purser. 'In any case, here is the passenger-list. You can have a look at it.'

Passepartout looked at the list. His master's name was not on it. A sudden thought flashed through his mind.

'I *am* on the *Carnatic*, am I not?' he cried.

'Yes,' replied the purser.

'Bound for Yokohama?'

'Yes indeed.'

For a moment Passepartout had been afraid that he was on the wrong ship. But, if he was on the *Carnatic*, it was nevertheless a fact that his master was not.

Passepartout flopped back into an armchair. He felt as if he had been struck by lightning. Then suddenly it dawned on him. He remembered that the sailing-time of the *Carnatic* had been brought forward and that he had been going to inform his master, but he had not done so! So it was his fault that Mr. Fogg and Mrs. Aouda had missed the boat!

His fault, yes, but, even more so, the fault of the traitor who had made him drunk in order to separate him from his master and keep the latter in Hong Kong. Now at last he understood the detective's stratagem. There was no doubt that Mr. Fogg was ruined, his bet was lost and he had been arrested and perhaps in prison! At that thought Passepartout tore his hair. Oh, if ever Fix fell into his clutches, he would settle accounts with him, once and for all!

After that first devastating moment Passepartout grew calm again and proceeded to examine the situation. It was not an enviable one. The Frenchman was on his way to Japan. He was sure to get there, but how could he get back? His pockets were empty. He had not a shilling, not a penny! But his passage and his food on board had been paid for in advance, so he had five or six days left in which to reach a

decision. He ate and drank an incredible amount during that trip. He ate for his master and for Aouda as well as for himself. He ate as if Japan, where he was soon to land, were a desert country devoid of any edible material.

On the thirteenth the *Carnatic* sailed into the port of Yokohama on the morning tide.

Yokohama is an important port of call on the Pacific. All the mail and passenger steamers sailing between North America, China, Japan and Malaya put in there. It is situated on Yeddo, or Tokyo, Bay, only a short distance from the immense city of Tokyo, the second capital of the Japanese Empire and formerly the residence of the *taikun*, or feudal sovereign, in the days when there was a civil emperor. It is the rival of Meako, or Kyoto, the great city where the *mikado*, the ecclesiastical emperor and descendant of the gods, has his abode.

The *Carnatic* came alongside the quay in Yokohama near the jetties and the Customs warehouses, amid many ships of all nationalities.

Passepartout set foot on this curious Land of the Rising Sun without any enthusiasm. He could do no better than let himself be guided by fate, and so he wandered idly through the streets of the city.

Passepartout found himself first of all in a completely European city where there were houses with low façades, adorned with verandahs, under which elegant peristyles had been constructed. Its streets and squares, its docks and warehouses covered all the space between Treaty Point and the river. There, as in Hong Kong and Calcutta, there was a swarming mixture of people of all races—Americans, British, Chinese, Dutch—and there were merchants willing to buy and sell anything. In the midst of all these people the Frenchman found himself just as much of a stranger as if he had been flung into the land of the Hottentots.

There was only one course open to Passepartout, and that was to appeal to the French or British Consul in Yokohama. But he would not care to tell his story, which was so closely bound up with that of his master. Before taking that extreme step he wanted to exhaust all the other possibilities.

So, after going through the European quarter of the city, where fate did not assist him in any way, he entered the Japanese quarter, determined, if necessary, to push on as far as Yeddo (Tokyo).

The native quarter of Yokohama is called Benten, after a goddess of the sea worshipped on the neighbouring islands. There he saw wonderful avenues of firs and cedars, sacred gateways built in a strange style of architecture, bridges lost amid bamboo and reeds, temples shaded by great melancholy cedars which must have been centuries old, monasteries in whose depths vegetated the *bonzes*, or priests, of the Buddhist religion and followers of Confucius, interminable streets where one could have gathered in a harvest of children with pink skins and red cheeks, little creatures who looked as if they had been carved on some native screen. They were playing among short-legged poodles and tailless yellow cats and looked very lazy and affectionate.

In the streets there was an incessant jostling and bustling to and fro. There were *bonzes* passing in procession, striking their monotonous tambourines, *yakunins*, or officers of the Customs or police, with pointed lacquered hats and carrying two swords in their belts, soldiers dressed in blue cotton uniforms with white stripes and armed with percussion guns, men-at-arms of the *mikado* stuffed into silken doublets, with hauberks and coats of mail, and a number of other soldiers of all types and conditions, for in Japan the military profession is just as highly esteemed as it is despised in China. Then there were mendicant friars, pilgrims in long robes, ordinary citizens with sleek hair as black as ebony and large heads and low waists and slender legs. They were not very tall and their complexions ranged from dark copper to dull white, but never yellow like the skin of a Chinaman. Indeed there is a great difference between the Chinese and the Japanese. Finally, among the carriages, palanquins, horses, porters, chairs with sails, sedan-chairs with lacquered sides, soft *cangos*, or portable chairs, and bamboo litters there were women walking about their tiny feet taking tiny steps. They wore canvas shoes or straw sandals or clogs made of carved wood, and they

were not pretty with their slits of eyes and flattened chests and their teeth blackened in keeping with the fashion of the day. But they wore the national dress, or *kirimon* which is like a dressing-gown, tied with a silk sash with an extravagant bow at the back, which the modern women of Paris appear to have borrowed from the Japanese.

Passepartout walked for some hours amid that variegated throng and looked at the strange, opulent-looking shops, the bazaars where all the showy Japanese jewellery is piled in profusion, the restaurants decorated with streamers and banners which he was forbidden to enter, and those tea-houses where cupfuls of hot scented water are drunk with *sake*, the liquor extracted from fermented rice, and those snug smoking-houses where one can smoke very fine tobacco, not opium, which is almost unknown in Japan.

Then Passepartout found himself in the open country, amid huge paddy-fields. There he saw brilliant camellias in bloom, putting forth their last colours and their last perfume. They were not growing on bushes, but on trees, and in enclosures he saw bamboo trees and cherry-trees, plum-trees and apple trees which the inhabitants cultivate for their blossom rather than for their fruit, and to defend them from the beaks of sparrows and pigeons and crows and other voracious birds there were grimacing scarecrows which creaked as they revolved. Every majestic cedar seemed to harbour a large eagle among its branches and every weeping willow seemed to be spreading its foliage over a heron which was standing lugubriously on one leg. There were rooks everywhere and ducks and sparrow-hawks and wild geese and a large number of those cranes which the Japanese address as lords and consider to be symbols of happiness and long life.

As he wandered on in this way Passepartout noticed some violets growing among the grass. 'Good!' he said. 'That will be my supper.' But, when he sniffed them, he found they had no perfume. 'No luck!' he thought.

Of course the good fellow had had as large a lunch as he could before leaving the *Carnatic*, just in case, but after walking about for a whole day he felt that his stomach was

very empty. He had noticed that there were no sheep or goats or pigs in the butchers' windows and, as he knew that it was sacrilegious to kill oxen, which are set aside entirely for farmwork, he concluded that meat was scarce in Japan. He was not mistaken, but, in the absence of butcher's meat, his stomach would have made do with a haunch of wild boar or venison, or partridge or quail, or poultry or fish, of which the Japanese diet consists more or less entirely, together with the produce of the paddy-fields. But he had to make the best of a bad job and he postponed the business of finding food till the following day.

Night came. Passepartout returned to the native quarter and roamed through the streets in the midst of multi-coloured lanterns and watched groups of mountebanks carrying out their amazing tricks and stargazers gathering crowds round their telescopes. Then he saw the roadstead again, dotted with the lights of fishermen who were luring fish with the glare of burning resin torches.

Finally the streets became deserted. The crowd gave way to *yakunins* going on their rounds. These officers in their magnificent costumes and accompanied by their retinues looked like ambassadors, and Passepartout would say jokingly every time he met one of those resplendent patrols:

'Bravo! There goes another Japanese ambassador and his staff on their way to Europe!'

In which Passepartout's nose grows to a fantastic length

The next day Passepartout, famished and exhausted, told himself that he would have to eat at all costs, the sooner the better. He could, of course, have sold his watch, but he would rather have starved. It was now or never—he would just have to make use of the strong, if not melodious, voice that nature had endowed him with.

He knew some French and English tunes and he determined to try them out. The Japanese must certainly be fond of music, as everything there is done to the sound of cymbals or drums or tom-toms and so they could not fail to appreciate the talents of a European virtuoso.

But it was perhaps a little too early in the morning to put on a concert and, if the dilettanti were awakened unexpectedly from their slumbers, they might not pay the singer with coins bearing the image of the *mikado*.

So Passepartout decided to wait for a few hours. But, as he walked, he reflected that he might seem too well dressed to be a strolling artist and he had the idea of exchanging his own clothes for older garments more in keeping with his station. The transaction would, moreover, leave him with some cash in hand which he could use to satisfy his hunger.

Having taken that decision, all that remained was to carry it out. Passepartout had to search for a long time before he found a dealer in secondhand goods to whom he could make his request. The dealer liked the European clothes and Passepartout soon walked out, dressed up in an old Japanese robe and with a kind of ribbed turban discoloured by the elements, but he now had a few silver coins jingling in his pocket.

'Good,' he thought. 'Now I shall just make believe it is carnival time.'

The first thing Passepartout did after turning himself into a Japanese was to go into an unassuming tea-house, where he had fragments of poultry and a few handfuls of rice for his lunch, in the knowledge that dinner would present yet another problem.

'Now,' he said to himself when he had built up his strength again, 'I must not lose my head. I shall have no chance of selling these old clothes in exchange for others that are even more Japanese in style. So I must think of a way of leaving this land of The Rising Sun as quickly as possible with all the unhappy memories it will evoke.'

Passepartout decided to visit the steamers going to America. He intended to offer his services as a cook or domestic in return for only his passage and his food. Once in San Francisco he would find a way of getting out of his difficulties. The important thing was to cross those four thousand seven hundred miles of the Pacific stretching between Japan and the New World.

Passepartout was certainly not the kind of man to let an idea grow cold on him, so he made his way to the harbour area of Yokohama. But, as he drew near to the docks, his scheme, which had seemed so simple when he first thought of it, now appeared impossible. People would not need a cook or a servant on board an American ship and what confidence would he, in any case, inspire, dressed up as he was? What testimonials could he give? What references could he quote?

As he was meditating thus, his eyes lighted on a huge placard which was being paraded through the streets of Yokohama by a kind of clown. The placard was worded as follows, in English:

THE JAPANESE ACROBATS
of
Mr. William Batulcar

Final Performances
*Before Their Departure For
The United States*
by the
LONG-NOSES — LONG-NOSES
Under The Direct Protection
of the God Tingu
Special Attraction!

'The United States!' exclaimed Passepartout. 'That is just what I am looking for!'

He followed the sandwich-man back into the Japanese quarter, and stopped a quarter of an hour later in front of a huge building with bunches of streamers fluttering from the top. On the outside walls a troupe of jugglers was portrayed in garish colours and with no sense of perspective.

This was the headquarters of Mr. Batulcar, a kind of American Barnum, who directed a troupe of mountebanks, jugglers, clowns, acrobats, balancing artistes and gymnasts who, according to the placard, were giving their final performance before leaving the Empire of the Rising Sun and going to the United States.

Passepartout went into the porch in front of the building and asked for Mr. Batulcar. Mr. Batulcar appeared in person.

'What do you want?' he said to Passepartout, whom he took to be Japanese to begin with.

'Do you require a servant?' asked Passepartout.

'A servant,' cried the showman, stroking the thick grey beard that sprang so luxuriantly from his chin. 'I have two and they are faithful and obedient and have never left me. They serve me for nothing provided I feed them . . . and here they are.' he added, displaying his two sturdy arms ridged with veins as thick as the strings of a double-bass.

'I am no good to you then?'

'None at all!'

'Dash it all! It would have been ideal if I could have left with you!'

'Now then,' said Mr. Batulcar, 'if you are a Japanese, then I am a monkey's uncle! Why are you dressed up like that?'

'One wears what one can.'

'True. You are a Frenchman, are you not?'

'Yes, a Parisian straight from Paris.'

'So you must know how to pull faces.'

'Oh yes,' replied Passepartout, but he was upset that his nationality should have given rise to that question. 'We Frenchmen can pull faces all right, but not any better than an American!'

'That is so. Well, if I do not take you on as a servant, I may take you on as a clown. You see, my good fellow, in France they show foreign clowns, but in other countries they show French clowns.'

'Oh!'

'Are you strong, by the way?'

'Oh yes, especially after a meal.'

'And can you sing?'

'Yes,' replied Passepartout, who had at one time taken part in street concerts.

'But can you sing standing on your head, with a spinning top on the sole of your left foot and a sword balanced on the sole of your right foot?'

'Of course I can!' replied Passepartout, recalling the first exercises he had had to practise in his youth.

'That is all there is to it,' said Mr. Batulcar.

Passepartout was taken on there and then. He had at last found a job. He was to be a general all-round performer in a famous Japanese troupe. That was not very flattering, but in less than a week he would be on his way to San Francisco.

The performance, noisily proclaimed by Mr. Batulcar, was due to start at three o'clock. Soon the formidable instruments of a Japanese orchestra with drums and tom-toms were thundering at the door. As one will realize,

Passepartout had not been able to rehearse his part, but he had to lend his strong shoulders for the great feat known as the 'human pyramid,' performed by the Long Noses of the god Tingu. That 'special attraction' was to be the final trick of the series.

By three o'clock the audience had come crowding into the huge building. There were Europeans and natives, Chinese and Japanese, men, women and children, rushing to take their places on the narrow benches or in the boxes facing the stage. The musicians had come inside and the full orchestra of gongs, tom-toms, clappers, flutes, tambourines and big drums was performing for all it was worth.

The performance was like any other display of acrobatics. But it must be admitted that the Japanese are the premier balancing artistes in the world. One, equipped with a fan and small pieces of paper, was doing the graceful trick of the butterflies and the flowers. Another was rapidly tracing out in the air with the perfumed blue smoke of his pipe a series of words intended as a compliment to the audience. One man juggled with lighted candles which he put out one by one as they passed in front of his lips and which he lit one from the other without interrupting his amazing juggling for a single instant. Another was doing the most fantastic things with spinning tops. In his hands those whirring machines seemed to be endowed with a life of their own as they went on turning interminably. They ran along the stems of pipes, along sword-blades, on wires and on actual hairs stretched across from one side to the other. They went round large glass vases, they climbed bamboo ladders, they scattered into every corner, producing strange and harmonious effects. The jugglers juggled with them and they spun in the air. They tossed them up like shuttlecocks with wooden racquets and they went on turning. They stuffed them into their pockets and when they took them out again they were still turning. Then a spring was released and they blossomed out into firework sprays.

It is unnecessary here to describe the wonderful feats of the acrobats and gymnasts in the troupe. The tricks with

ladders, poles, balls, casks and so on were executed with remarkable precision. But the main attraction was the display by the long Noses, amazing balancing artistes who had not yet been shown in Europe.

Those Long Noses were a special body of men who came under the direct protection of the god Tingu. They were dressed like heroes of the Middle Ages and wore a splendid pair of wings on their shoulders. But their special distinguishing feature was the long nose that adorned their faces and, above all, the use they made of it. These noses were in actual fact bamboo canes five, six, or ten feet long, some straight and others curved, some smooth and others gnarled. It was on these appendages, which were securely attached to their faces, that they carried out all their balancing feats. A dozen of these followers of the god Tingu lay down on their backs and their companions pranced about on their noses, which stuck up like lightning conductors. They jumped and vaulted from one to the other and performed the most improbable tricks.

To end the performance the human pyramid was announced. In this about fifty Long Noses were to represent the Car of Juggernaut. But, instead of using their shoulders as supports for the pyramid, Mr. Batulcar's troupe were to use their noses. One of the men who made up the base of the car had left the troupe and, as all that was required was to be strong and adroit, Passepartout had been chosen to replace him.

That worthy fellow felt very sorry for himself when—as a sad reminder of his early days—he put on his mediaeval costume, adorned with multi-coloured wings, and a nose six feet long was stuck on his face! But the nose was, after all, what he earned his living by, and so he made the best of it.

Passepartout came on to the stage and lined up with those of his colleagues who were to form the base of the Car of Juggernaut. They all lay down on the floor with their noses pointing upwards. A second band of acrobats took up their positions on these long appendages, and a third went above, then a fourth. And so on these noses, of which only

the tips were touching, a human edifice soon rose up to the frieze.

The applause grew louder and the instruments in the orchestra burst forth in deafening clamour. But just at that moment the pyramid tottered, the balance became upset and one of the noses at the bottom was pulled out. The whole edifice crumbled like a castle of cards . . .

It was all Passepartout's fault. He abandoned his post and crossed the footlights without the help of his wings and then climbed up the right-hand gallery and fell at the feet of a member of the audience, crying:

'Oh, Master! Master!'

'Is it you?'

'Yes, it is.'

'Well, in that case, off to the ship with you, my lad!'

Mr. Fogg, Aouda who was with him, and Passepartout rushed along the corridors and out of the building. But there they found Mr. Batulcar who was very angry and demanded compensation for the collapse of the pyramid. Phileas Fogg appeased his wrath by throwing him a handful of banknotes. And at half past six, just as she was about to sail, Mr. Fogg and Aouda boarded the American steamer, followed by Passepartout, with his wings still fastened to his back and on his face that six-foot nose which he had not had time to wrench off.

In which they cross the Pacific Ocean

The reader will realize what happened within sight of Shanghai. The signals sent out by the *Tankadere* were seen by the steamer going to Yokohama. The captain, noticing the flag at half-mast, sailed towards the small schooner. A few moments later Phileas Fogg, paying for his passage at the agreed price, put five hundred and fifty pounds in the pocket of her owner, John Bunsby. Then he, Aouda and Fix climbed on board the steamer which at once set her course for Nagasaki and Yokohama.

Reaching there on the morning of 14th November at the scheduled time, Phileas Fogg left Fix to attend to his own business and went on board the *Carnatic*, where he learned to the great joy of Aouda—and possibly of himself, although he gave no sign of it—that the Frenchman Passepartout had indeed reached Yokohama the day before.

Phileas Fogg was to be leaving for San Francisco that very evening and he set out at once in search of his servant. He inquired in vain at the French and British Consulates and, after wandering fruitlessly through the streets of Yokohama, he despaired of ever meeting Passepartout again. Then fate, or perhaps a sort of presentiment, made him go into Mr. Batulcar's theatre. He certainly would not have recognized his servant in the extraordinary herald's outfit, but the latter, lying in a recumbent position, noticed his master in the gallery. He could not help moving his nose. and that upset the balance of the group and caused the pyramid to collapse.

Passepartout learned all this from the lips of Aouda, who told him how they had crossed from Hong Kong to Yokohama on the schooner *Tankadere* in the company of Mr. Fix. Passepartout did not bat an eyelid when he heard Fix's

name. He felt that the time had not yet come for him to tell his master what had passed between the police inspector and himself. So in the version he gave of his own adventures he blamed himself entirely and apologized for having succumbed to the intoxicating effects of opium in the smoking house in Hong Kong.

Mr. Fogg listened calmly to his tale without comment. Then he gave his servant sufficient money to buy more suitable clothing on board. And so, in less than an hour, the good fellow had cut off his nose and clipped off his wings and there was nothing left to remind one of the follower of the god Tingu.

The steamer crossing from Yokohama to San Francisco belonged to the Pacific Mail Steam Company and was called the *General Grant*. She was a huge paddle-steamer of two thousand five hundred tons, well fitted out and capable of great speed. A huge beam rose and fell above the deck. At one end a piston-rod was attached and at the other the stem of a connecting-rod which was secured to the axle of the wheels and changed the rectilinear movement into a circular movement. The *General Grant* was rigged as a three-masted schooner and had a large spread of canvas which provided a powerful addition to her steam power. Travelling at her usual speed of twelve miles per hour, the steamer would not take more than twenty-one days to cross the Pacific. So Phileas Fogg had good reason to believe that he would arrive in San Francisco on 2nd December and would be in New York on the 11th and in London on the 20th, a few hours in advance of that fateful date—21st, December.

There were a fair number of passengers on board—British subjects, many Americans and a great contingent of coolies emigrating to America, also some officers of the Indian Army who were using their leave to go round the world.

That crossing was without incident. The steamer, supported by her broad wheels and helped along by her great spread of canvas, rolled very little. The Pacific Ocean was living up to its name. Mr. Fogg was just as calm and

uncommunicative as ever. And his young companion was growing more and more attached to him, by ties other than those of gratitude. His silent, generous disposition was making a greater impression on her than she realized and, almost without her knowledge, certain feelings were growing within her, but they seemed to have no effect at all on the enigmatic Mr. Fogg.

Aouda was very much interested in the gentleman's plans. She worried about the various mishaps that might affect his success. She often chatted with Passepartout, who was well able to read between the lines as far as Aouda's heart was concerned. That worthy fellow now had an unquestioning faith in his master. He could not praise him enough for his integrity, his generosity and his devotion. And he reassured Aouda about the outcome of the journey and told her again and again that the most difficult part of it was over and they had left those fantastic countries of China and Japan and were returning to civilized lands, and all that he had to do now to complete that seemingly impossible journey round the world in the time stipulated was to catch a train from San Francisco to New York and a liner from New York to London.

Nine days after leaving Yokohama, Phileas Fogg had gone round exactly half of the globe.

On 23rd November the *General Grant* passed the 180th meridian, the one on which the antipodes of London in the southern hemisphere are situated. Out of the eighty days at his disposal Mr. Fogg had, it was true, used up fifty-two and had only twenty-eight left. But it should be remembered that, although the gentleman was only half-way round if one subtracted the meridians, he had in reality covered more than two-thirds of the total distance. He had been obliged to make vast detours, from London to Aden, from Aden to Bombay, from Calcutta to Singapore, and from Singapore to Yokohama. If he had gone round the fiftieth parallel in a circle, for that is the parallel on which London is situated, the distance would only have been about twelve thousand miles, whereas Phileas Fogg had, owing to the whims of public transport, to cover twenty-six thousand, of

which he had done about seventeen thousand up to 23rd November. But the route was direct now and Fix was no longer there to pile obstacles in his path.

On 23rd November Passepartout felt really delighted. You will recall that the obstinate fellow had insisted on keeping London time on his famous family watch and thought that all the countries he passed through were wrong. And on that day, although he had never put his watch forward or back, it was in agreement with the chronometers on board.

One can understand how triumphant he felt. He would have liked to have known what Fix would have said, if he had been there.

'Fancy that rascal telling me all those tales about the meridians and the sun and the moon!' Passepartout said to himself. 'Clocks would be in a fine state if you listened to people like that! I was positive the sun would take it into its head to follow my watch some time or other!'

Passepartout did not know one thing. If the face of his watch had been divided up into twenty-fours, as some Italian clocks are, he would have had no reason to feel triumphant, as the hands of his watch would have been pointing to nine o'clock in the evening, that is, the twenty-first hour after midnight, when it was only nine o'clock in the morning on board—a difference equal to that between London and the 180th meridian.

But, if Fix had been able to explain that purely physical effect, Passepartout would doubtless have been unable, if not to understand it, at least to admit it. And, in any case, if the impossible did happen and the police inspector unexpectedly appeared on board at that moment, it is likely that Passepartout, who had every reason to bear him a grudge, would have discussed quite a different subject with him, and in a completely different manner.

Where was Fix at that moment? At that very moment he was, in fact, on board the *General Grant*. On reaching Yokohama, the detective had left Mr. Fogg, whom he intended to meet again in the course of that day, and had gone straight to the British Consul. There he had at long

last found the warrant which had followed him from Bombay and had been dated forty days previously. The warrant had been sent to him on the *Carnatic*, the very ship he was thought to be on. You can imagine how disappointed the detective felt. The warrant was useless now. Mr. Fogg had left British territory. Now an extradition order was necessary before he could be arrested.

'All right!' Fix said to himself after his first moment of anger had passed. 'My warrant is not valid here, but it will be in England. The rogue is giving every sign of returning home. He believes he has thrown the police off the scent. Very well then, I shall follow him there. But I only hope some of the money will be left. What with travelling expenses, bonuses, lawsuits, fines, paying for an elephant, and all kinds of outlays, my man has disposed of over five thousand pounds on the way so far. But the Bank is wealthy.'

Having reached that decision, he boarded the *General Grant* immediately. He was on board when Mr. Fogg and Aouda arrived and in amazement he recognized Passepartout in his herald's costume. He hid at once in his cabin in order to avoid explanations. That might have spoilt everything. Owing to the large number of passengers, he relied on not being observed by his enemy, but on that very day he found himself face to face with him in the forepart of the ship.

Passepartout flung himself at Fix's throat, without explanation and to the great delight of some Americans who began to place bets on him at once, and he gave the unfortunate inspector a sound thrashing, thereby demonstrating the superiority of French boxing over British boxing. When Passepartout had finished, he appeared calmer, as if his feelings had been relieved. Fix rose to his feet in rather poor shape and, surveying his adversary, he said coldly:

'Have you finished?'

'Yes, for the time being.'

'Well then, come and have a word with me!'

'I . . .'

'It is in the interests of your master.'

Passepartout, as if dominated by the inspector's composure, followed him and they both sat down in the bows.

'You have given me a good thrashing,' said Fix. 'All right. Now listen to me. Up to now I have been against Mr. Fogg, but now I am on his side.'

'At long last!' cried Passepartout. 'You think he is an honest man then, do you?'

'No,' replied Fix coldly, 'I think he is a rogue. Sh! Let me speak! As long as Mr. Fogg was on British soil, it was in my interest to detain him till a warrant arrived. I did everything I could to bring this about. I sent out the priests in Bombay against him, I made you drunk in Hong Kong, I separated you from your master, I made him miss the steamer to Yokohama . . .'

Passepartout listened with clenched fists.

'Now,' Fix went on, 'it looks as if Mr. Fogg is going back to England. Very well, I will follow him. But from now on I shall take as much trouble and interest in removing obstacles from his path as I used to do in putting them there. You see, I am playing a different game now, and it is different because that it is my interest. I would add that your interest is the same as mine. It is not until you get back to England that you will find out if you are serving a criminal or an honest man.'

Passepartout had listened to Fix very carefully and was convinced that the latter was sincere.

'Are we friends?' asked Fix.

'Not friends,' replied Passepartout, 'but we are allies, but only conditionally. At the least sign of treachery I will wring your neck.'

'Agreed,' said the police inspector calmly.

Eleven days later, on 3rd December, the *General Grant* sailed into the bay of the Golden Gate and reached San Francisco.

So far Mr. Fogg had neither gained nor lost a single day.

*In which we are given a brief glimpse of San
Francisco on a Convention Day*

It was seven o'clock in the morning when Phileas Fogg,
Aouda and Passepartout set foot on the American continent—if one can give that name to the floating wharf on
which they landed. These landing-stages rise and fall with
the tide and facilitate the loading and unloading ships.
Clippers of all sizes come alongside and steamers of every
nation and those multi-storeyed steamboats that ply on the
Sacramento and its tributaries. Products of the trade
carried on with Mexico and Peru, Chile and Brazil, Europe
and Asia are piled up there.

In his joy at landing on American soil at last, Passepartout
decided to turn a somersault in the grandest style as he
went ashore. But the planking on the wharf was worm-
eaten, so when he came down on his feet he nearly went
through it. Quite put out by the way in which he had 'set
foot' on the New World the good fellow uttered a mighty
cry which sent a great flock of cormorants and pelicans,
the denizens of those floating wharves, flying off into the
air.

As soon as Mr. Fogg landed, he inquired about the time
when the first train left for New York. It was at six o'clock
in the evening. So Mr. Fogg had a whole day before him in
the Californian city. He ordered a carriage for Aouda and
himself. Passepartout climbed up on the box and the
vehicle, which cost three dollars per trip, went off in the
direction of the International Hotel.

From his high seat Passepartout looked curiously at the
great American city. There were broad streets, low houses
set in neat lines, churches built in the Anglo-Saxon Gothic
style, immense docks, warehouses that looked like palaces,

some built of brick and the others of wood. In the streets he saw many carriages and buses and trams, and on the crowded pavements there were not only Americans and Europeans, but also Chinese and Indians—in short, all the elements needed to make up a population of over two hundred thousand.

Passepartout was rather surprised at what he saw. He had been thinking of the legendary city of 1849 with its bandits and firebrands and murderers who had come rushing out there in search of gold nuggets—a vast conglomeration of down-and-outs. There men had gambled with gold dust, with a revolver in one hand and a knife in the other. But those 'good old days' had passed. San Francisco gave the appearance of a large trading city. The high tower of the city hall overlooked that whole network of streets and avenues, crossing at right angles, with green squares stretching between them. And there was a Chinese quarter that looked as if it had been imported from the Celestial Empire in a toy box. There were no sombreros or the red shirts of miners, no Indians with feathered head-dresses, but silk hats and dark clothes, worn by the large number of gentlemen who were bustling energetically about. Certain streets, including Montgomery Street—which is like Regent Street in London or the Boulevard des Italiens in Paris or Broadway in New York—were lined with magnificent shops which displayed the products of the whole world in their windows.

When Passepartout reached the International Hotel he felt as if he had never left England. The ground floor of the hotel was occupied by a huge bar, a sort of buffet open *free* to all passers-by. There were smoked meat, oyster soup, biscuits and Cheddar cheese being served there, and the customer did not have to put his hand in his pocket. He only paid for his drink—ale, port or sherry—if he felt inclined for some refreshment. Passepartout thought it all seemed very American.

The hotel restaurant was very comfortable. Mr. Fogg and Aouda settled themselves at a table and were lavishly served from Lilliputian dishes by negroes with jet-black skins.

After lunch Phileas Fogg, accompanied by Aouda, left the hotel and went to the British Consulate to have his passport stamped. On the pavement he found his servant who asked if he thought it would be a good idea to buy a few dozen Enfield rifles or Colt's revolvers before going on the Pacific Railroad. Passepartout had heard about Sioux and Pawnees who held up trains like ordinary Spanish brigands. Mr. Fogg said it was an unnecessary precaution, but he left it to him to do as he thought fit. Then he went to the Consulate.

Phileas Fogg had gone less than a hundred yards when, 'by the greatest coincidence', he bumped into Fix. The inspector gave signs of extreme surprise. What! Mr. Fogg and he had travelled across the Pacific together and had not met on board? But Fix was honoured to meet again the gentleman to whom he owed so much. His business was taking him back to Europe and he would be delighted to resume the journey in such agreeable company.

Mr. Fogg replied that the honour was his and Fix, who was anxious not to lose sight of him, asked if he might go round that curious city of San Francisco with him. His wish was granted.

So there were Aouda, Phileas Fogg and Fix strolling along the streets. They soon found themselves in Montgomery Street where there were tremendous crowds. There were people on the pavements, in the middle of the roadway, on the tram rails, in spite of the coaches and buses that were passing constantly in shop doorways and at the windows of all the houses and even on the roofs. Sandwich-men were moving among the groups. Banners and streamers were fluttering in the breeze. Shouts rang out from all sides.

'Hurrah for Kamerfield!'

'Hurrah for Mandiboy!'

It was a convention. At least, that was what Fix thought and he passed on the idea to Mr. Fogg, adding:

'We would be well advised, sir, not to mingle with this rabble. We might get a few nasty knocks.'

'Yes indeed,' replied Phileas Fogg, 'and fisticuffs are still fisticuffs even if they are politically inspired.'

Fix thought he was intended to smile at that remark. So that they could see, without being caught up in all the scuffling, Aouda, Phileas Fogg and he took up their positions on the top landing of a flight of steps connecting with a terrace at the top end of Montgomery Street. In front of them, on the other side of the street, between a coal merchant's wharf and a petroleum dealer's store, there was a huge open-air convention centre upon which the various streams of the crown appeared to be converging.

Why was that convention taking place ? What was it being held for ? Phileas Fogg had no idea. Was a senior military or civil official being nominated, or the governor of a state or a member of Congress ? One might suppose it was some-thing of the kind, judging by the extraordinary excitement in the city.

At that moment there was a great movement in the crowd. All hands were raised. Clenched fists appeared to shoot up and then down again just as quickly in the midst of shouting. Votes were no doubt being recorded. There were eddying movements in the crowd which was now flowing back. The banners wavered, disappeared for a moment and then reappeared in tatters. The crowd surged as far as the stairway, with their hands moving like white horses on the surface, of a sea suddenly whipped up by a squall. The number of black hats diminished preceptibly and most of them seemed to have lost their normal height.

'It is obviously a convention,' said Fix, 'and the issue being decided must be an important one. I would not be at all surprised to find it was that business of the s.s. *Alabama* cropping up again, although it has been settled.'

'Perhaps,' was all that Mr. Fogg said.

'At any rate,' Fix went on, 'there are two champions facing each other, Mr. Kamerfield and Mr. Mandiboy.'

Aouda, holding Phileas Fogg's arm, was gazing in sur-prise at that turbulent scene and Fix was just about to ask one of the people beside him what had caused this upsurge of popular feeling when a more definite movement could be detected in the crowd. The hurrahs, accompanied by insults, redoubled in vigour. The staffs of the banners were

turned into offensive weapons. Hands were no longer to be seen—only fists. Fighting was carried on from the tops of the carriages and from the buses that had been brought to a standstill. Everything was used as missiles. Boots and shoes travelled long distances through the air and a few revolver shots mingled with the shouting of the crowd.

The rabble approached the stairway and flowed back on to the bottom steps. One of the factions had obviously been driven back, although the ordinary spectator could not see if it was Mandiboy or Kamerfield who held the advantage.

'I think it would be wise to leave,' said Fix who did not want 'his man' to be knocked about or get into any scrape. 'If this business has any bearing on Britain and they recognize us, we shall become involved in the scuffle!'

'A British subject . . .' replied Phileas Fogg.

But the gentleman was not able to finish his sentence. From behind him, from the terrace leading to the stairway, came terrifying hurrahs. 'Hip, hip hurrah for Mandiboy!' came the cry. It was a group of electors coming to the rescue and attacking the supporters of Kamerfield on the flank.

Mr. Fogg, Aouda and Fix found themselves between two fires. It was too late to escape. That torrent of men, armed with loaded sticks and bludgeons, could not be held off. Phileas Fogg and Fix were jostled terribly as they tried to protect the young woman. Mr. Fogg, just as phlegmatic as ever, tried to defend himself with those weapons that nature has fixed at the end of every Englishman's arms, but all to no avail. A huge fellow with a red beard and a florid complexion and broad shoulders, who seemed to be the leader of the band, raised his formidable fist against Mr. Fogg and he would have done that gentleman great harm if Fix, out of loyal devotion, had not received the blow on his behalf. A huge bump formed at once under the detective's silk hat, which had been reduced to a toque.

'Yankee!' said Mr. Fogg with a glance of profound contempt for his adversary.

'Englishman!' replied the other. 'I will see you about this.'

'Whenever you like.'

'What is your name?'

'Phileas Fogg. And yours?'

'Colonel Stamp W. Proctor.'

Then the tide of humanity swept past. Fix was knocked down and picked himself up again, his clothes torn, but without any serious bruises. His overcoat had been torn into two unequal parts and his trousers were like the breeches worn by certain Indians—this is a matter of fashion—from which they first of all remove the seat. But Aouda was safe and Fix, who had been punched, was the only victim.

'Thank you,' said Mr. Fogg to the inspector as soon as they were out of the crowd.

'It was nothing,' replied Fix, 'but come with me.'

'Where?'

'To an outfitters.'

That visit was indeed necessary. Phileas Fogg and Fix had their clothes in tatters. One would have thought they had been fighting on behalf of Kamerfield or Mandiboy.

One hour later they were suitably provided with clothes and hats. Then they returned to the International Hotel.

There Passepartout was waiting for his master. He was armed with half a dozen revolvers with spring-daggers in the stocks. They were six-shooters with a central firing system. When he noticed Fix in the company of Mr. Fogg his brow darkened. But Aouda told him briefly what had happened, whereupon Passepartout brightened up. Fix was obviously no longer an enemy, but an ally. He had kept his word.

When dinner was over a coach came to take the travellers and their luggage to the station. As they were getting into the coach, Mr. Fogg said to Fix:

'You have not seen that Colonel Proctor again, have you?'

'No,' replied Fix.

'I shall return to America and seek him out,' said Phileas Fogg calmly. 'It would not be right for a British subject to let himself be treated in that way.'

The inspector smiled and did not answer. But it could be seen that Mr. Fogg belonged to that breed of Englishmen

who do not tolerate duelling in their own country, but fight abroad if it is a case of upholding their honour.

At a quarter to six the travellers reached the station and found the train ready to leave.

As Mr. Fogg was climbing aboard, he espied a railway official and he went up to him and asked:

'Tell me, my friend, have there not been some disturbances in San Francisco today?'

'It was a convention, sir,' replied the official.

'But I thought I noticed a certain amount of uproar in the streets.'

'It was just a convention to do with an election.'

'Oh, the election of a commander-in-chief, no doubt?' said Mr. Fogg.

'No, sir, the election of a Justice of the Peace.'

On receiving that reply, Phileas Fogg climbed into the carriage and the train departed at great speed.

---

*In which they all go on an express train on the
Pacific Railroad*

'Ocean to ocean' is how the Americans put it, and these
three words should be the general title of the 'grand
trunk' which crosses the United States at her widest
point. But the Pacific Railroad is, in reality, divided into
two separate parts: the Central Pacific between San
Francisco and Ogden and the Union Pacific between
Ogden and Omaha. Five separate lines join up there,
establishing a frequent communication between Omaha
and New York.

So New York and San Francisco are at present linked by
an uninterrupted ribbon of metal no less than three
thousand seven hundred and eighty-six miles long. Between Omaha and the Pacific the railway line crosses an
area still frequented by Indians and wild animals—a vast
expanse which the Mormons began to colonize around
1845 after they were chased out of Illinois.

In earlier days it took six months to go from New York to
San Francisco if conditions were really favourable. Now it
can be done in seven days. In spite of opposition from the
Congressmen of the South, who wanted the line to be
farther south, the course of the railway was fixed between
the 41st and 42nd parallel in 1862. The late lamented
President Lincoln made the town of Omaha in the state of
Nebraska the terminus of the new railway system. Work was
begun at once and pursued with typically American vigour,
untrammelled by red tape or bureaucracy. The speed at
which the work was carried out was not detrimental in any
way to good workmanship. In the prairie land they ad-
vanced at the rate of a mile and a half per day. An engine,
trundling along the rails that had been laid the day before,

brought up the rails for the next day and ran along them as soon as they were put in position.

The Pacific Railroad sends out several branch-lines along the way in the states of Iowa, Kansas, Colorado and Oregon. On leaving Omaha, it runs along the left bank of the Platte River as far as the junction with its northern branch, then it follows the southern branch and crosses the territories of Laramie and the Wasatch Mountains, goes round the Great Salt Lake, reaches Salt Lake City, the capital of the Mormons, plunges into the Tooele valley, skirts the desert, the Cedar and the Humboldt Mountains, the Humboldt River and the Sierra Nevada and goes down to the Pacific again via Sacramento, without the gradient ever exceeding one hundred and twelve feet per mile even when the line is crossing the Rocky Mountains.

Along that long artery the trains could pass in seven days and it was going to enable Phileas Fogg—or, at least, he hoped so—to catch the steamer for Liverpool in New York, on the 11th.

The carriage occupied by Phileas Fogg was like a kind of long omnibus resting on two trucks consisting of four wheels each. The mobility of this stock is ideal for taking sharp curves. There were no compartments inside. There were two lines of seats, one on either side, perpendicular to the axle, and between them was a corridor leading to the lavatories, etc., with which each carriage was supplied. Along the whole length of the train the carriages were connected with one another by means of gangways, and the travellers could go from one end of the train to the other and visit the saloons, observation platforms, restaurant cars and cafes. All that was missing was a theatre, but that will be provided some day, too.

Vendors of books and newspapers were crossing those gangways constantly, selling their wares, also dealers in liquor, foodstuffs and cigars, and there was no lack of customers.

The travellers had left Oakland station at six o'clock in the evening. It was dark already—a cold, gloomy night with an overcast sky, in which the clouds were threatening to

turn to snow. The train was not travelling very fast. Allowing for stops, it was not covering more than twenty miles per hour, but that speed was nevertheless sufficient to allow the train to cross the United States in the scheduled time.

There was little conversation in the carriage. The travellers would, in any case, soon be asleep. Passepartout found himself seated beside the police inspector, but he did not speak to him. As a result of recent events their friendship had cooled considerably. There was no longer any feeling of warmth or liking. Fix had not changed at all as a person, but Passepartout was being extremely reserved and was ready to throttle his former friend at the least suspicion of treachery.

One hour after the train left it began to snow. It was fine snow which fortunately could not affect the speed of the train. All that one could now see through the windows was an immense expanse of white against which the coils of steam from the engine looked a greyish colour.

At eight o'clock a steward came into the carriage and told the travellers that it was time for bed. The carriage was a sleeping-car and in a few minutes it had been transformed into sleeping quarters. The backs of the seat were folded up and carefully parcelled berths were spread out by an ingenious system and cabins were improvised in a few moments. Soon each traveller had at his disposal a comfortable bed shielded from indiscreet eyes by thick curtains. The sheets where white and the pillows soft. All the passengers could do now was lie down and go to sleep— which they all proceeded to do, just as if they had been in comfortable steamer cabins—and the train went steadily on through the state of California.

In the area between San Francisco and Sacramento there are few undulations in the ground. That part of the railway, which is called the Central Pacific Railroad, originally took Sacramento as its starting-point and went east to meet the line coming from Omaha. From San Francisco to the capital of California the line ran due north-east, skirting the American River, which flows into the Bay of San Pablo.

The hundred and twenty miles between these two important cities were crossed in six hours, and around midnight, as they were having the first part of their night's sleep, the travellers reached Sacramento. So they saw nothing of that large city, seat of the legislature of the state of California, or of its fine wharves, its broad streets and splendid mansions, its squares and its churches.

Leaving Sacramento, the train passed the stations of Junction, Roclin, Auburn and Colfax and plunged into the mountains of the Sierra Nevada. It was seven o'clock in the morning when they went through the station of Cisco. One hour later the dormitory became an ordinary carriage again and the travellers saw through the windows the picturesque scenery of that mountainous area. The railway line followed the irregularities of the Sierra. In some places it clung to the mountain sides, in others it hung over chasms, using bold curves to avoid sharp angles, and rushed into narrow gorges that one would have thought had no way out. The engine, glittering like some shrine, with its large headlight sending out a lurid gleam and its silvery bell and its cow-catcher which stuck out like a spur, added its whistles and roars to the sounds of the mountain streams and waterfalls and twined its smoke round the dark branches of the fir-trees.

There were few tunnels, if any, and no bridges on that stretch of line. The railway went round the side of the mountains, not attempting to take the shortest way from one point to another by going in a straight line, and so not going against nature.

Around nine o'clock the train went along the Carson valley into the state of Nevada, still travelling to the north-east. At noon it left Reno where the travellers had twenty minutes for lunch.

After that the railway skirted the Humboldt River and went up to the north for a few miles, following the river's course. Then it bent round towards the east and did not leave the water till it reached the Humboldt Ranges, where it has its source, almost on the eastern edge of the state of Nevada.

168

After lunch, Mr. Fogg, Aouda and their companions sat down in the carriage again. Seated comfortably, they looked out at the varied scenery drifting past them—vast prairies, mountains outlined against the horizon, creeks with rolling, foaming waters. Sometimes a large herd of bison would mass in the distance, looking like a moving wall. These vast armies of ruminants often present an insurmountable obstacle on the railway. Thousands of these animals might be seen passing over the line in serried ranks for hours on end. The engine has to stop and wait until the track is clear again.

That is exactly what happened on this occasion. About three o'clock in the afternoon a herd of ten to twelve thousand head blocked the line. The engine reduced speed and tried to work the cow-catcher into the flank of that immense column, but it had to stop, because the mass was impenetrable.

The passengers saw these ruminants—buffaloes as the Americans call them incorrectly—walking along in their placid way and emitting powerful bellows from time to time. They were larger than European bulls and had short legs and tails and protruding withers which formed a hump of muscle. Their horns were far apart at the base and their heads, necks and shoulders were covered with a long-haired mane. There could be no question of stopping the migration. When bison are going in a particular direction, nothing is capable of arresting or altering their course. It is like a torrent of living flesh that no dike could ever hold back.

The passengers, scattered along the gangways, were watching this odd spectacle. But the man who should have been in the greatest hurry of all, Phileas Fogg, had stayed in his seat and was waiting philosophically till it pleased the bison to let him pass. Passepartout was furious at the delay caused by that horde of animals. He would have liked to have discharged his arsenal of revolvers at them.

'What a country!' he cried. 'You see ordinary oxen stopping trains and going along in procession without hurrying, just as if they were not holding up the traffic at

all. I wonder if Mr. Fogg allowed for this delay in his programme. And the engine-driver will not dare to make a rush through all these animals blocking the line!'

The driver had made no attempt to thrust the obstacle aside and in this he acted wisely. He would no doubt have crushed the first bison struck by the cow-catcher, but, powerful though it was, the engine would soon have been brought to a standstill and the train would have been derailed and left stranded there.

So the best thing to do was to wait patiently and then try to make up the time lost by increasing the speed. The procession of bison went on crossing for three solid hours and the track was not clear till nightfall. As the last of the herd were going across the rails, the first were already disappearing below the southern horizon.

So it was eight o'clock before the train went through the passes of the Humboldt Ranges and half past nine when it entered the territory of Utah, the region of the Great Salt Lake and the curious land of the Mormons.

*In which Passepartout attends a course of Mormon
history while travelling at twenty miles per hour*

During the night of 5th to 6th December the train ran in a
south-easterly direction for about fifty miles, then went up
to the north-east for the same distance and drew near to the
Great Salt Lake.

Around nine o'clock in the morning Passepartout went out
to take the air on the gangways. The weather was cold and
the sky grey, but it had stopped snowing. The disc of the
sun, magnified by the haze, looked like an enormous gold
piece and Passepartout was busy trying to calculate its
value in pounds sterling when his mind was taken off that
useful occupation by the appearance of a rather strange-
looking person.

The man had joined the train at Elko station. He was tall
and very swarthy with a black moustache, black stockings,
a black silk hat, a black waistcoat, black trousers, a white
cravat and dog-skin gloves. One would have taken him for
a clergyman. He was going from one end of the train to the
other and on the door of each carriage he was sticking up
hand-written notices with sealing-wax.

Passepartout went up and read on one of the notices that
Elder William Hitch, a Mormon missionary, was taking
advantage of his presence on train No. 48 to conduct a
lecture on Mormonism from 11 a.m. to 12 noon in car
No. 117, and he invited all gentlemen anxious to receive
information about the mysteries of the religion of their
Latter-Day Saints to attend.

'I will certainly go,' said Passepartout to himself. He
knew nothing of Mormonism except its custom of polygamy, which formed the basis of Mormon society.

The news spread quickly through the train which was

carrying about a hundred passengers. Of that number thirty at most, attracted by the prospect of the lecture, were in their places by eleven o'clock in car No. 117. Passepartout was sitting in the front row. Neither his master nor Fix had troubled to come.

At the appointed hour Elder William Hitch rose to his feet and in rather a cross voice, as if he had been contradicted before he started, he shouted:

'I tell you that Joseph Smith is a martyr and his brother Hyrum is a martyr too and the persecutions of the prophets, as carried out by the Government of the Union, are going to make Brigham Young a martyr too! Will anyone dare to say otherwise?'

No one ventured to contradict the missionary, whose excitement contrasted with the naturally calm expression on his face. But his anger was doubtless accounted for by the fact that Mormonism was going through a very trying period. The Government of the United States had just subdued these independent fanatics after some difficulty. They had taken control of Utah and subjected it to the laws of the Union, after imprisoning Brigham Young, who was accused of polygamy. Since then the disciples of the prophet had been redoubling their efforts and, until action could be taken, they were resisting the claims of Congress verbally.

As we can see, Elder William Hitch was proselytizing even on the railway.

And then he gave them the history of Mormonism from Biblical times and enlivened his tale by raising his voice and gesticulating vigorously. He told them how in Israel a prophet of the tribe of Joseph published the annals of the new religion and bequeathed them to his son Moroni; how, many centuries later, a translation of that precious book, written in Egyptian characters, was made by Joseph Smith Jr., a farmer in the state of Vermont, who revealed himself as a mystical prophet in 1825; and how, in the end, a Heavenly messenger appeared to him in a forest of light and handed him the annals of the Lord.

At that stage a few members of the audience, who were not interested in the missionary's historical account, left the

carriage. But William Hitch went on and related how Joseph Smith Jr. gathered together his father, his two brothers and a few disciples and founded the religion of the Latter-Day Saints, a religion adopted not only in America, but in Britain, Scandinavia and Germany and including among its followers workers and professional people. He told them how a colony was founded in Ohio and a temple was built at a cost of two hundred thousand dollars and a town was constructed at Kirtland, and how Smith became an enterprising banker and how he obtained from an ordinary man who exhibited mummies a papyrus containing a story written by the hand of Abraham and other celebrated Egyptians.

As the story was growing rather long the audience began to thin out a little more and only about twenty people were left.

But the Elder went on unconcernedly to give details of how Joseph Smith went bankrupt in 1837, of how his ruined shareholders tarred and feathered him, and how he turned up gain a few years later, more honourable and more honoured than ever, at Independence, Missouri, where he became the head of a flourishing community, comprising no less than three thousand disciples, and then, pursued by the hatred of the Gentiles, he was obliged to flee to the Far West.

There were still ten people in the audience, including the worthy Passepartout, who was all ears. He learned how, after long periods of persecution, Smith reappeared in Illinois and founded in 1839 on the banks of the Mississippi Nauvoo the Beautiful, whose population amounted to twenty-five thousand souls. Then he heard how Smith became the mayor, the supreme judge and the commander-in-chief and in 1843 handed in his candidature for the Presidency of the United States and how, in the end, he was led into an ambush at Carthage and was thrown into prison and murdered by a gang of masked men.

At that moment Passepartout was quite alone in the carriage and the Elder, looking him full in the face and almost mesmerising him with his words, reminded him

that, two years after the murder of Smith, his successor, the inspired prophet Brigham Young, left Nauvoo and established himself on the shores of the Great Salt Lake and there, in that fine territory, surrounded by fertile land which was on the route of emigrants crossing Utah on their way to California, the new colony grew to vast proportions, thanks to the Mormon principle of polygamy.

'And that,' added William Hitch, 'that is why the jealousy of Congress has descended upon us! That is why the soldiers of the Union have trampled the soil of Utah! And why our leader, the prophet Brigham Young, has been imprisoned in defiance of every concept of justice! Will we yield to force? Never! Hunted out of Vermont, hunted out of Illinois, and out of Ohio and Missouri and Utah, we will, in spite of that, find some independent territory where we can pitch our tents . . . And you, brother,' added the Elder, fixing his wrathful gaze upon his solitary hearer, 'will you pitch yours in the shadow of our flag?'

'No,' replied Passepartout bravely and fled in turn, leaving the fanatic to preach to the desert air.

But during the lecture the train had been travelling fast and about half past twelve it touched the north-west tip of the Great Salt Lake. From there they obtained an extensive view of that inland sea which is also called the Dead Sea. Into it flows the American Jordan. It is a fine lake, framed in beautiful rugged rocks, with broad strata, which are encrusted with white salt. This superb expanse of water used to cover a larger area, but, as time went on, its shores rose little by little and reduced its area, at the same time increasing its depth.

The Great Salt Lake is about seventy miles long and thirty-five wide and lies three thousand eight hundred feet above sea-level. It is quite different from the Asphaltites, or Dead Sea, which is twelve hundred feet below sea-level. It has a considerable degree of salinity and the solid matter dissolved in its waters represents a quarter of their weight. Their specific gravity is 1170, that of distilled water being 1000. So fish cannot live there. Those which are flung into it by the Jordan and the Weber and other creeks soon

perish. But it is not true that the density of the water is such that a man cannot dive into it.

The countryside round the lake was very well cultivated. The Mormons are well versed in agriculture. Six months later, there would have been ranches and corrals for livestock, fields of wheat, maize and sorghum, lush prairies, hedges of brier-roses, everywhere and clumps of acacias and euphorbia. But at that time of year the earth was hidden under a light covering of snow, which was coming down like fine powder.

At two o'clock the travellers got out at Ogden station. As the train was not due to leave till six o'clock, Mr. Fogg, Aouda and their two companions had time to go to the City of the Saints along the small branch-line running off from Ogden station. Two hours were adequate for visiting that completely American city. It was built on the pattern of all the towns of the Union in the form of vast chequerboards with cold straight lines and the 'sombre sadness of right angles', as Victor Hugo put it. The founder of the City of the Saints could not escape from that need for symmetry which is a distinguishing feature of the 'Anglo-Saxons'. In that odd country, where the men do not come up to the level of the institutions, there is something four-square about everything—towns, houses and even acts of stupidity.

At three o'clock the travellers were walking along the streets of the city, which is built between the bank of the Jordan and the foothills of the Wasatch Mountains. They noticed that there were few, if any, churches. The monuments of interest were the house of the Prophet, the Court House and the arsenal. There were houses built of bluish bricks with verandahs and galleries, surrounded by gardens and fringed with acacias, palm-trees and carob-trees. A wall of clay and pebbles, built in 1853, encircled the city. In the main street, where the market is held, were a few large buildings decked with flags, including Salt Lake House.

Mr. Fogg and his companions did not find the city very thickly populated. The streets were almost deserted, except for the precincts of the Temple, which they were only able to reach after crossing several areas surrounded by fences.

175

There was a fair abundance of women, accounted for by the unusual composition of Mormon households. But one must not think that all Mormons practise polygamy. They are free to do so, but it should be pointed out that it is, above all, the female citizens of Utah who are anxious to marry as, according to their religion, the Mormon Heaven does not allow spinsters to partake of its blessings. The poor creatures did not seem either well off or happy. Some of them, the wealthiest no doubt, wore a black silk jacket open at the waist under a hooded cloak or a very modest shawl. The others were dressed just like Indian women.

Passepartout, a confirmed bachelor, looked in awe at those Mormon women who have to band together to bring happiness to one Mormon man. He was sensible enough to pity the husband most of all. He thought it was terrible to have to guide so many ladies simultaneously through all the vicissitudes of life and lead them in a group to the Mormon Paradise, with the prospect of meeting them again and being with them to all eternity, in the company of the glorious Joseph Smith who would be the leading person in that blessed land. He felt it was definitely not his vocation and he thought—but he was perhaps mistaken in this—that the ladies of Salt Lake City cast rather disquieting glances at him.

Fortunately his stay in the City of the Saints did not have to be a long one. At a few minutes before four the travellers were back at the station and returned to their places in the carriages.

The whistle was blown, but, just as the driving wheels of the engine began to slip along the rails and send the train quickly on its way, they heard someone cry, 'Stop! Stop!'

One does not stop a moving train. The gentleman who was shouting was obviously a Mormon who had arrived late. He was running so fast that he was out of breath. Fortunately for him, the station had no gates or barriers. So he rushed on to the track, jumped on to the foot-board of the last carriage and flopped breathlessly on to one of the seats.

Passepartout, who had been watching those gymnastic

feats excitedly, looked at the latecomer and was interested when he learned that that citizen of Utah had fled because of domestic trouble.

When the Mormon had got his breath back, Passepartout ventured to ask him how many wives he had. Judging by the way he had been running, he would have assumed that he had a score of them at least.

'One, sir!' replied the Mormon, raising his arms heaven-wards. 'One, and one was quite enough!'

*In which Passepartout cannot make anyone listen
to reason*

Leaving the Great Salt Lake and the station of Ogden, the train travelled up towards the north for an hour as far as the Weber River. It had now gone about nine hundred miles from San Francisco. After that it went in an easterly direction again through the irregular range of the Wasatch Mountains. It is in the area between those mountains and the Rocky Mountains proper that American engineers have had to tackle the most serious difficulties. So along that stretch subsidies from the United States Government have amounted to forty-eight thousand dollars per mile, whereas they came to only sixteen thousand dollars in the plain. But, as we have said, the engineers have not gone against nature and despoiled her, but have handled her with cunning. They have gone round the difficult parts. In fact, in order to reach the great basin, only one single tunnel fourteen thousand feet long was bored along that whole stretch of the railway.

It was actually at the Great Salt Lake that the line gained its greatest height so far. From then onwards, viewed from the side, it took the form of a very long curve going down towards the valley of Bitter Creek and then climbing up again to the watershed of the Atlantic and the Pacific. There were numerous streams in that mountain area. The Muddy, the Green and others had to be crossed by means of small bridges. Passepartout had become increasingly impatient as he drew nearer to his destination. Fix would have been glad to have been out of this difficult region. He was afraid of delays and he dreaded accidents. In fact, he was in more of a hurry than Phileas Fogg himself to set foot on English soil!

At ten o'clock in the evening the train stopped at Fort Bridger station, which they left almost at once, and twenty miles farther on they entered the state of Wyoming—formerly Dakota—following the entire valley of the Bitter Creek, from which come some of the waters forming the hydrographic system of Colorado.

On the next day, 7th December, there was a stop of a quarter of an hour at Green River station. A fair amount of snow had fallen during the night, but, as it was mixed with rain and was half melted, it did not impede the progress of the train. But this bad weather was a constant source of worry to Passepartout as any accumulation of snow would certainly be detrimental to the journey, as it would clog the wheels.

'What an idea of my master's,' he said to himself, 'to travel in winter! Could he not have waited for the fine weather to add to his chances?'

But, while he was worrying only about the appearance of the sky and the drop in the temperature, Aouda was tormented by even sharper anxieties, caused by something quite different.

Some of the passengers had stepped down from their carriages and walked about on the platform at Green River station till the train was due to leave. And, through the window, the young woman recognized among them Colonel Stamp W. Proctor, the American who had behaved so boorishly towards Phileas Fogg at the time of the convention in San Francisco. Not wishing to be seen, Aouda leaned back in her seat.

That episode had made a deep impression on the young woman. She had grown attached to the man who daily gave her tokens of the greatest consideration and devotion, albeit with an air of cold indifference. No doubt she did not realize the full depth of feeling that her rescuer had awakened within her. She still called it gratitude, but, unknown to her, it had become more than that. So her heart missed a beat when she recognized that boorish person from whom Mr. Fogg intended, sooner or later, to demand satisfaction. It was mere chance that had brought Colonel Proctor on to

the same train, but the point was that he was there and Phileas Fogg would have to be prevented at all costs from observing his adversary.

When the train had got under way again, Aouda took advantage of a moment when Mr. Fogg was dozing to tell Fix and Passepartout of the situation.

'So that man Proctor is on the train, is he?' cried Fix. 'Well, do not worry, madam. Before he deals with Mr. Fogg, he will have to deal with me. After all, I am the person he insulted most.'

'And, what is more,' added Passepartout, 'I will take care of him, colonel or no colonel!'

'Mr. Fix,' went on Aouda, 'Mr. Fogg will not allow anyone to avenge him. He has told me that he is the type of man who would return to America and seek out the man who had insulted him. So, if he notices Colonel Proctor, we shall not be able to prevent a duel, and that may have disastrous consequences. So he must not see him.'

'You are right, madam,' replied Fix. 'A duel might spoil everything. Whether he won or lost, Mr. Fogg would be delayed . . . '

'And,' added Passepartout, 'that would be playing into the hands of the gentlemen of the Reform Club. In four days we shall be in New York. Well, if during those four days my master does not leave the carriage, there is a good chance that he will not meet that accursed American face to face, confound him! We must find a way of preventing him . . . '

The conversation was broken off. Mr. Fogg had awakened and was looking out through the snow-spattered window. But later on Passepartout said to the police inspector, without being overheard by his master or Aouda:

'Would you really fight on his behalf?'

'I shall do everything in my power to bring him back to Europe alive!' Fix replied simply in a very determined voice.

Passepartout felt a kind of shudder run down his spine, but his faith in his master never wavered.

Was there any way of keeping Mr. Fogg in the carriage

and guarding against a meeting between the Colonel and himself? That should not be too difficult as the gentleman was not inquisitive by nature and did not move about much. In any case, the police inspector thought he had found a way and a few moments later he said to Phileas Fogg:

'The hours seem very long on a railway journey, sir, and they pass very slowly.'

'Yes, indeed,' replied the gentleman, 'but they do pass.'

'On board ship,' went on the inspector, 'you used to play whist, did you not?'

'Yes,' replied Phileas Fogg, 'but that would be difficult here. I have no cards and no partners.'

'Oh, as for cards, we would certainly be able to buy some. They sell everything on American trains. And, as regards partners, if you, madam . . .'

'Certainly, sir,' replied the young woman eagerly. 'I know how to play whist. It is part of an English upbringing.'

'And I,' Fix went on, 'may lay some claim to being a good player. Now if we three play with a dummy . . .'

'As you wish, sir,' replied Phileas Fogg, delighted at being able to resume his favourite game, even on the railway.

Passepartout was sent in search of the steward and he soon returned with two complete packs of cards and markers and counters and a little board covered with cloth. They had all they required. And so play began. Aouda was quite a good player and even received a few compliments from the severe Phileas Fogg. As for the inspector, he was really a first-class player, worthy of competing with the gentleman.

'Now,' said Passepartout to himself, 'we have got him where we want him. He will not move from here.'

At eleven o'clock in the morning the train reached the watershed of the two oceans. This was at Bridger Pass, at a height of seven thousand five hundred and twenty-four feet above sea-level, one of the highest points reached by the railway line on its route through the Rocky Mountains. About two hundred miles from there the travellers would find themselves at last on the vast plains extending as far as the Atlantic which nature has made so suitable for the building of a railway.

On the slope of the Atlantic basin the first streams, tributaries of the North Platte River, were forming. The whole of the northern and eastern horizon was blocked by that immense semi-circular barrier, which constitutes the northern portion of the Rocky Mountains, dominated by the peak of Laramie. Huge well-watered plains stretched between that curve and the railway line. On the right of the railway the first slopes of the mountain ridge rose up in tiers. And the ridge swelled out to the south as far as the sources of the Arkansas River, one of the great tributaries of the Missouri.

At half past twelve the travellers had a momentary glimpse of Fort Halleck which dominates the area. In just a few more hours they would have finished crossing the Rocky Mountains. So they could but hope that the train would not suffer any accident in that difficult region.

It had stopped snowing. The weather was now cold and dry. Large birds, frightened by the engine, flew off into the distance. No wild beasts, no bears or wolves, were to be seen on the plain. It was like a desert in its immense bareness.

After a fairly comfortable lunch, served in the actual carriage, Mr. Fogg and his partners had just resumed their interminable games of whist when loud whistles could be heard. The train stopped. Passepartout put his head out of the carriage door and saw nothing that could have caused the stoppage. There was no station in sight.

Aouda and Fix were afraid for a moment that Mr. Fogg would think of stepping down on to the track. But the gentleman merely said to his servant:

'Go and see what is the matter!'

Passepartout dashed out of the carriage. About forty passengers had already left their seats, including Colonel Stamp W. Proctor.

The train had stopped in front of a signal which was at red, closing the line. The driver and the guard had got out and were having a lively discussion with a railwayman whom the stationmaster at Medicine Bow, the next station, had sent out to intercept the train. Some passengers had gone up to

them and were taking part in the discussion—amongst others, the said Colonel Proctor, with his loud voice and imperious gestures.

Passepartout joined the group and heard the railwayman say: 'No! There is no way of passing! The Medicine Bow bridge is insecure and it would not bear the weight of the train.'

The bridge in question was a suspension bridge across rapids, a mile from the spot where the train had stopped. According to the railwayman, it was threatenin to gcollapse and several of the wires were broken, so it was not possible to risk a crossing. It was no exaggeration on the part of the railwayman to say that they could not go over it. What is more, bearing in mind the free and easy ways of the Americans, one might say that when they do start being cautious, it would be sheer madness not to be.

Passepartout, not daring to go and tell his master, listened with clenched teeth. He was as stiff as a statue.

'Now then!' cried Colonel Proctor. 'We are surely not going to stay here and just take root in the snow.'

'Colonel,' replied the guard, 'we have telegraphed to Omaha station asking for a train, but it probably will not reach Medicine Bow until six o'clock.'

'Six o'clock!' cried Passepartout.

'Probably,' repled the guard, 'and we will need the time to walk to the station in any case.'

'Walk!' cried all the travellers.

'But how far away is the station, then?' one of them asked the guard.

'Twelve miles away, on the other side of the river. We will have to make a detour . . . '

'Twelve miles in the snow!' cried Stamp W. Proctor.

The Colonel let fly a volley of oaths and blamed the railway company and the guard. Passepartout, who was furious, felt inclined to join in. This was a physical obstacle against which all his master's banknotes could not prevail.

There was widespread disappointment among the passengers who, quite apart from the delay, found themselevs obliged to walk all those miles across a snow-covered plain.

So there was a tremendous uproar and shouting that would certainly have attracted Phileas Fogg's attention if he had not been absorbed in his game.

However, Passepartout would have to let him know and, with head bowed, he was making his way towards the carriage when the driver—a real Yankee called Forster—shouted out:

'We might be able to cross after all.'

'The bridge?' replied one passenger.

'Yes, the bridge.'

'In our train?' asked the Colonel.

'Yes, in our train.'

Passepartout had stopped and was positively devouring the driver's words.

'But the bridge is threatening to collapse!' persisted the guard.

'No matter!' replied Forster. 'I think that if I sent the train over at its maximum speed there would be some chance of crossing it.'

'Good Heavens!' cried Passepartout.

But a certain number of the passengers found the suggestion attractive at once. It appealed to Colonel Proctor in particular. That hothead found it a perfectly practicable proposition. He even recalled how engineers had had the idea of crossing small rivers 'without a bridge', in rigid trains sent across at top speed, and so on. In the end all those interested sided with the driver.

'The chances of crossing are fifty-fifty,' said one of them.

'Sixty in favour,' said another.

'Eighty—or ninety out of a hundred!'

Passepartout was flabbergasted, although he was prepared to try anything to get across Medicine Creek. But it all seemed a little too 'American' in his eyes.

'But,' he reflected, 'there is something far simpler we could do and these people have not even thought of it! Sir', he said to one of the passengers, 'the way suggested by the driver seems a bit risky to me, but . . . '

'The chances are eighty out of a hundred!' retorted the passenger turning his back on him.

'I know,' replied Passepartout, turning to another gentleman, 'but if you consider for a minute . . . '

'Consider? That does not bring results!' said the American whom Passepartout had addressed and he shrugged his shoulders. 'The driver assures us that we will get over it.'

'No doubt we shall get over,' replied Passepartout, 'but it would perhaps be wiser . . . '

'What! Wiser!' shouted Colonel Proctor. The word he had just happened to hear made him see red. 'It will be at top speed! Do you understand? At top speed! Do you understand? At top speed!'

'I know . . . I understand . . . ' repeated Passepartout. No one would let him finish his sentence. 'But it would be, if not wiser, for I see the word shocks you, at least more natural . . . '

'Who? What? What does the fellow mean? Natural?' they all cried.

The poor fellow did not know where he could get a hearing.

'Are you scared?' Colonel Proctor asked him.

'Me, scared?' cried Passepartout. 'Very well then! I will show these people that a Frenchman can be just as American as they are!'

'All aboard! All aboard!' shouted the guard.

'Yes! All aboard!' repeated Passepartout. 'All aboard! And right away! But no one can stop me thinking that it would have been more natural to make the passengers walk over the bridge first and then let the train over!'

But no one heard that wise reflection and, in any case, they would not have been willing to admit how reasonable it was.

The passengers had returned to their carriages. Passepartout sat down in his seat again without saying a word about what had happened. The players were wholly absorbed in their game.

The engine gave a powerful whistle. The driver reversed his engine and sent the train nearly a mile back down the line—like an athlete taking his run-up before jumping.

Then, at a second whistle-blast, they began to move forward again. The speed increased—soon it was terrifyingly fast. The only sound that could be heard was a single snort from the engine. The pistons were doing twenty strokes per second and the axles of the wheels were smoking in their grease-boxes. It felt as if the train, going along at a hundred miles per hour, was not weighing down upon the rails at all. The speed seemed to be eating up the weight.

And they crossed over! It all happened in a flash. They saw nothing of the bridge. It was as if the train had jumped from one bank to the other, and the driver was only able to stop his runaway engine five miles beyond the station.

But, no sooner had the train crossed the river, than the bridge, damaged beyond repair, crashed into the rapids of Medicine Bow.

In which we shall relate various incidents that could only have taken place on a United States railroad

That evening the train went on its way without encountering any obstacles, passed Fort Sanders, went though the Cheyenne Pass and reached Evans Pass. There the railway climbed to the highest point on the route, that is, eight thousand and ninety-one feet above sea level. All that the travellers had to do now was to go down to the Atlantic over limitless plains levelled by nature.

On the 'Grand Trunk' there was a branch line running to Denver City, the main city of Colorado. There is an abundance of gold and silver mines in that area and over fifty thousand people have settled there already.

They had now travelled thirteen hundred and eighty-two miles from San Francisco, in three days and three nights. It was estimated that they would take four nights and four days to reach New York, so Phileas Fogg was keeping to the scheduled times.

During the night they passed Walbach Camp on the left. Lodge Pole Creek ran parallel to the track, following the straight line of the boundary between the states of Wyoming and Colorado. At eleven o'clock they entered Nebraska, passed close to Sedgwick and touched Julesburgh, which is situated on the southern branch of the Platte River.

That is where the Union Pacific Railroad was inaugurated on 23rd October, 1867. The chief engineer was General G. M. Dodge. There the two powerful locomotives pulling the nine carriages stopped. They included the Vice-President, Mr. Thomas C. Durant. Cheering resounded through the air and the Sioux and Pawnees staged an Indian war in miniature. Fireworks exploded and the first issue of the publication *Railway Pioneer* was run off a

portable printing-press. Those were the celebrations marking the opening of the great railway, which was to be an instrument of progress and civilization. It had been flung across the desert and would link up towns and cities not yet in existence. The whistle of the engine, more powerful than Amphion's lyre, was soon to make them spring up from the soil of America.

At eight o'clock in the morning they left Fort MacPherson behind them. It is three hundred and fifty-seven miles from there to Omaha. On the left bank the railway followed the capricious twists and curves of the southern branch of the Platte River. At nine o'clock they reached the important town of North Platte, built between these two branches of the river which meet round it, joining to form one single artery. It is a large tributary and its waters flow into the Missouri a little above Omaha.

The 101st meridian had been crossed.

Mr. Fogg and his partners had resumed play. None of them complained of the length of the route—not even the dummy. Fix had begun by winning a few guineas and was now in the process of losing them again, but he showed just as much keenness as Mr. Fogg. During that morning fortune really seemed to smile on that gentleman. Trumps and honours came flooding into his hands. At a certain point in the game he had planned a bold manoeuvre and was just about to play spades when a voice was heard from behind his seat:

'I would play diamonds . . . '

Mr. Fogg, Aouda and Fix raised their heads. Colonel Proctor was standing there beside them.

Stamp W. Proctor and Phileas Fogg recognized each other at once.

'Oh, so it is you, Mr. Englishman,' cried the Colonel. 'You are the man who wants to play spades.'

'And who is going to play spades,' replied Phileas Fogg coldly, laying down a ten of that suit.

'Well, I would like it to be a diamond,' retorted Colonel Proctor in an irritated voice. And he made a move to grab the card that had been played, adding: 'You do not understand a thing about the game.'

'Perhaps I may be cleverer at another,' said Phileas Fogg, rising.

'It is up to you to find out, you son of John Bull!' rejoined that boorish individual.

Aouda had turned pale. All her blood was flowing to her heart. She had grasped Phileas Fogg by the arm, but he pushed her gently away. Passepartout was ready to hurl himself at the American, who was looking most insultingly at his opponent. But Fix rose to his feet and, going up to Colonel Proctor, he said:

'You seem to forget that I am the man you have to deal with, sir. You did not merely insult me—you struck me.'

'Mr. Fix,' said Mr. Fogg, 'I beg your pardon, but this matter concerns me alone. In claiming that I made a mistake in playing spades, the Colonel has insulted me once again and he will have to give me satisfaction for it.'

'Whenever you like and where you like,' replied the American, 'and with whatever weapons you please.'

Aouda tried in vain to restrain Mr. Fogg and the inspector tried in vain to take up the quarrel again on his own account. As for Passepartout, he wanted to fling the Colonel through the carriage door, but a sign from his master stopped him. Phileas Fogg left the carriage and the American followed him on to the gangway.

'Sir,' said Mr. Fogg to his adversary, 'I am in a great hurry to return to Europe and any delay would greatly prejudice my interests.'

'What concern is that of mine!' retorted Colonel Proctor.

'Sir,' Mr. Fogg went on politely, 'after our meeting in San Francisco I had planned to come back and see you again in America as soon as I had concluded the business taking me to Europe.'

'Really!'

'Will you agree to meet me in six months from now?'

'Why not in six years?'

'I said six months,' replied Mr. Fogg, 'and I shall arrive punctually for our meeting.'

'You are just making excuses!' cried Stamp W. Proctor. 'Straight away or not at all.'

'Very well,' replied Mr. Fogg. 'Are you going to New York?'

'No.'

'Chicago?'

'No.'

'Omaha?'

'It is none of your business! Do you know Plum Creek?'

'No.' replied Mr. Fogg.

'It is the next station. The train will be there in an hour. It will stop there ten minutes. In ten minutes we will have time to exchange a few shots.'

'Very well,' replied Mr. Fogg. 'I shall stop at Plum Creek.'

'And I think you will stay there!' added the American with outrageous insolence.

'Who knows, sir?' replied Mr. Fogg and he went back into his carriage, as cool and composed as ever.

There the gentleman first of all tried to reassure Aouda and told her that bullies were never to be feared. Then he asked Fix to act as his second in the duel about to take place. Fix could not refuse and Phileas Fogg went on calmly with his interrupted game, playing spades with perfect aplomb.

At eleven o'clock the whistle of the engine announced that they were approaching Plum Creek station. Mr. Fogg rose and, followed by Fix, went out on to the gangway. Passepartout accompanied him, carrying a pair of revolvers. Aouda had stayed behind in the carriage, as pale as a corpse.

At that moment the door of the other carriage opened and Colonel Proctor also appeared on the gangway, followed by his second, a Yankee of his own stamp. But, just as the two adversaries were about to step down on to the track, the guard came running up and shouted to them:

'No one is to get off, gentlemen.'

'Why not?' asked the Colonel.

'We are twenty minutes late and the train is not stopping.'

'But I have to fight this gentleman.'

'I am sorry,' replied the official, 'but we are leaving again at once. There goes the bell now!'

The bell was indeed ringing and the train started off again.

'I am truly sorry, gentlemen,' said the guard. 'In any other circumstances I would have been able to oblige you. But, seeing you did not have time to fight here, what is to prevent you from fighting on the way?'

'Perhaps that will not suit the other gentleman!' said Colonel Proctor with a mocking air.

'It will suit me perfectly,' replied Phileas Fogg.

'Well, well, we certainly are in America!' thought Passepartout. 'And the guard is a real gentleman.'

So saying, he followed his master.

The two adversaries and their seconds, led by the guard, went through the carriages, one after the other, to the back of the train. There were only about ten passengers in the last carriage. The guard asked them if they would be willing to vacate it for a few moments because there were two gentlemen who had to settle a matter of honour.

Why, of course! The passengers were only too happy to oblige the two gentlemen and withdrew to the gangway.

The carriage was about fifty feet long and was ideally suitable for the purpose. The two men could walk towards each other between the seats and shoot at will. Never had a duel been so easy to arrange. Mr. Fogg and Colonel Proctor, each armed with two six-shooters, entered the carriage. Their seconds, who had remained outside, shut them in. At the first whistle-blast from the engine they were to start firing . . . Then, after an interval of two minutes, they would remove from the carriage what was left of the two gentlemen.

Nothing could really be simpler. It was, in fact, so simple that Fix and Passepartout felt their hearts beating as if they would burst.

They were waiting for the agreed whistle-blast when suddenly there came the sound of savage cries. They were accompanied by shots, but these did not come from the

carriage set aside for the use of the duellers. These shots came from all along the train, as far as the front of it. Cries of terror could be heard from inside the train.

Colonel Proctor and Mr. Fogg, their revolvers at the ready, left the carriage at once and rushed to the front of the train, where the reports and the shouting were loudest. They realized that the train was being attacked by a band of Sioux.

It was not the first time these bold Indians had attempted such a thing. They had held up trains more than once. As was their practice, they did not wait for the trains to stop, but rushed on to the foot-boards and climbed up the carriages like a clown vaulting on to a galloping horse. There were about a hundred of them.

The Sioux were armed with rifles. That accounted for the shots, which the travellers, nearly all of whom were armed, answered with revolver fire. First of all, the Indians rushed on to the engine. The driver and firemen were partly knocked out. Then a Sioux chief, wishing to stop the train, but not knowing how to operate the regulator handle, opened it, instead of closing it, and now the engine was running along at a terrifying speed.

At the same time the Sioux had invaded the carriages. They ran like frantic monkeys over the roofs, breaking open the doors and fighting with the passengers at close quarters. From the luggage van, which had been forced open and looted, packages had been thrown down on to the track. The shouting and firing were going on unceasingly.

But the passengers were defending themselves bravely. Certain of the carriages were barricaded and were being besieged like moving fortresses, travelling along at a hundred miles an hour.

From the start of the attack Aouda had behaved courageously. With a revolver in her hand she was defending herself heroically, shooting through the broken windows whenever some savage appeared there beside her. About a score of mortally wounded Sioux had fallen on to the track and the carriage wheels squashed like worms any who slipped on to the rails from the gangways.

Several passengers, seriously injured by bullets or toma-hawks, were lying on the seats.

But it had to be brought to an end. The fighting had been going on for ten minutes and would end in a Sioux victory if the train did not stop. Fort Kearny station was less than two miles away. There was an American army post there, but once they passed it the Sioux would become masters of the train between Fort Kearny and the next station.

The guard was fighting by Mr. Fogg's side when a bullet brought him down. As he fell, the man cried:

'We are lost if the train does not stop in under five minutes.'

'It will stop!' said Phileas Fogg, who made a move to leave the carriage.

'Stay here, sir!' cried Passepartout. 'I will attend to it.'

Phileas Fogg had no time to stop the brave fellow. He opened a door, without being seen by the Indians, and managed to slip along underneath the carriage. And, as the fight went on and bullets criss-crossed over his head, he moved along under the carriages with all the old agility and suppleness he had had as a clown. He clung on to the chains, grasped the brake lever and the buffer beams and so crawled from one carriage to the next with remarkable dexterity. And so he reached the front of the train. He had not been seen—in fact, he could not be seen.

There, hanging by one hand between the luggage van and the tender, he unhooked the safety chains with his other hand. But, because of the pull that was being exerted, he would never have managed to unfasten the coupling if the engine had not given a violent jerk, which made the coupling jump. And so the train, detached from the engine, fell farther and farther behind, whilst the engine raced on faster than ever.

Carried on by its own momentum, the train went trund-ling along for a few more minutes, but the brakes were applied inside the carriages and the train finally stopped less than a hundred feet away from Kearny station.

There the soldiers from the fort, whose attention had been attracted by the gunfire, came running up to the train. The

Sioux had not been expecting them and, before the train had stopped completely, the whole band had made off.

But when the passengers were counted on the station platform it was discovered that some of them were not there, and they included the daring Frenchman whose devotion to duty had just saved them from certain death.

In which Phileas Fogg merely does his duty

Three passengers, including Passepartout, had disappeared. Had they been killed in the struggle? Were they prisoners of the Sioux? No one knew. There were a fair number of wounded, but it was found that there had been no fatal casualties. One of the most seriously injured was Colonel Proctor, who had fought bravely and had been hit by a bullet in the groin. He was carried to the station with other travellers requiring immediate attention. Aouda was safe and sound. Phileas Fogg, who had not spared himself, did not have a scratch. Fix was wounded in the arm, but the injury was slight. However, Passepartout was missing and tears were running down the young woman's face.

All the passengers had left the train. The carriage wheels were spattered with blood. Formless shreds of human flesh hung from the naves and spokes of the wheels. As far as the eye could see over the white plain there were long red streaks. The last Indians were disappearing southwards, in the direction of the Republican River.

Mr. Fogg stood motionless with folded arms. He had a serious decision to take. Aouda was standing beside him. She was looking at him in silence and he knew what that look meant. If his servant had been taken prisoner, ought he not to risk everything in an attempt to rescue him from the Indians?

'I shall find him, dead or alive,' he said simply to Aouda.

'Oh, sir . . . Mr. Fogg!' cried the young woman, seizing her companion's hands and bathing them with tears.

'Alive!' added Mr. Fogg. 'If we do not lose a single moment.'

In making that decision Phileas Fogg was sacrificing everything. He had just spelt out his ruin. One single day's

delay would make him miss the ship in New York. His bet would be irrevocably lost. But he did not hesitate, for it was his duty.

The captain commanding Fort Kearny was there. His soldiers—about a hundred—had placed themselves on the defensive in case the Sioux launched a direct attack on the military post.

'Sir,' said Mr. Fogg to the captain, 'three passengers have disappeared.'

'Are they dead?' asked the captain.

'Dead or taken prisoner,' replied Phileas Fogg. 'We must put an end to this uncertainty. Do you intend to go out after the Sioux?'

'That is a serious matter, sir.' said the captain. 'These Indians may well go off beyond the Arkansas. I cannot abandon the fort entrusted to my care.'

'The lives of three men are at stake,' replied Phileas Fogg.

'True, but can I risk the lives of fifty men to save three?'

'I do not know if you can, but you ought to.'

'Sir,' replied the captain, 'I need no one to teach me my duty.'

'Very well,' said Phileas Fogg calmly. 'I shall go alone!'

'You, sir!' exclaimed Fix who had just come up. 'You go off alone in pursuit of the Indians?'

'Do you expect me to let that poor fellow die? All the people here owe their lives to him. I mean to go.'

'Well, you will not go alone!' cried the captain, who felt moved in spite of himself. 'No! You are a brave man . . . I want thirty volunteers,' he added, turning to his soldiers.

The whole company stepped forward to a man. So all the captain had to do was to select thirty of those brave soldiers. This was duly done and an old sergeant was put in command of them.

'Thank you, captain!' said Mr. Fogg.

'Will you permit me to accompany you?' Fix asked the gentleman.

'You will do as you please, sir,' replied Phileas Fogg, 'but if you want to do me a favour, please stay with Aouda. Should some misfortune befall me . . . '

A sudden pallor spread over the police inspector's face. Part with the man whom he had followed so persistently step by step! Let him venture into the wilderness like that! Fix gave Mr. Fogg a searching look, but, for some reason or other, in spite of his prejudices and the conflict going on inside him, he lowered his eyes when confronted by that frank, untroubled gaze.

'Very well, I shall stay,' he said.

A few moments later Mr. Fogg shook the young woman by the hand, then, after handing over to her his precious carpet-bag, he departed with the sergeant and his small band of men. But, before leaving, he said to the soldiers:

'My friends, there will be a thousand pounds for you if we manage to rescue the prisoners.'

It was then a few minutes after noon.

Aouda had withdrawn to a room at the station and there she waited alone, thinking of Phileas Fogg and of his generosity, which was simple and yet on a grand scale, and of his calm courage. Mr. Fogg had sacrificed his fortune and now he was risking his life, all without hesitation, from a sense of duty, without fine phrases. Phileas Fogg was a hero in her eyes.

Inspector Fix's thoughts were not running along those lines. He could not restrain his agitation. He walked feverishly up and down the station platform. For a moment his real self had given way, but now it was returning. Now that Fogg had left, he realized how foolish he had been to let him go. What! The man whom he had just followed round the world—and he had agreed to part company with him! His own true nature was coming out on top now. He accused himself, he blamed himself, he spoke to himself as if he had been the chief of the Metropolitan Police admonishing a policeman whom he had caught behaving like a naïve simpleton.

'I have been incompetent!' he thought. 'The other fellow will have told him who I am! He has gone away and he will not be coming back. Where can I find him now? How ever could I let myself be persuaded like that—me, Fix? And I

have the order for his arrest in my pocket. Oh, I have certainly been a fool!'

The police inspector went on arguing like this with himself as the hours went slowly by. He did not know what to do. Sometimes he felt like telling Aouda the whole story. But he knew the reception he would get from her! What was he to do? He was tempted to go off across those endless white plains in pursuit of Fogg. He did not think it would be impossible to find him. The footmarks of the detachment were still imprinted on the snow. But soon all trace of them would be blotted out, if there were a fresh fall of snow.

Then Fix became despondent. He felt an unconquerable desire to give up the whole scheme. In fact, he did have an opportunity of leaving Kearny Station and going on his way.

About two o'clock in the afternoon, as the snow was coming down in large flakes, long whistle-blasts could be heard coming from the east. A huge shadowy object, with a glaring light in front of it, was moving slowly forward, magnified by the haze which made it seem quite unreal.

But they were not expecting any train from the east yet. The help for which they had telegraphed could not have come so soon, and the train from Omaha to San Francisco was not due to arrive till the next day. But they soon found out what it was.

The engine which was advancing so slowly and emitting loud whistles was the one that had become detached from the train and had proceeded on its way at such a terrifying speed, carrying the unconscious driver and fireman with it. It had run along the rails for several miles, then the fire had gone down for lack of fuel. The steam had eased off and one hour later it had slowed down little by little and stopped at last twenty miles beyond Kearny station.

Neither the driver nor the fireman had succumbed to their injuries and, after lying unconscious for a fair time, they finally came round.

The engine was at a standstill by that time. When he saw that he was out in the open country with only the engine and none of the carriages following on behind, the driver

realized what had happened. He could not understand how the engine had become detached from the train, but he was in no doubt that the train, which had been left behind, would be in difficulties.

The driver did not hesitate. The wise thing to do would be to continue in the direction of Omaha. It would be dangerous to return to the train, which the Indians were perhaps still looting . . . But no matter! Shovelfuls of coal and wood were swallowed up by the firebox, the fire was rekindled, pressure rose once more and about two o'clock in the afternoon the engine backed along the line in the direction of Kearny station. And it was the engine that was sending out those whistle-blasts through the mist.

The passengers were delighted when they saw the engine coming up to the head of the train. They would be able to continue after that unfortunate interruption.

When the engine arrived, Aouda went out and had a word with the guard.

'Are you going to start?' she asked him.

'At once, madam.'

'But what about the prisoners . . . our unfortunate companions?'

'I cannot hold up the railroad service,' replied the guard. 'We are three hours late already.'

'And when will the next train from San Francisco be coming through?'

'Tomorrow evening, madam.'

'Tomorrow evening! But that will be too late. You must wait . . . '

'That is out of the question,' replied the guard. 'If you wish to leave, you must go aboard now.'

'I am not leaving,' replied the young woman.

Fix had heard the conversation. A few moments earlier, when there was no transport available, he had been determined to leave Kearny, but, now that the train was there and ready to depart and all he had to do was to sit down in his seat again, an irresistible force seemed to be keeping him rooted to the spot. The station platform was burning his feet and he could not tear himself away from it. The struggle

inside him began all over again. He was choking with anger at his failure. He wanted to fight to the end.

The travellers, including some of the injured, were back in the carriages. Colonel Proctor, who was in a grave condition, was among them. One could hear the booming of the overheated boiler. Steam was escaping from the valves. Then the driver whistled and the train moved off and was soon out of sight, its white smoke mingling with the flurries of snow.

Inspector Fix had stayed behind.

A few hours had passed. The weather was very bad and the cold was intense. Fix sat motionless on a bench in the station. One would have thought he was asleep. In spite of the weather Aouda every few minutes left the room that had been placed at at her disposal. She went to the end of the platform, trying to peer through the blizzard and penetrate the haze which made the horizon shrink around her, and she listened. But there was nothing. Then she went in, numb with cold, and came out again a few moments later, but always in vain.

Evening came. The small detachment of men had not returned. Where were they at moment ? Had they been able to overtake the Indians ? Had there been a battle, or were the soldiers lost in the mist and just wandering about aimlessly ? The captain of Fort Kearny was very worried, although he did not want to show it.

Night came. The snow was not falling so heavily now, but the cold had become more intense. The boldest of men would not have been able to view the dark immensity of the plain without fear. There was absolute silence. There were no birds flying or wild beasts moving about to disturb the infinite peace of it all.

Throughout that night Aouda, her mind full of sinister forebodings, her heart filled with anxious fears, roamed about on the edge of the prairie. Her imagination carried her afar off and revealed to her a thousand dangers. What she suffered during those long hours cannot be described. Fix stayed in his place without moving, but he did not sleep either. At one point a man came up to him and spoke to him,

but the detective sent him away with a shake of his head.

And so the night passed. At dawn the pale disc of the sun rose above the misty horizon, but the eye could see over a distance of two miles. Phileas Fogg and the detachment had gone off in a southerly direction . . . but the plain to the south was absolutely deserted. It was then seven o'clock in the morning.

The captain, extremely worried, did not know what to do. Should he send a second detachment out to the assistance of the first? Should he sacrifice fresh men with so little chance of saving those who had been sacrificed at the start? But he did not hesitate for long. He beckoned to one of his lieutenants and ordered him to send out a reconnaissance patrol to the south. At that moment there was a sound of gunfire. Was it a signal? The soldiers rushed out of the fort and half a mile away they observed a small body of men returning in an orderly fashion.

Mr. Fogg was marching at their head, and beside him Passepartout and the two other passengers rescued from the Sioux. There had been fighting ten miles to the south of Kearny. A few moments before the arrival of the detachment Passepartout and his two companions had already been struggling with their captors and the Frenchman had knocked out three with his fists by the time his master and the soldiers came to their assistance.

They were all acclaimed, both rescuers and rescued, with shouts of joy and Phileas Fogg handed out to the soldiers the bonus he had promised them. Passepartout kept on saying to himself, not without some justification:

'I am certainly costing my master a great deal of money!'

Fix looked at Mr. Fogg without a word and it would have been hard to analyse the feelings struggling within him at that moment. As for Aouda, she had grasped the gentleman's hand and was holding it tightly in hers, unable to utter a single word!

Since arriving, Passepartout had been looking for the train. He expected to find it there, all ready to move off to Omaha, and he hoped they would still be able to make up for the time lost.

'The train, the train!' he cried.

'Gone!' replied Fix.

'And when will the next train be coming through?' asked Phileas Fogg.

'Not until this evening.'

'Oh,' was all that the impassive gentleman said.

In which Inspector Fix takes Phileas Fogg's interests very much to heart

Phileas Fogg was twenty hours behind time. Passepartout, the involuntary cause of the delay, was in despair. He had unquestionably brought about his master's downfall! Just then the inspector went up to Mr. Fogg and, looking him straight in the face, said:

'Seriously, sir,' he asked, 'you are in a hurry, are you not?'

'Very much so,' replied Phileas Fogg.

'I will put it another way,' Fix went on. 'You are anxious to be in New York by nine o'clock in the evening of the 11th, when the ship sails for Liverpool?'

'Very anxious indeed.'

'And if your journey had not been interrupted by the Indian attack you would have reached New York on the morning of the 11th?'

'Yes, twelve hours before the ship was due to sail.'

'So you are twenty hours behind time. Twelve from twenty is eight. You have eight hours to make up. Do you want to try and do it?'

'On foot?' asked Mr. Fogg.

'No, by sledge,' replied Mr. Fix, 'on a sledge with sails. A man came along and suggested it to me.'

It was the man who had spoken to the police inspector during the night and whose offer Fix had refused.

Phileas Fogg did not answer Fix, but the latter pointed out the man in question, who was walking about outside the station, and so the gentleman went up to him. A moment later Phileas Fogg and the American, whose name was Mudge, went into a hut at the bottom Fort Kearny.

There Mr. Fogg inspected a rather odd-looking vehicle,

a kind of frame resting on two long beams, slightly raised in front like the runners of a sledge. Five or six people could sit on it. A third of the way along the frame, towards the front, rose a very high mast on which a huge spanker sail was bent. From this mast, strongly held by metal shrouds, stretched an iron stay used for hoisting a large jib. At the rear there was a sort of steering oar enabling one to steer the craft.

As one can realize, it was a sledge rigged like a sloop. In winter, when the trains are stopped by snow, these vehicles can travel extremely fast over the frozen plain from one station to another. They are, moreover, provided with a wonderful spread of canvas—with more sails even than a racing cutter can have, because it would be in danger of capsizing. With the wind behind them, they glide over the surface of the prairies as fast as, or even faster than an express train.

In a few moments a bargain was made between Mr. Fogg and the owner of the land craft. The wind was favourable. A stiff breeze was blowing from the west. The snow had become hard and Mudge was confident that he could take Mr. Fogg to Omaha station in a matter of a few hours. There are frequent trains and plenty of tracks from there to Chicago and New York. There was a chance that they would be able to make up the time lost. So they should make the attempt without delay.

Not wishing to expose Aouda to the ordeal of travelling across the snow in the open air under cold conditions which would be rendered even more unbearable by the speed at which they would be going, Mr. Fogg suggested that she should stay behind at Kearny station, guarded by Passepartout. He would bring the young woman safely to Europe by a better route and under more acceptable conditions.

Aouda refused to part from Mr. Fogg and Passepartout was delighted at her decision. Indeed nothing in the world would have made him want to leave his master, because Fix would be accompanying him.

It would be difficult to say what thoughts were running through the inspector's mind. Had his firm belief been

shaken by the return of Phileas Fogg, or did he consider him to be an extremely clever rogue who, after going on his trip round the world, thought he would be absolutely safe in England? Perhaps Fix's opinion of Phileas Fogg had indeed changed. But he was no less determined to do his duty and was more impatient than any of them to return to England as soon as possible.

At eight o'clock the sledge was ready to leave. The travellers—one might be tempted to say the passengers—took their seats and huddled themselves up tightly in their travelling-rugs. The two immense sails were hoisted and, with the wind driving it along, the vehicle sped over the hardened snow at the rate of forty miles per hour.

The distance between Fort Kearny and Omaha is, in a straight line, or in a beeline, as the Americans say, two hundred miles at most. If the wind held, that distance could be covered in five hours. Barring accident, the sledge should reach Omaha at one o'clock in the afternoon.

What a journey it was! The travellers, pressed close together, could not speak to one another. The cold, intensified by the speed at which they were travelling, made them absolutely speechless. The sledge slid as lightly over the surface of the plain as a craft skimming over the water—and here there was no swell to contend with. When the breeze came sweeping over the ground, it seemed as if the sledge was being lifted off the ground by its sails. They were like great wings with an immense span. Mudge, at the steering-oar, kept going in a straight line and with a movement of the oar corrected the yawing of the craft. All the canvas was drawing. The jib was no longer screened by the spanker. A topmast was put up and a topsail, spread out to the breeze, added its own driving power to that of the other sails. It could not be estimated mathematically, but certainly the speed of the sledge could not have been less than forty miles per hour.

'If nothing gives way,' said Mudge, 'we will get there!'

Mudge was anxious to arrive within the time stipulated as Mr. Fogg, faithful to his system, had tempted him with a large bonus.

The prairie, which the sledge was cutting across in a straight line, was as flat as the sea. It was like a huge frozen pond. The railway serving that part of the territory climbed up from the south-west to the north-west via Grand Island, Columbus, an important town in Nebraska, Schuyler, Fremont, then Omaha. Throughout its course it followed the right bank of the Platte River. The sledge took a shorter route and followed the chord of the arc traced out by the railway. Mudge had no fear of being halted by the Platte River at the small bend it makes before Fremont, as its waters were covered with ice. So the route was completely free from obstacles and Phileas Fogg had only two things to fear—damage to the craft and a change or drop in the wind.

But the breeze did not slacken. On the contrary, it blew so hard that it bent the mast, which was kept secure by iron shrouds. These metal ropes, like the strings of a musical instrument, were making sounds, just as if they had been set vibrating by the bow of a violin. So the sledge sped along to the accompaniment of a plaintive melody of unusual intensity.

'These strings are playing fifths and octaves,' said Mr. Fogg.

And those were the only words he uttered during the entire journey. Aouda, snugly wrapped in the furs and travelling-rugs, was protected as far as possible from the biting cold.

As for Passepartout, his face was as red as a fiery sun setting in a haze and he was sniffing up that keen air. An incorrigible optimist, he had begun to hope once more. Instead of reaching New York in the morning, they would arrive in the evening, but there was still a chance that they would be there before the ship sailed for Liverpool.

Passepartout had even felt strongly inclined to shake his ally Fix by the hand. He did not forget that it was the inspector himself who had secured the services of the sledge with sails, which was the only means of reaching Omaha in time. But some strange foreboding made him maintain his usual reserve. In any case, there was one thing that Passe-

partout would never forget and that was the sacrifice Mr. Fogg had unhesitatingly made in order to rescue him from the Sioux. Mr. Fogg had risked his fortune and his life. No, his servant would never forget that!

As the travellers abandoned themselves to their own very different thoughts, the sledge continued to skim over the immense carpet of snow. Any creeks there were, tributaries of the Little Blue River, were passed unnoticed. Fields and water-courses alike had disappeared under the uniform carpet of white. The plain was completely deserted. It formed, as it were, a large uninhabited island between the Union Pacific Railroad and the branch linking Kearny and St. Joseph. There was not a village, not a station to be seen, and not even a fort. From time to time they saw some grimacing tree flash past, its white skeleton writhing in the breeze. Sometimes flocks of wild birds rose as one. And sometimes prairie wolves, great packs of thin, famished beasts, driven by fierce hunger, tried to race the sledge. On those occasions Passepartout, revolver in hand, held himself in readiness to fire at the nearest wolves. If the sledge had broken down then, the travellers would have been attacked by these ferocious carnivores and would have been in danger of their lives. But the sledge kept going and soon sped on ahead, leaving the whole howling pack behind.

At noon Mudge realized from certain signs that they were crossing the frozen Platte River. He said nothing, but he was sure that Omaha station was only twenty miles farther on.

And, sure enough, in less than an hour, the skilful guide left the helm and rushed to the halliards of the sails and brought them in. The sledge, carried on by its own momentum, went on for another half mile under bare poles. Finally it stopped and Mudge, pointing to a cluster of roofs white with snow, said:

'We are there.'

They were there! They had arrived at the station which is linked with the east of the United States by a frequent daily service of trains. Passepartout and Fix had jumped down and were shaking their numbed limbs. They helped Mr.

Fogg and the young woman to get down from the sledge. Phileas Fogg settled up generously with Mudge, and Passepartout shook him by the hand as if he were a real friend, and then they all rushed towards Omaha station.

It is at that important city of Nebraska that the Pacific Railroad, properly speaking, ends, that is, the railway connecting the basin of the Mississippi with the great ocean. To go from Omaha to Chicago the railway, which is called the Chicago—Rock Island Road, runs due east and serves fifty stations.

A through train was about to leave. Phileas Fogg and his companions just had time to dash into a carriage. They had seen nothing of Omaha, but Passepartout had no regrets about this as sight-seeing was not what they had come there for.

The train entered the state of Iowa at tremendous speed by way of Council Bluffs, Des Moines and Iowa City. During the night it crossed the Mississippi at Davenport and came into Illinois via Rock Island. At four o'clock in the afternoon of the next day, the 10th, it reached Chicago, which had already risen up from its ruins and was standing more proudly than ever on the shores of beautiful Lake Michigan.

It is nine hundred miles from Chicago to New York. There were plenty of trains in Chicago. Mr. Fogg went from one train to the other at once. The fast engine of the Pittsburgh—Fort Wayne—Chicago Railroad rushed off full steam ahead, as if it realized that the gentleman had no time to lose. It crossed Indiana, Ohio, Pennsylvania, and New Jersey in a flash, passing through towns with ancient names, some of which had streets and tramlines, but as yet no houses. Finally the Hudson came into view and at eleven fifteen in the evening of 11th December the train stopped at the station situated on the right bank of the river in front of the very pier from which the steamers of the Cunard Line, known also as the British and North American Royal Mail Steam Packet Co., depart.

The *China*, bound for Liverpool, had sailed forty-five minutes earlier.

In which Phileas Fogg comes to grips with his bad luck

As she sailed away, the _China_ seemed to be carrying with her the last hopes of Phileas Fogg.

Indeed, none of the other steamers sailing direct between America and Europe, the French transatlantic liners, the ships of the White Star Line, or those of the Inman Company or the Hamburg Lines, or any others could assist the gentleman in his plans.

The _Pereire_, belonging to the French company—whose ships equal in speed and surpass in comfort all those belonging to the other lines, without exception—was sailing two days later, on 14th December. And, like those of the Hamburg Company, she was not going direct to Liverpool or London, but to Le Havre, and that extra crossing from Le Havre to Southampton would have delayed Phileas Fogg and rendered his final efforts fruitless.

As for the Inman steamers, one of which, the _City of Paris_, was putting to sea the next day, they were not to be thought of. They are used mainly for carrying emigrants. Their engines are not powerful and they sail just as much under canvas as by steam, and so their speed is poor. To cross from New York to England they took more than the amount of time that Mr. Fogg had left in order to win his bet.

The gentleman was perfectly aware of all this as he consulted his Bradshaw, which gave the day-to-day movements of ocean-going vessels.

Passepartout was absolutely devastated. The knowledge that they had missed the steamer by only forty-five minutes positively bowled him over. It was his fault. Instead of helping his master, he had scattered obstacles along his

path the whole time. And when he went over all the various incidents of the journey in his mind and reckoned up the sums that had been spent without any return and entirely on his behalf, and when he reflected that that huge bet, together with the considerable outlays made on the journey, which had now become quite pointless, was going to ruin his master completely, he called himself all the names he could think of.

But Mr. Fogg did not reproach him in any way and, as he left the pier used by the transatlantic steamers, he merely said:

'We shall see to the matter tomorrow. Come along!'

Mr. Fogg, Aouda, Fix and Passepartout crossed the Hudson in the Jersey City ferry-boat and climbed into a cab which took them to the St. Nicholas Hotel on Broadway. Rooms were placed at their disposal and the night passed. It was a short night for Phileas Fogg, who slept soundly, but very long for Aouda and the others, who could not rest because of the state of agitation they were in.

The next day was 12th December. From seven o'clock in the morning of the 12th to eight-forty-five in the evening of the 21st amounted to nine days, thirteen hours and forty-five minutes. If Phileas Fogg had left on the day before on the *China*, one of the fastest ships of the Cunard Line, he would have reached Liverpool, and then London, within the time stipulated.

Mr. Fogg left the hotel on his own, instructing his servant to wait for him there and warn Aouda to be prepared to depart at any moment.

Mr. Fogg made his way to the banks of the Hudson and searched among the ships moored at the quayside or anchored in the river for those that were about to sail. The Blue Peter was flying on several vessels that were preparing to go out on the morning tide. In that large and wonderful port of New York not a day goes by without a hundred ships or so departing for places all over the world. But the majority were sailing ships and were unsuitable for Phileas Fogg's purpose.

It seemed as if the gentleman was going to fail in his

final attempt when he noticed a merchant ship with a propeller that was built on graceful lines. She was anchored in front of the Battery, a cable's length away at most. Great plumes of smoke were emerging from her funnel, which showed that she was ready to put to sea.

Phileas Fogg hailed a small boat, climbed into it and was soon rowed up to the ladder of the *Henrietta*, a steamer with an iron hull and the upper works in wood.

The captain of the *Henrietta* was on board. Phileas Fogg went up on deck and asked to see him. He came forward at once.

He was a man of fifty, an old sea-dog with a grumbling nature who would not be easy to deal with. He had large eyes and his skin was the colour of oxidised copper, and he had red hair and a powerful neck and not at all the appearance of a gentleman!

'Are you the captain?' asked Phileas Fogg.

'I am.'

'I am Phileas Fogg from London.'

'And I am Andrew Speedy from Cardiff.'

'You are about to sail?'

'In an hour.'

'And you are loaded for ... ?'

'Bordeaux.'

'What is your cargo?'

'A load of stones. No freight. I am sailing in ballast.'

'Have you any passengers?'

'No passengers. Never carry them. They get in the way and they argue.'

'Does your ship move fast?'

'She does between eleven and twelve knots. The *Henrietta* is known for that.'

'Will you take me to Liverpool with three other persons?'

'To Liverpool? Why not to China?'

'I said Liverpool.'

'No!'

'No?'

'No. I am ready to sail to Bordeaux and that is where I am going.'

'Irrespective of the price?'

'Irrespective of the price.'

The captain had spoken in a tone that brooked no reply.

'But the owners of the *Henrietta* . . . ' went on Phileas Fogg.

'I am the owner,' replied the captain. 'The ship belongs to me.'

'I will charter her from you.'

'No.'

'I will buy her from you.'

'No.'

Phileas Fogg did not move a muscle. But the situation was a serious one. New York was not like Hong Kong and the captain of the *Henrietta* was not like the owner of the *Tankadere*. So far the gentleman's money had conquered every obstacle. But this time his money had no effect.

But he had to find a way of crossing the Atlantic by ship, unless he went over it by balloon, which would have been a great adventure, and not an impossibility either.

It seemed, however, as if Phileas Fogg had had an idea, for he said to the captain:

'Well, will you take me to Bordeaux?'

'No, not even if you paid me two hundred dollars.'

'I will offer you two thousand.'

'Per head?'

'Per head.'

'And there are four of you?'

'Yes, four.'

Captain Speedy began to scratch his brow as if he wanted to tear the skin right off. There were eight thousand dollars to be earned without any change of route. It was certainly worth his while to set aside the strong dislike he had of carrying passengers. But passengers at two thousand dollars per head were not just passengers. They were a valuable cargo.

'I am sailing at nine o'clock,' said Captain Speedy bluntly. 'And if you and your folks are here . . . '

'We shall be on board by nine o'clock,' replied Mr. Fogg no less bluntly.

It was half past eight. Mr. Fogg landed from the *Henrietta*, climbed into a carriage, went to the St. Nicholas Hotel, fetched Aouda and Passepartout and even the inseparable Fix, to whom he graciously offered a passage. And all this was done with his customary calm, which never left him no matter what happened.

Just as the *Henrietta* was preparing to sail, all four went on board.

When Passepartout learned what this last sea-crossing would cost, he uttered one of those long drawn-out 'Ohs' that go down through the whole chromatic scale.

As for Inspector Fix, he told himself that the Bank of England would not come out of this whole business scot-free. Indeed, by the time they arrived, assuming that Mr. Fogg did not throw a few more handfuls of them into the sea, the bag of banknotes would be lighter by over seven thousand pounds!

In which Phileas Fogg shows himself equal to the situation

One hour later the s.s. *Henrietta* passed the lightship marking the entrance to the Hudson, went round the headland of Sandy Hook and put out to sea. During that day she skirted Long Island, off the Fire Island beacon, and sailed rapidly eastwards. At noon on the next day, 13th December, a man went up on the bridge to take their bearings. One might have imagined it to be Captain Speedy. Not at all! It was Mr. Phileas Fogg. Captain Speedy was safely locked in his cabin and was letting out yells which showed that he was, quite pardonably, in a paroxysm of rage.

What had happened was very simple. Phileas Fogg wanted to go to Liverpool, but the captain did not want to take him there. So Phileas Fogg had agreed to take a passage for Bordeaux and in the thirty hours he had been on board he had managed things so well, with the help of banknotes, that the crew—the sailors and stokers—a scratch crew who were on rather bad terms with the captain, were completely won over. And that is how Phileas Fogg came to be in command in place of Captain Speedy and why the captain was shut in his cabin and why, finally, the *Henrietta* was making for Liverpool. Judging by the way in which Mr. Fogg handled things, it was quite clear that he was an experienced sailor.

How the adventure would end they would not know until later. Aouda worried the whole time without saying a word, and Fix was utterly dumbfounded to begin with. As for Passepartout, he found the whole business thoroughly delightful.

'Between eleven and twelve knots,' Captain Speedy had

said, and that was the average speed that the *Henrietta* was maintaining.

So if—and how many 'ifs' there still were—the sea did not become too rough, if the wind did not shift to the east, if nothing happened to the ship and if the engine did not break down, the *Henrietta* would cross the three thousand miles between New York and Liverpool in the nine days from 12th to 21st December. Of course, once they arrived there, the affair of the *Henrietta*, coming on top of the Bank affair, might take the gentleman a little farther than he wished.

During the first few days they had excellent sailing conditions. The sea was not too rough and the wind appeared to be fixed in the north-east. The sails were set and under her try-sails the *Henrietta* was speeding on like a real transatlantic liner.

Passepartout was delighted. His master's final exploit, the possible consequences of which he shut out of his mind, filled him with enthusiasm. Never had the crew seen such a lively, agile fellow. He was on extremely good terms with the sailors and astonished them with his acrobatic feats. He always had a friendly word or a drink for them. For him they handled the ship like true gentlemen and the stokers stoked the fires like heroes. His good humour and talkativeness were infectious. He had forgotten all about the past and their dangers and worries. He thought only of the goal which they had almost reached and at times he simmered with impatience as if he had been heated up by the boilers of the *Henrietta*. He often hovered round Fix and gave him looks which spoke volumes, but he never talked to him, as there was no longer any warm feeling between these two former friends.

Fix was mystified by it all. The commandeering of the *Henrietta*, the buying-over of the crew and Fogg handling everything as if he were a skilled sailor—he was dazed by it all. He did not know what to think. But, after all, a gentleman who started off by stealing fifty-five thousand pounds could well end up by stealing a ship. And Fix was naturally inclined to believe that the *Henrietta* under Fogg's command was not going to Liverpool at all, but to some spot in

the world where the robber, who had now turned into a pirate, would calmly set about finding a safe refuge. This really seemed quite likely and the detective began to regret ever having become involved in the business.

As for Captain Speedy, he went on yelling in his cabin and Passepartout, whose task it was to keep him supplied with food, took the greatest precautions when he gave him his meals, in spite of his great strength. As for Mr. Fogg, he behaved as if he never suspected there was a captain on board.

On the 13th they reached the tail of the Newfoundland Bank. These are stormy parts. In winter, in particular, there are often fogs there and terrible gales. Since the day before, the barometer, which had fallen abruptly, led them to suspect an early change in the weather. And, sure enough, the temperature changed during the night, the cold became keener and at the same time the wind shifted to the south-east.

It was unfortunate. In order not to deviate at all from his course, Mr. Fogg had to take in his sails and increase steam. Nevertheless the ship slowed down because of the state of the sea. Long waves were breaking against her stem. She was pitching violently and that reduced her speed. The breeze was gradually turning into a hurricane and it was anticipated that the *Henrietta* might not be able to keep head on to the sea. But, if they had to run from it, they would be exposed to all the hazards of the unknown.

Passepartout's face darkened simultaneously with the sky and for two days the good fellow was absolutely on tenterhooks. But Phileas Fogg was a bold seaman who knew how to stand up to the sea, and he kept on his course and did not reduce steam. When the *Henrietta* could not rise with the waves, she went through them and her deck was swept from stem to stern, but she got through. Sometimes the propeller emerged, its blades beating the air wildly, when a mountain of water raised the stern out of the sea, but the ship still went forward.

However, the breeze did not freshen as much as they might have feared. It was not one of those hurricanes which

pass at the rate of ninety miles an hour. It kept at half a gale, but unfortunately it blew obstinately from the south-east quarter and did not allow them to use any canvas. And, as we shall see, it would have been very useful to help out the steam.

On 16th December, the 75th day had passed since Mr. Fogg's departure from London. The *Henrietta* had not been seriously delayed. They had completed almost half of the crossing and the worst areas were behind them. In summer they could have been certain of success. But in winter one is at the mercy of the weather. Passepartout would make no predictions. Deep down in his heart he was hopeful and, even if the wind did not serve them, at least they could count on the steam.

On that particular day the engineer had come up on deck and met Mr. Fogg and had rather an animated conversation with him.

Without knowing why—as a result of some presentiment, no doubt—Passepartout had a vague feeling of anxiety. He would have given one of his ears to have known what the man was saying. However, he was able to catch a few words, including something said by his master:

'You are sure of what you say?'

'Quite sure, sir,' replied the engineer. 'You must not forget that we have had the boilers going hard ever since we sailed and, although we had enough coal to go from New York to Bordeaux under easy steam, we do not have enough to go full-steam ahead from New York to Liverpool.'

'I shall give the matter due consideration,' replied Mr. Fogg.

Passepartout understood what had happened. He was seized with mortal anxiety.

They were going to run out of coal!

'Oh, if my master can cope with that,' he said to himself, 'he must be a great man.'

And, when he met Fix, he could not help telling him what had happened.

'So,' replied the detective between clenched teeth, 'you think we are going to Liverpool?'

'Of course we are!'

'You fool!' replied the inspector and he went off with a shrug of his shoulders.

Passepartout was on the point of tackling him about that insulting epithet, the true significance of which he could not understand. But he told himself that the unfortunate Fix must be very disappointed and his pride must be hurt after stupidly following a false scent right round the world, and so he decided not to press the point.

And now what was Phileas Fogg going to do? It was hard to imagine. But it did seem as if the phlegmatic gentleman had come to a decision because he sent for the engineer that very evening and said to him:

'Make all steam and keep on course until the fuel is completely exhausted!'

A few moments later the funnel of the *Henrietta* was belching out torrents of smoke.

So the ship kept on going at full steam ahead. But two days later, on the 18th, the engineer informed him that they would run out of coal in the course of that day, as he had warned him might happen.

'Do not let the fires down!' replied Mr. Fogg. 'And charge the valves!'

Towards noon on that day, after taking their bearings and calculating the position of the ship, Phileas Fogg sent for Passepartout and instructed him to fetch Captain Speedy. It was like ordering the good fellow to go and unchain a tiger and, as he went down to the poop, he said to himself:

'He will be in a blind fury.'

A few minutes later shouting and oaths could be heard. It seemed as if a bomb had been dropped on the poop, and that bomb was Captain Speedy. It was obvious that it was going to explode at any minute.

'Where are we?' Those were the first words he said. He was choking with anger and if he had had the least tendency to apoplexy he would never have got over it.

'Where are we?' he repeated, purple in the face.

'Seven hundred and seventy miles from Liverpool,' replied Mr. Fogg with his usual imperturbably calm.

'Pirate!' shouted Andrew Speedy.

'I have sent for you, sir . . .'

'Thief!'

'. . . sir,' went on Phileas Hogg, 'to ask you to sell me your ship.'

'No, by all the devils in Hell, no!'

'The fact of the matter is that I shall be compelled to burn her.'

'Burn my ship?'

'Yes, at least the upper works. We are short of fuel.'

'Burn my ship!' cried Captain Speedy, hardly able to get his tongue round the words. 'A ship that is worth fifty thousand dollars!'

'Here are sixty thousand!' replied Phileas Fogg, offering the captain a bundle of banknotes.

That had an amazing effect on Andrew Speedy. The sight of sixty thousand dollars does something to one. In a moment the captain had forgotten his anger and his imprisonment and all his grievances against his passenger. His ship was twenty years old. But it had become a gold mine. The bomb could not explode now, for Mr. Fogg had removed the fuse.

'And you will leave me with the iron hull?' he said in an oddly gentle voice.

'The iron hull and the engine, sir. Is that a bargain?'

'It is.'

And Andrew Speedy seized the bundle of banknotes, counted them and tucked them into his pocket.

During that episode Passepartout had turned pale. As for Fix, he nearly had a stroke. Fogg had spent almost twenty thousand pounds and yet he was abandoning the hull and engine to the seller, the parts which represented almost the entire value of the ship. True, the sum stolen from the Bank had been fifty-five thousand pounds, but . . . ! When Andrew Speedy had pocketed the money, Mr. Fogg said to him:

'You must not be surprised at all this, sir. I shall lose twenty thousand pounds if I am not in London by 8.45 p.m. on 21st December. I missed the steamer from New York and as you refused to take me to Liverpool . . .'

'And I acted wisely, by all the devils in Hell,' cried Andrew Speedy, 'for now I have earned forty thousand dollars at least.' Then, more seriously: 'Do you know something, Captain . . . ?'

'Fogg.'

'Captain Fogg? Well, you seem a bit of a Yankee to me.'

And, after paying his passenger what he thought was a compliment, he was just going away when Phileas Fogg said to him:

'So the ship now belongs to me?'

'Of course, from the keel to the truck of the masts. Everything that is made of wood, I mean.'

'Good! Have the internal fittings demolished and use them to stoke the boilers!'

One can imagine how much dry wood had to be consumed to maintain the steam at a high enough pressure. That day the poop, the deck-houses, the cabins, the quarters, the spar-deck were all burned.

On the next day, 19th December, they burned the masts, the rafts and the spars. The masts were brought down and chopped up with axes. The crew set to work with a will. Passepartout went on cutting and hewing and sawing and did the work of ten men. Demolition was proceeding fast and furious.

On the next day, the 20th, the netting, the bulwarks, the topsides and the greater part of the deck were devoured. The *Henrietta* was now stripped down to the hull.

But that day they had sighted the coast of Ireland and the light on Fastnet.

But at ten o'clock in the evening the ship was still only abreast of Queenstown. Phileas Fogg had just twenty-four hours in which to reach London. And that was the amount of time the *Henrietta* needed to reach Liverpool—even if she sailed full-steam ahead. And they were going to run out of steam before the end of the voyage.

'Sir,' Captain Speedy said to him, for he was now taking an interest in his schemes, 'I am truly sorry for you. Everything is against you. We are only off Queenstown.'

'Oh,' said Mr. Fogg, 'so it is the lights of Queenstown we are seeing.

'Yes.'

'Can we go into the harbour?'

'Not for three hours. Only at high water.'

'Let us wait then,' Phileas Fogg replied calmly. His face did not reveal that he had had one final inspiration and was going to try and conquer his ill-luck once again.

Queenstown is a port on the coast of Ireland where transatlantic steamers coming from the United States leave their mail-bags as they pass. These letters are carried to Dublin by express-trains which are always in readiness to depart. From Dublin they go to Liverpool on very fast steamers—arriving twelve hours ahead of the fastest vessels of the ordinary shipping lines.

Phileas Fogg was hoping to take advantage of those twelve hours gained by the mail from America. Instead of arriving in Liverpool on the evening of the following day on board the *Henrietta*, he would be there at noon and so would have time to reach London by 8.45 p.m.

About one o'clock in the morning the *Henrietta* sailed into the harbour of Queenstown at high water and, after receiving a vigorous handshake from Captain Speedy, Phileas Fogg left him on the stripped carcase of his ship which was worth half the price he had sold her for.

The passengers landed at once. At that moment Fix had a fierce desire to arrest Mr. Fogg on the spot. But he did not do so. Why? What conflict was going on inside him? Had he changed his mind about Mr. Fogg? Did he realize at last that he had made a mistake? However, Fix did not leave Mr. Fogg. With Mr. Fogg, Aouda and Passepartout, who did not even give himself time to breathe, he climbed into the train at Queenstown at one-thirty in the morning and reached Dublin as day was dawning. At once they boarded one of those steamers, which looked like steel spindles and were all engine. They scorn the idea of rising with the waves and invariably pass through them.

At twenty minutes to twelve on 21st December Phileas

Fogg finally landed on the quayside in Liverpool. He was only a six hours' journey away from London.

But at that very moment Fix came up to him, laid a hand on his shoulder and said, showing his warrant:

'You *are* Mr. Phileas Fogg?'

'Yes.'

'I hereby arrest you in the name of the Queen!'

34

*Which gives Passepartout the opportunity of making
a dreadful, but perhaps original, pun*

Phileas Fogg was in prison. He had been shut up in the
Customs House lock-up in Liverpool and was to spend the
night there till his transfer to London.

At the moment of his arrest Passepartout felt like hurling
himself at the detective, but policemen held him back.
Aouda, horrified by the brutality of it all and not knowing
a thing about it, could not understand what was happening,
Passepartout explained the situation to her. Mr. Fogg the
honourable and courageous gentleman to whom she owed her
life, had been arrested as a common thief. The young woman
protested against that allegation and her heart was filled with
indignation and tears flowed from her eyes when she saw that
she could do nothing to help the man who had rescued her.

As for Fix, he had arrested the gentleman because duty
compelled him to do so, whether he was guilty or not. The
courts would decide the issue.

But then a thought struck Passepartout—the terrible
thought that he himself had been the cause of all this misfortune. Why had he concealed the affair from Mr. Fogg?
When Fix had revealed that he was a police inspector and
told him of his mission, why had he taken it upon himself
not to warn his master? If the latter had been informed, he
would doubtless have given Fix proofs of his innocence. He
would have pointed out his error. At any rate the unfortunate detective would not have followed him about at his
expense and then have arrested him as soon as he set foot
on United Kingdom soil. Reflecting on his own mistakes
and imprudence, the poor fellow was seized with over-
whelming remorse. He burst into tears and looked a
pathetic sight. He felt like dashing out his brains.

In spite of the cold, Aouda and he had remained under the porch of the Customs House. Neither was prepared to leave the spot. They wanted to see Mr. Fogg again.

As for the gentleman himself, he was really ruined now, just when he was about to achieve his goal. His arrest had spoilt his chances completely. He had reached Liverpool at twenty minutes before noon on 21st December and had until eight-forty-five to put in an appearance at the Reform Club, that is, he had nine hours and fifteen minutes left, and he only needed six to reach London.

Anyone going inside the Customs House would have found Mr. Fogg sitting motionless on a wooden bench, not angry at all, but quite composed. One might say he was resigned to the situation. The final blow had not roused his emotions at all, at least not visibly. Had one of those secret rages developed inside him—terrible because they are held in check and do not burst out until the last moment fierce and powerful eruption? No one could tell. But Phileas Fogg was sitting there calmly waiting—for what? Did he still have some hope? Did he still believe he would be successful even after the prison door had closed behind him?

Be that as it may, Mr. Fogg had carefully placed his watch on the table and was watching the hands go round. Not a word came from his lips, but there was a strange fixed look in his eyes.

He was in a terrible position: if he was an honest man he was ruined, and if he was a dishonest man he was caught.

Had he any thought of escaping? Did it occur to him to look and see if there was a way out of his prison? Did he think of running away? One might feel tempted to believe he did, because, at a certain point, he rose and walked round the room. But the door was securely fastened and the window was fitted with iron bars. So he sat down again and took out of his wallet the itinerary for the journey. On the line bearing the words: '21st December, Saturday, Liverpool,' he added, '80th day. 11.40 a.m.' And he waited.

One o'clock struck on the Customs House clock. Mr.

Fogg discovered that his watch was two minutes ahead of that clock.

Then two o'clock! Assuming that he could climb into an express train at that very moment, he would still be able to reach London and be at the Reform Club by 8.45 p.m. A slight furrow appeared on his brow . . .

At two-thirty-three a loud noise could be heard outside. There was a clash of doors opening. He could hear the voice of Passepartout, and the voice of Fix.

There was a momentary gleam in Phileas Fogg's eye.

The cell door opened and Aouda, Passepartout and Fix came rushing towards him. Fix was out of breath and his hair was dishevelled . . . He could not speak.

'Sir,' he stammered, 'sir . . . I am sorry . . . dreadfully like you . . . robber . . . he was arrested . . . three days ago . . . you . . . you are free!'

Phileas Fogg was free! He went up to the detective. He looked him straight in the eye and, performing the only rapid movement he had ever made or would ever make in his life, he brought back both his arms and then, with the precision of an automaton, he hit the unfortunate inspector with both fists.

'Well hit!' cried Passepartout, then, indulging in an atrocious pun worthy of a Frenchman, he added: 'Well, well! That is what you might call a good skinful of English wallop!'

Fix had been knocked down and could not say a word. He had merely got what he deserved. Then Mr. Fogg, Aouda and Passepartout left the Customs House at once. They flung themselves into a carriage and in a few minutes they were at the station.

Phileas Fogg asked if there was an express ready to leave for London . . .

It was two-forty . . . The express had left thirty-five minutes before.

Then Phileas Fogg ordered a special train.

There were several very fast locomotives under steam, but, owing to service requirements, the special train could not leave the station till three o'clock.

After saying a few words to the driver about earning a bonus, Phileas Fogg went speeding off in the direction of London, accompanied by the young woman and his faithful servant.

He had to cover the distance between Liverpool and London in five and a half hours, which was perfectly feasible if they had a clear run all the way. But there were unavoidable delays and, when the gentleman reached the station, all the clocks in London were pointing to ten minutes to nine.

Phileas Fogg had gone round the world and had arrived five minutes late!

He had lost the bet.

*In which Passepartout does not need to be told twice
by his master*

The next day the inhabitants of Savile Row would have been very much surprised if anyone had told them that Mr. Fogg had returned home. All the doors and windows were closed. No change was visible from outside.

After leaving the station, Phileas Fogg had instructed Passepartout to buy some provisions and he had then returned home.

The gentleman had withstood the blow with his usual composure. He was ruined—thanks to that bungling police inspector! After going steadily on for all those miles, overcoming a thousand obstacles and braving a thousand dangers, and still finding time to do some good on the way, he had foundered on reaching port because of a brutal stroke of fate that he could not have foreseen and against which he was powerless. It was terrible! Of the considerable sum he had taken away with him, only an insignificant residue remained. His fortune now consisted merely of the twenty thousand pounds deposited with Baring Brothers, and he owed these twenty thousand pounds to the gentlemen at the Reform Club. After incurring so much expense, winning the bet would not have made him any richer—in fact he had probably never set out to make any money, being one of those men who bet for the sake of honour—but losing the bet meant that he was utterly ruined. He had made his decision. He knew what he had to do now.

A room in the house in Savile Row had been set aside for Aouda. The young woman was in despair. From certain words spoken by Mr. Fogg she realized that he was contemplating some tragic scheme.

We know the terrible extremes to which Englishmen are

driven by a mono-mania or obsession. So Passepartout was watching his master, without appearing to do so.

But first of all the worthy fellow had gone up to his room and turned out the gas-jet which had been burning for eighty days. He had found a bill from the Gas Company in the letter-box and he thought it was high time to put an end to all the expense he was incurring.

The night passed. Mr. Fogg had gone to bed, but had he slept? As for Aouda, she was unable to get any rest. And Passepartout kept guard outside his master's door like a dog.

The next day Mr. Fogg sent for him and told him briefly to attend to Aouda's breakfast. He himself would merely have a cup of tea and a slice of toast. Aouda would please excuse his absence at lunch and dinner as all his time would be devoted to putting his affairs in order. He would not be coming downstairs. In the evening he would ask leave to talk to Aouda for a few moments.

Having heard the programme for the day, Passepatrout could merely comply with it. He looked at his master, who was as impassive as ever, and could hardly bring himself to leave the room. His heart was filled with emotion and his conscience was stricken with remorse. Now, more than ever, he blamed himself for being the cause of this final disaster. Yes, if he had warned Mr. Fogg, if he had revealed the detective's plans to him, Mr. Fogg would certainly not have dragged him as far as Liverpool, and then . . .

Passepartout could stand it no longer.

'My dear master! Mr. Fogg!' he cried. 'Curse me! It is my fault . . . '

'I am not accusing anyone,' replied Phileas Fogg very quietly. 'Go now!'

Passepartout left the room and went to see the young woman. He told her of his master's intentions.

'Madam,' he added, 'I cannot do anything on my own at all—I have no influence over my master. Perhaps you . . . '

'What influence do I have? replied Aouda. 'Mr. Fogg responds to none. Has he ever seen that my gratitude to him was ready to overflow at any moment? Has he ever

read what is in my heart? My friend, you must not leave him, not for a single instant. You said he intended to speak to me this evening?'

'Yes, madam. It is no doubt to do with safeguarding your position in England.'

'We must wait and see,' replied the young woman, who had grown very thoughtful.

So throughout that Sunday the house in Savile Row looked as if it was unoccupied, and for the first time since he had gone to live there Phileas Fogg did not leave for the Club when Big Ben struck eleven-thirty.

And why should the gentleman have put in an appearance at the Reform Club? The others were not expecting him now. As Phileas Fogg had not appeared in the drawing-room of the Reform Club on the previous evening—on that fateful Saturday, 21st December, at 8.45—he had lost his bet. It was not even necessary for him to go to his bankers and take out the sum of twenty thousand pounds. His opponents were already in possession of a cheque signed by him and a straightforward entry in the book of Baring Brothers was all that was needed before the twenty thousand could be made over to them.

So Mr. Fogg had no reason to go out and he did not do so. He stayed in his room and put his affairs in order. Passepartout kept on going up and downstairs. The hours seemed to drag. He listened at his master's door, but he did not feel he was committing any indiscretion in so doing. He looked through the key-hole because he imagined he had a right to do so. Passepartout was afraid that there might be a catastrophe at any moment. He sometimes thought of Fix, but his outlook had changed. He no longer bore a grudge against the police inspector. Fix had made a mistake, as anyone is liable to do, and in shadowing and arresting Phileas Fogg he had merely been doing his duty, whereas he himself . . . That thought overwhelmed him. He felt the most miserable of mortals.

When at last Passepartout felt too unhappy to be alone, he knocked at Aouda's door and went into her room, where he sat down in a corner and looked at the young woman

without saying a word. She still seemed very thoughtful.

Around half past seven in the evening Mr. Fogg asked to speak to Aouda and a few moments later he and the young woman were alone in the room.

Phileas Fogg took a chair and sat down near the fireplace, facing Aouda. His face revealed no emotion. The Mr. Fogg who had come back was just the same as the Mr. Fogg who had gone away. Just as calm, just as impassive.

He was silent for five minutes. Then, raising his eyes to look at Aouda, he said:

'Madam, you will forgive me for having brought you to England, I trust?'

'Yes, Mr. Fogg . . . ' replied Aouda, trying to check the pounding of her heart.

'Please allow me to finish,' went on Mr. Fogg. 'When I had the idea of taking you far away from a country that was so full of danger for you I was rich and I intended to place a part of my fortune at your disposal. You would have led a free and happy life. Now I am ruined.'

'I know, Mr. Fogg,' replied the young woman, 'and I shall in my turn ask you to forgive me for having followed you—and who knows?—for having delayed you perhaps and helped to bring about your downfall.'

'Madam, you could not stay in India. Your safety could only be guaranteed by going far enough away for those fanatics not to be able to catch you again.'

'So, Mr. Fogg,' went on Aouda, 'not content with saving me from a horrible death, you also felt under an obligation to guarantee my position abroad, did you?'

'Yes, madam,' replied Mr. Fogg, 'but events have gone against me. However, what little remains to me I would ask leave to place at your disposal.'

'But what will become of you, Mr. Fogg?' asked Aouda.

'I need nothing,' replied the gentleman distantly.

'But how do you view the fate that awaits you, sir?'

'As it is fitting that I should,' replied Mr. Fogg.

'In any case,' went on Aouda, 'a man like you could never experience hardship. Your friends . . . '

'I have no friends, madam.'

'Your relatives . . .'

'I have no relatives left.'

'Then I am sorry for you, Mr. Fogg. Loneliness is a sad state to be in. What! Have you no one to whom you can pour out your sorrows? They say that even poverty is bearable if it is shared.'

'So they say.'

'Mr. Fogg,' Aouda then said, getting up and stretching out her hand towards him, 'will you accept a relative and a friend combined in one? Will you have me as your wife?'

At those words Mr. Fogg rose, too. There was an unaccustomed light in his eyes and his lips seemed to be trembling. Aouda was looking at him. He was astonished to begin with by the sincerity and directness, and the firmness and gentleness expressed in that noble woman's lovely eyes, for this was a woman who dared everything to save the man to whom she owed everything. Then understanding dawned. He closed his eyes for a moment, as if to stop those other eyes boring deeper into his . . . when he opened them again, he said simply:

'I love you! Yes, it is true. By all that is most sacred in the world, I love you and I am yours.'

'Oh!' cried Aouda, lifting her hand to her heart.

Passepartout was rung for. He came at once. Mr. Fogg was still holding Aouda's hand in his. Passepartout saw what had happened and his broad face beamed like a tropical sun at the zenith.

Mr. Fogg asked him if it would not be too late to go and notify the Reverend Samuel Wilson, the incumbent of the parish of Marylebone.

Passepartout put on his best smile.

'It is never too late,' he said.

It was only five minutes past eight.

'Is it to be for tomorrow, Monday?' he said.

'Is tomorrow, Monday, all right?' asked Mr. Fogg, looking at the young woman.

'Tomorrow, Monday, it is!' replied Aouda.

And Passepartout ran out of the house.

In which Phileas Fogg is once more at a premium on the Stock Market

I should mention at this stage how public opinion in the United Kingdom changed when it was learned that the real Bank robber—a certain James Strand—had been arrested in Edinburgh on 17th December.

Three days earlier Phileas Fogg had been a criminal hunted down by the police and now he was the most honest gentleman in the kingdom, methodically accomplishing his eccentric journey round the world.

What an effect that had! What turmoil there was in the press! All those who had betted for or against him and had forgotten all about the whole thing in the meantime came back to life again as if by magic. All the transactions were considered valid once more. All the undertakings were renewed and betting started up again with renewed vigour. The name of Phileas Fogg was once more at a premium on the Stock Market.

The gentleman's five acquaintances at the Reform Club felt a certain amount of anxiety during those three days. Phileas Fogg, whom they had forgotten, was back in the limelight. Where was he at that moment? On 17th December—the day when James Strand was arrested—Phileas Fogg had been away for seventy-six days and there was no news of him. Was he dead? Had he given up the struggle, or was he still carrying on in accordance with the agreed itinerary? And would he appear on Saturday, 21st December at 8.45 p.m. in the doorway of the drawing-room at the Reform Club, the personification of punctuality?

I shall not attempt to describe the state of anxiety in which English society lived during the space of those three days. Telegrams were sent to America and Asia to find out

about Phileas Fogg. The house in Savile Row was watched night and morning. But there was nothing to report. And the police did not know what had become of the detective Fix who had gone off on such a wild-goose chase. All this did not prevent the betting from being started up on an even vaster scale. Phileas Fogg was like a race-horse reaching the final bend. He was no longer quoted at 100, but at 10 or 5, and the old paralytic, Lord Albemarle, laid even odds on him.

So on Saturday evening there was a crowd in Pall Mall and the adjacent thoroughfares. It was like some great concourse of brokers, permanently established beside the approaches to the Reform Club. The traffic was held up. There were discussions and arguments and the market price of 'Phileas Foggs' was called out as if he were a British security. The police found it hard to restrain the populace and as the hour approached at which Phileas Fogg was due to arrive the excitement grew to fantastic proportions.

That evening the gentleman's five colleagues had been in the large drawing-room of the Reform Club for some hours. The two bankers, John Sullivan and Samuel Fallentin, the engineer Andrew Stuart, Gauthier Ralph, a director of the Bank of England, and the brewer Thomas Flanagan were all waiting anxiously.

When the clock in the great drawing-room pointed to eight-twenty-five Andrew Stuart rose to his feet and said:

'Gentlemen, in twenty minutes the time agreed between Mr. Phileas Fogg and ourselves will be up.'

'When did the last train come in from Liverpool?' asked Thomas Flanagan.

'At seven-twenty-three,' replied Gauthier Ralph, 'and the next train does not arrive till twelve-ten.'

'Well, gentlemen,' said Andrew Stuart, 'if Phileas Fogg had come on the seven-twenty-three train he would be here by now. So we can take it that we have won the bet.'

'Let us wait! We must not say anything definite yet,' replied Samuel Fallentin. 'You know how very eccentric

our friend is. His accuracy in all matters is common knowledge. He never arrives either too early or too late, and so I would not be unduly surprised if he were to appear here at the last minute.'

'And I would not believe it even if I saw him,' said Andrew Stuart, who was, as always, in a state of nerves.

'Phileas Fogg's plan was certainly a mad one,' declared Thomas Flanagan. 'However precise and punctual he is, he could not avoid certain delays, and a delay of only two or three days would be enough to upset his whole journey.'

'You will notice, moreover,' added John Sullivan, 'that we have had no news from our friend although there have been plenty of telegraph wires along the route.'

'He has lost, gentlemen,' went on Andrew Stuart. 'He has definitely lost! The *China*, the only ship from New York that he could have travelled on if he wanted to reach Liverpool in time, docked yesterday. And here is the passenger list published in the *Shipping Gazette*. The name of Phileas Fogg is not on that list. Assuming that everything was in his favour, our friend can barely have reached America. I would estimate that he will arrive twenty days at least after the agreed date and old Lord Albemarle will have to lose his five thousand pounds, too!'

'That is perfectly obvious,' replied Gauthier Ralph, 'and tomorrow all we need to do is to present Mr. Fogg's cheque to Baring Brothers.'

At that moment the clock in the drawing-room was pointing to eight-forty.

'Five minutes still to go,' said Andrew Stuart.

The five friends eyed one another. One could imagine that their hearts would be beating a little faster as, even for seasoned gamblers, the contest was an exciting one. But they gave no sign of this and, at Samuel Fallentin's suggestion, took their places at a card-table.

'I would not give up my four thousand pounds share,' said Andrew Stuart, sitting down, 'even if I were offered three thousand nine hundred and ninety-nine pounds!'

At that moment the hands of the clock were at eight-forty-two.

The players had picked up their cards, but they kept on looking at the clock as each moment passed. No matter how secure they might feel in their victory, never had minutes seemed so long.

'Eight-forty-three,' said Thomas Flanagan, cutting the pack held out to him by Gauthier Ralph.

Then there was a moment of silence. The vast drawing-room of the Club was absolutely quiet. But from outside they could hear the uproar of the crowd, with shrieks rising above it from time to time. The pendulum of the clock was beating out the seconds with mathematical regularity. Every one of the players could count the sixtieths reverberating in his ears.

'Eight-forty-four!' said John Sullivan, and there was a hint of involuntary emotion in his voice.

There was just a minute to go and then the bet would be won. Andrew Stuart and his friends had stopped playing. They had abandoned their cards. They were counting the seconds.

At the fortieth second nothing happened. At the fiftieth, still nothing.

At the fifty-fifth there was a noise like thunder coming from outside—clapping and cheering and even oaths, surging into one continuous roar.

The players rose to their feet.

At the fifty-seventh second the door of the drawing-room opened and, before the pendulum had beaten out the sixtieth second, Phileas Fogg appeared, followed by a delirious crowd who had forced their way into the Club.

'Here I am, gentlemen!'

*In which it is proved that Phileas Fogg gained
nothing by going round the world, except happiness.*

Yes! It was Phileas Fogg in person.

You will recall that at eight-five in the evening—about
twenty-five hours after the travellers reached London—
Passepartout was instructed by his master to notify Rev.
Samuel Wilson about a certain marriage that was to be
solemnized on the following day.

Passepartout set out delighted. He walked at a brisk pace
to the residence of the Reverend Samuel Wilson, but the
latter had not yet returned home. Of course Passepartout
waited, but he had to wait twenty full minutes at least.

In short, it was eight-thirty-five when he left the clergyman's house. But what a state he was in! His hair was
dishevelled and he was hatless and he ran and ran and ran
as nobody had ever been seen to run in living memory—
pushing over passers-by and rushing like a whirlwind along
the pavements.

In three minutes he was back at the house in Savile Row
and he tumbled breathlessly into Mr. Fogg's room.

He could not speak.

'What is wrong?' asked Mr. Fogg.

'Master . . .' stammered Passepartout, 'the marriage . . .
it is impossible.'

'Impossible?'

'Impossible . . . tomorrow.'

'Why?'

'Because tomorrow . . . is . . . a Sunday!'

'Monday,' replied Mr. Fogg.

'No . . . today . . . is Saturday.'

'Saturday? Impossible!'

'Yes, yes, it is,' cried Passepartout. 'You are a day

wrong. We arrived twenty-four hours ahead of time . . . but there are only ten minutes left . . . '

Passepartout had seized his master by the collar and was dragging him away with all his strength. Pulled along in that way, Phileas Fogg had no time to think and so he hurried out of the room and out of the house, jumped into a cab, promised the driver a hundred pounds and, after running over two dogs and colliding with five carriages, he reached the Reform Club.

The clock was pointing to eight-forty-five when he appeared in the great drawing-room.

Phileas Fogg had gone round the world in eighty days!

And now, how could such a precise and meticulous man have been one day wrong? Why did he think it was the evening of Saturday, 21st December, when he arrived in London, whereas it was only Friday, 20th December, just seventy-nine days after his departure?

The reason for the mistake is very simple. Without suspecting it, Phileas Fogg had gained one day, merely because he had gone round the world from west to east, and he would have lost a day if he had gone in the opposite direction, i.e., from east to west. By travelling towards the east Phileas Fogg had gone to meet the sun and consequently the days were reduced by four minutes every time he crossed a degree in that direction. Now, the circumference of the earth measures three hundred and sixty degrees, and these three hundred and sixty degrees multiplied by four minutes come to twenty-four hours exactly, and that is the day he unwittingly gained. In other words, Phileas Fogg, as he travelled eastwards, saw the sun pass the meridian *eighty times*, but the people he left behind in London saw it pass only *seventy-nine times*. That is why the men were waiting for him in the drawing-room of the Reform Club on that particular day, which was a Saturday and not, as Mr. Fogg had thought, a Sunday.

And that would have been shown by Passepartout's famous watch—which had kept London time throughout— if it had indicated the days as well as the hours and minutes.

So Phileas Fogg had won the twenty thousand pounds.

But, as he had spent about nineteen thousand on the way, the pecuniary result was poor. However, as we said before, the eccentric gentleman had merely looked on the bet as a contest, not as a means of winning a fortune. As for the remaining thousand pounds, he actually shared them between the worthy Passepartout and the unfortunate Fix, as he found it impossible to bear a grudge against the latter. But, to keep matters straight, he deducted from his servant's money the cost of nineteen hundred and twenty hours of gas consumed as a result of his oversight.

That very evening Mr. Fogg, just as impassive and phlegmatic as ever, said to Aouda: 'Are you still happy about this marriage, madam?'

'Mr. Fogg,' replied Aouda, 'I am the one who should be asking you that question. You were a poor man and now you are rich.'

'You will pardon me, madam, but that fortune belongs to you. If you had not had the idea of marrying me, my servant would not have gone to the the Reverend Samuel Wilson and I would not have discovered my mistake and...'

'Dear Mr. Fogg...' said the young woman.

'Dear Aouda...' replied Phileas Fogg.

The marriage was celebrated forty-eight hours later and Passepartout, a magnificent, nay, a dazzling figure, acted as the young woman's witness. Had he not saved her life, thereby deserving that honour?

At dawn on the following day Passepartout rapped loudly on his master's door.

The door opened and the impassive gentleman appeared.

'What is the matter, Passepartout?'

'The matter, sir? I have just discovered this very minute...'

'What?'

'That we could go round the world in only seventy-eight days.'

'No doubt,' replied Mr. Fogg. 'If we did not go across India. But if I had not gone across India, I would not have rescued Aouda and she would not be my wife and...'

And Mr. Fogg quietly closed the door.

So Phileas Fogg had won his bet. He had gone round the world in eighty days! To do so he had used all the available forms of transport—steamers, railways, carriages, yachts, merchant vessels, sledges, and an elephant. The gentleman had displayed throughout remarkable qualities of *sang-froid* and accuracy. But, over and above that, what had he gained by leaving home? What had he brought back from his journey?

'Nothing,' you will say. Nothing? Perhaps not, except for a charming wife who, however unlikely it may seem, made him the happiest of men!

And surely a man would go round the world for less than that.

OTHER TITLES IN THIS SERIES